An Elusive Hero

'You know that we are the Croix de Guerre village?' Mourass said.

'Yes, one can hardly miss it.'

'Do you know what it is for?' I nodded. 'Do you know that we were also given the Belgian *Medaille du Roi Albert* and the American Medal of Honour, Special Category?'

'And from Britain?' I said, knowing the answer.

'Nothing.'

'And so you went to buy one.'

Mourass pulled a tassel on a cord at one side of the display box and the little purple curtain parted. The medals were behind glass on black velvet and my father's VC was in the middle.

'I can understand how you feel,' I said. 'I can even understand you buying my father's medal. What I cannot understand is the booklet which describes the action.'

'I wrote that,' he said.

'You don't mention my father at all.'

'That is what we have to explain,' he said.

Point of Honour

ALAN SCHOLEFIELD

BALLANTINE BOOKS • NEW YORK

Originally published in Great Britain in 1979 by William Heinemann Ltd.

 Published in the United States by Ballantine Books, a division of Random House, Inc., New York.

Library of Congress Catalog Card Number: 79-51250

ISBN: 0-345-28713-4

This edition published by arrangement with William Morrow and Company, Inc.

Manufactured in the United States of America

First Ballantine Books Edition: October 1980

FOR GUY SLATER

London

My involvement in what follows began on a spring day when I attended a sale of medals at Sotheby's in Bond Street. Until that time I had not made up my mind whether to become involved or not. I needed the money—most authors do—but it is not often one is asked to investigate one's father, which is what it amounted to, and I had felt uneasy at the prospect, not so much for what I expected to turn up—and I had no idea what I *would* turn up—but simply that his dead presence had dominated our family for so long that I was in awe of his memory; even that is putting it mildly.

With the fortieth anniversary of Dunkirk only a year or two away my publishers, like many others, had decided their lists would be incomplete without some work on the subject. They had approached me with the idea that instead of a general history of the event—the usual type of book—why not write something more personal and tell a story about one man's Dunkirk? Who better than a VC to pin one's story to? And who better than the VC's son, already an author of some half-dozen books, to write it for them? So they had asked me to write about a very brave man, someone who had lifted British spirits when they were at a low ebb in World War II, a man who had been awarded a posthumous Victoria Cross and whose memory was a flame at which my mother had warmed herself for many lonely years; even if a trifle uncomfortably at times.

I stood at one of the pillars in Sotheby's sale-room listening to the dealers bid for Boer War medals and Crimean medals, Polar medals and Peninsular medals and medals which had been won in the Punjab and in

Syria, at the Taku forts and the Alma, in the Kaffir Wars and the Ashanti Wars, in Somaliland and Abyssinia and Afghanistan—a drum-roll from the Imperial past—and as I watched and listened I could not have imagined in my wildest moments what I was about to embark upon.

Looking back I am tempted to think that had I had the slightest hint of what was to come I would have stopped right then. But I hadn't, and what started as a search for my father and continued as a search for Stefan Granek became also, in a sense, a search for myself.

'Lot Number 32,' said the voice of the auctioneer. 'The Carib war medal, 1773. Seven hundred pounds?' I glanced around the room. The Carib war medal, according to Sotheby's list of prices, was expected to sell well. We were in one of the smaller galleries in the warren of passages that leads from Bond Street. The room was split by pillars which, like the walls, were covered in hessian. The auctioneer's desk was on a small platform and below it was a table at which most of the dealers were seated. There was a fair sprinkling of buyers standing about the room but nothing like the crowds which one sees at a televised auction when a famous Old Master comes under the hammer; medal-collecting is a recondite occupation.

'Come, ladies and gentlemen. Six hundred then. I don't have to tell you how rare a Carib war medal is.' An assistant in a long brown coat held up the medal in its original shagreen case and turned it so everyone could see it. 'A very fine example,' the auctioneer said. The bidding began at £550 and quickly ran up to £800 when it was knocked down to one of the dealers.

I noticed that several folding chairs at the back of the room had become vacant and I made my way over and sat down. I was interested in Lot 264 which I had been told would not come up before the middle of the afternoon. It was the last item of all and was expected to be the climax of the day. Sotheby's catalogue, which described the sale in somewhat orotund upper case, as IMPORTANT MILITARY and NAVAL CAMPAIGN MEDALS, GALLANTRY AWARDS and OTHER

ENGLISH and FOREIGN ORDERS, MEDALS and DECORATIONS, had a good deal to say about Lot 264.

An outstanding Posthumous Victoria Cross awarded to Captain Geoffrey Baines Turner, Royal Hampshire Fusiliers, 1 June 1940. Virtually mint state.

> *** *London Gazette:* The King has been graciously pleased to approve the grant of the Victoria Cross to Captain Geoffrey Baines Turner in recognition of the following act of most conspicuous gallantry during the evacuation of Dunkirk. On 1 June 1940 Captain Turner, though badly wounded by shrapnel, organised the perimeter defences of the village of St Claude-sur-Mer, thereby halting the advancing German forces for more than three hours during which time several hundred stretcher cases were evacuated from the nearby estuary. Twice during the action Captain Turner left the safety of his defensive position to bring in wounded civilians. Though rescued himself he died before reaching hospital in England.

I can vouch for that, he was dead when I saw him. As with all childhood memories it is difficult to know what one actually saw and heard and what has been built up over the years from reading or from hearing the story over and over again until the picture is formed slowly like a coral reef. *Did* I actually see the body? Or did my mother tell me of the wound? Did I let in the doctor? Did I take the undertaker a cup of tea? All these things are dimly perceived through the haze of memory; I accept the experience but can't quite remember it. My mother told me so many things about him, so many details, that I cannot now winnow the real experience from the pattern of her memories.

We lived then in Petersford in Hampshire in a bungalow in Wellington Close called 'Pentland' by my mother after the hills outside Edinburgh, from which city she originally came. My father was a cashier in a local bank. My memory of the house is that it was rather dark with a huge hedge of hydrangeas on one side of the narrow path to the front door. The hedge was lovely in summer but lank and spindly and depressing at other times. All the years we lived in that house my mother wanted fitted carpets but she never managed to get them.

We had a front parlour and a kitchen/living-room rather in the style of an Edinburgh tenement, a bedroom for my mother and father, a room for me, and another smaller room which ultimately became mine. The one I originally had was let to an old man called Adey-Watson, who had invented a machine for making wire staples; it could not have been a very good machine for he did not seem to have much money. He owned a little Flying Standard car and sometimes he would take mother and me for runs to the Downs and we would look out over the sea through a telescope and try to spot the names of ships. I always thought mother might marry Mr Adey-Watson but she never did. She told me years later that remarriage would have insulted my father's memory.

But that was in the future. They brought my father's body home in an ambulance from Newhaven. My mother told me the story many times and I shall put it down now in her own words: 'I was out the back taking in the washing,' she said. 'It was a good drying day. They had phoned me that morning and said he'd been brought into Newhaven and that he was dead and they told me what he'd done. How brave he had been—not everything, just a bit—and that he was being recommended for a medal. And they said they were going to bury him in the Army cemetery at Dover. No, you're not, I said. He's my husband, I shall bury him myself. I didn't cry just then. I went and got on with my work and I was taking in the washing—I was always first out with my washing in Wellington Close, always—when I heard a motor in the front.

'He was wrapped in a blanket and someone had sewn the sides together. The blanket was all stained rusty brown. They said it was oil from the boat that had brought him back but it was a mixture of blood and sea water, you could tell that. I meant to keep the blanket with his other things but I think the undertaker must have burnt it. He denied it, but I think he must have. It was a deep blue blanket and good quality and it had a label on it saying it was made in Belgium, I remember being surprised because I had never thought you could get a good quality blanket like that from a foreign country.

'"Where do you want him, missus?" the ambulance driver asked and I said the front parlour, please. There were two of them. It was an army ambulance, khaki with a red cross on the side, and they took him into the house and put him on the gate-legged table.' (I remember that table: mock oak, mock Jacobean. When I started smoking I burnt the top with a cigarette butt and my mother was as angry as I have ever seen her in her life, not because I had been smoking but because it was the table on which my father's body had lain.)

She gave the ambulance driver and his mate a cup of tea in the kitchen. She would never have let them into the parlour even if my father's body had not been resting there for she had been brought up in Morningside, herself the daughter of a bank official, and knew her place in the scheme of things. It must have been an embarrassing few minutes for the ambulance men. She had probably given them mugs, not cups, and wouldn't have joined them. So they would have had to sip at their tea in silence, knowing about the body in the parlour but unable to bring themselves to say any words of comfort to this granite-faced, iron-haired Scottish woman who waited with obvious impatience for them to be gone. I know that feeling; she was able to generate a pervasive hostility that often made the house uninhabitable to me.

'After they'd gone,' she said, 'I took you next door to Mrs West to play and I got out my bike and went to see the bank and the undertakers.'

She could have used the telephone, we were one of the few families in Wellington Close to possess the instrument, an expense she justified because my father was a 'professional man,' but she wanted to know what money the bank was holding for him and once that was established she could order the coffin—'the best we could afford', she always said.

I can't remember anything about the day, what I can recall came later. It was June and the summer of 1940 is said to have been a lovely one so I imagine the evening to have been golden, with sunshine streaming through the parlour window. The undertaker must have brought the coffin and would have been laying out my father's body when the row took place. I never knew what it was about. I asked my mother once but she cut me short, saying that it had to do with the quality of the coffin; he had apparently brought one that she had not ordered. It was an explanation that never really satisfied me, for if that was the case why did the doctor come? I remember him clearly, old Dr March. In those days doctors made house calls more frequently than they do today and he would often have a small packet of boiled sweets in his waistcoat pocket and would give me one. Why I remember him so clearly on *this* evening is that he gave me the whole packet and then sent me out into the garden. When I heard raised voices I looked through the window and saw that an argument was in progress with all three, the undertaker, the doctor and my mother, gesticulating. If it had been only a matter of the coffin why had Dr March taken such a vigorous part? Why, in fact, had he been there at all?

'Lot 115,' said the auctioneer. 'Arctic Medal 1875–76. Three hundred pounds?' I looked down at the catalogue and read the inscription. The medal had been won by Able Seaman Richards in HMS *Alert*. He had been a member of a sledging party that had reached to within four hundred miles of the North Pole. He had suffered scurvy and frostbite and one of his feet had had to be amputated. It all seemed a long way away from Sotheby's on a spring day or even the coffin in the parlour of our house in Petersford.

As bids were awaited a voice said, 'Excuse me, is this chair taken?' I looked up and saw a middle-aged woman in country tweeds and strong brogues. She was heavy set, with grey hair and a high colouring. She spoke in a deep, almost a mannish voice. I said no and she sat down next to me. After a moment she said, 'Have they sold the VC yet?'

'No.'

She did not have a catalogue so I passed her mine, showing her Lot 264. 'We're here now,' I said, and pointed to Able Seaman Richards' Arctic Medal, which had been knocked down for £620. She looked at the catalogue for some moments, then passed it back to me. 'What will it make?' she said.

I smiled. 'I'm no expert, but Sotheby's have estimated twelve thousand.'

She turned sideways in her chair and stared into my face. A look of astonishment had spread into her eyes. 'Pounds?'

'Yes. Pounds. It's supposed to be a "good" VC.' My voice had dropped to a whisper.

She remained silent for some little while as the sale went on and then she said something I did not catch. 'I beg your pardon?'

'I said it was wicked. I mean to pay that much. Just to have it lie in a collection somewhere. Or a bank.'

'I suppose some people collect them as a hedge against inflation,' I said, lowering my voice even further. Some of the buyers were beginning to look at us.

'Never those who really need it,' she said obliquely. 'Not the people who suffer from real poverty.'

I nodded. I tried to visualize what £12,000 would have meant to us in 1940. There would have been no need to worry about the quality of my father's coffin, no need to take in lodgers. In those days the Government awarded a pension of £50 a year, but not to an officer. I believe it is double that now—still not a fortune. Even the medal itself had not been worth much. When my mother sold it in the late forties—the wrench had been almost too much for her to bear—to pay my school fees, she only made £150, and here they were talking in terms of five figures.

It was the medal sale and the estimate of what my father's VC might fetch that had first given my publishers the idea for the book. Victor Granville had had the catalogue on his desk when he had first mentioned it to me.

'Twelve thousand?' I had said with much the same air of astonishment as the lady in the country tweeds.

'But you knew that,' Victor said.

'I'm not a numismatist. I didn't know you were either.'

'Just a beginner,' he said, strolling over to the window.

The publishing house of Granville and Baker was in one of those elegant houses in Charles Street, from the windows of which you can see the plane trees and lawns of Berkeley Square. The room was very quiet, expensive, all dark, shiny rosewood, cut-glass and a gas-log fire flickering in the Victorian grate; it looked more like someone's drawing-room than the office of the managing director of a successful publishing company.

I had known Victor Granville for more than ten years, ever since I had given up daily journalism and written my first book. It was one of those analytical tomes of instant social history so popular in the sixties and had had a certain success. For a time I had been Victor's bright-eyed boy: lunches at the Savage, dinners at the Connaught with visiting New York publishers, a weekend or two at his cottage in Essex and five very long days after trout in Wales. I think he had hoped to turn me into a media guru, popping up regularly on 'Any Questions' or TV chat shows, but no one had bothered very much with my next book, nor the one after that. There had been enough money, enough critical acclaim for me to live on physically and emotionally, but not enough for Victor. Now he treated me with an air of faint disappointment, as though I had let him down.

He stood by the window staring out at the traffic, fiddling with the gold watch chain that looped across his waistcoat. He was a big man, as tall as I but broader, with dark hair and heavy proconsul features. Once he had been a tremendous sportsman. He had played county tennis and hockey for England but he was going to seed a bit. He had put on weight and there were flecks of dandruff on the dark collar of his suit. Winning was what had always mattered to Victor.

'Medals are more trouble than they're worth really,' he said. 'The insurance alone is crippling.' I thought of something like insurance crippling Victor and smiled to myself. One of his characteristics was that of boasting by denigration. He was the sort of person to whom it was important to be first in the field. When the new Rover car was announced and was unobtainable in Britian, Victor managed to buy one. I heard about it when he complained of a rattle in the door. 'You'd think they'd iron out those problems before putting them on the road,' he said. Then there had been quadrophonic sound. He had it before I had even heard of it. In fact it was from Victor, who complained that it gave him a buzzing in the ears, that I did hear about it. His fifteenth-century cottage in Essex, which was everyone's dream of beams and thatch, was often brought into the conversation, especially with visiting Americans, as a place where anyone over five feet in height was certain to get concussion. And there had been his power boat, which he had driven in the Biscay Race in 1969. I had heard of that because of the punishment which his kidneys had taken. 'I'm too old for this sort of thing,' he had said. Now he was deprecating the fact that he collected, and probably had an excellent collection of, medals.

'Who's putting it up?' he said.

'Thc VC? I don't know.'

'I thought you'd have kept up with it.'

'I was only a kid when my mother sold it.'

We went on to talk about the Dunkirk book. It was a good idea, but I wasn't keen. There was the question of my father and my relationship with his ghost, and there was another factor much tossed about between Victor and myself: 'I thought I'd do my novel next,' I said, and saw a slight stiffening of his well-padded cheeks. He came back, sat down at his rosewood table and fiddled with a silver paper knife.

'Still on that?' he said.

'You know me.'

'It's not a good time for novels.' There never had been a good time for novels as far as I could make out. 'You're known as a non-fiction writer. You've made a reputation. There'll be money in this one, David. We'll sell it in France and Germany and in the United States. A good paperback deal. There'll be appearances on TV and radio both as the author and the VC's son. Tremendous publicity. Do you no end of good.'

I knew he was trying again with me because he couldn't help trying. He was trying for Granville and Baker and for my sake and for his sake. He was trying because he was a trier, in the same way he had tried in tennis and hockey and in the acquisition stakes. But the reason I had given up daily journalism in the first place was to write a novel. He had put me off then—he and Fay between them.

'I'll think about it,' I said.

'All right. Don't take too long.' He picked up the Sotheby's catalogue and handed it to me. 'Why don't you go along? It might get you started.' At the door he said, 'How's . . . uh . . . ?'

'Christina.' He was never able to remember her name, or at least that is the impression he liked to give. 'Fine,' I said.

'And Fay?'

'Haven't seen her for a long time.'

'And now, ladies and gentlemen, we come to Lot 264,' the auctioneer said. 'The posthumous Victoria Cross won by Geoffery Baines Turner at Dunkirk. The citation is in your catalogues. Before we start I should like to say one thing: this Victoria Cross was last sold thirty years ago. It is very rare that a "good" VC comes up for sale. We do not expect to see another during this decade.'

There was a shuffle of anticipation and several people who had been standing against the walls moved into the centre of the room.

'Now, ladies and gentlemen, where shall we start? Twelve thousand?' Twelve thousand was the top limit in the estimate of prices issued by Sotheby's. There was no offer.

'Eleven five? Eleven? On my right. Eleven thousand.' Having started slowly the bidding now rose in leaps of five hundred pounds and as it did so I began to identify the interested parties. It jumped to twelve. Twelve five. Thirteen. Thirteen five. Fourteen. Fourteen five. Fifteen, where it stayed for several seconds.

'At fifteen thousand,' the auctioneer said. 'Fifteen five. Sixteen. Sixteen five. Seventeen. At seventeen thousand.'

The lady in the country tweeds whispered, 'Who is bidding?'

'Dealers,' I whispered back.

Most of the bids were coming from the table in front of the auctioneer. Some were so subtle that I could hardly catch them. Then I began to recognize the signals and realized, as the amount climbed to eighteen and nineteen thousand pounds, that only two men were in it. The first was a short, plump, bald-headed man who kept an index finger to his temple, and I assumed that as long as it was there, he was bidding. Two seats to his left was another dealer. In contrast to the first he had a shock of grey hair and wore a woolly scarf and coat. He stared down at his hands and his bid was an almost imperceptible nod. When the bidding reached twenty thousand, the rate at which the amount increased began to slow down and it crept by hundreds through twenty-one thousand and into twenty-two thousand.

'Twenty-two thousand four hundred pounds,' said the auctioneer. The VC was now almost double what Sotheby's had estimated. 'At twenty-two thousand four hundred pounds. Are you all done? At twenty-two . . .'

'Twenty-three thousand.'

The voice came from somewhere on the left of the room near the door and took everyone by surprise. We all swung around. I saw a man of about fifty, square, of middle height and with fair hair thinning on top. He was expensively dressed and stood with his legs apart, hands thrust deep into his coat pockets. He stared straight at the auctioneer ignoring all our craning heads. He gave an impression of self-possession bordering on arrogance that is often the hallmark of the very rich.

'Twenty-three thousand. At the back on the right. At twenty-three thousand pounds.' The dealers were not challenging now. 'At twenty-three thousand pounds then.' A tap. The sale was made.

For a moment there was dead silence, then came a buzz of speculation. Everyone turned to stare at the buyer but he had already vanished through the doorway. There was a noise of chairs being pushed back. People began to collect coats and umbrellas. The sale was over. I was still somewhat dazed at the final figure. Twenty-three thousand pounds for an act of bravery nearly forty years ago. Invested at ten per cent it would have brought in over £2,000 a year which in those days would have allowed us to live in comparative luxury. I wanted to know who he was, *why* he had bought the medal. I turned to follow him. At that moment the woman next to me shouted, 'It's a disgrace!' Her voice rose over the conversational hum and the auctioneer looked up like a startled deer. 'Shame!' she shouted. 'What about the old?' Two assistants in brown coats moved towards her. She had her heavy handbag in her right hand and menaced them. A big woman with broad shoulders, she was a formidable sight.

'Is she with you?' one of the men said to me.

'Me? Certainly not!'

'Come along now, madam.'

'Don't you touch me!'

'Please . . .'

'Let go!'

He took her by the arm and she hit him with her handbag. 'Leave go!' she cried. 'I'm not going to stand . . . ! Let me alone!'

A crowd had collected around us and people were looking at me as though I might be her son or at the very least her nephew. I tried to pretend that she had nothing to do with me but the crush had forced us close together. She turned to me and said, 'It's criminal to waste money when so many people are in need!'

One of the assistants managed to grip her right arm and they began to move her towards the door. I lagged behind. In the passage, a narrow dark place with glass show-cases along one side, she managed to break loose again and in the scuffle one of the cases was smashed. The noise of breaking glass seemed to sober everyone. I saw she had been cut on the hand. 'It's all right,' she said. 'I'm not dying!' They hustled her along the corridor and into the street.

I looked for the man who had bought the medal but he was nowhere to be seen and by the time I reached the door I knew I had lost him, for Bond Street at that time in the afternoon was choked with traffic and shoppers. The woman was standing on the pavement as if undecided what to do next. I did not want to get involved with her again so I turned back into Sotheby's and asked to see the Public Relations Officer.

I had to wait a few minutes before I was taken to his office. He was a young man with a purple tie and matching handkerchief. I told him what I was doing and he seemed interested. He was also firm. No, he could not under any circumstances disclose the name of the buyer.

'What about the seller?' I said.

'I'm sorry. Sometimes the people involved don't mind, but in this case we've had instructions from both parties that they don't want any publicity.'

'My God,' I said, 'you people buy and sell acts of courage like sausages. You're not even involved! Why pretend to some false ethic at this point?'

He was a good Public Relations Officer; he managed to control his anger and looked merely irritated. 'And why should you be concerned with our ethics?' he said. 'You'll make money out of your book. Aren't you feeding off the carcass as well?'

'Since he was my father I think I have a prior case,' I said.

'I'm sorry. I didn't realize that.' He smiled tentatively. 'I can understand your frustration. And your curiosity. But my hands are tied. I'll tell you this much, though: the man who bought it isn't a collector and he isn't a dealer. He's someone we've never heard of. And he isn't even British.'

When I arrived home late that afternoon I had to walk up the stairs because the lift was out of action as usual. Halfway up I was met by a blast of music which meant that Christina was home and had left the front door open. We lived on the third floor in a block of mansion flats—there were still the servants' bells above the kitchen door—with large rooms, high ceilings, moulded cornices and big bay windows. It was too big for us, though Christina's habits did have a diminishing effect. It was just off Haverstock Hill and I suppose strictly speaking was within the bailiwick of Belsize Park, but we told ourselves it was Hampstead. Fay would never have stood for that sort of dissembling, she despised people who pretended. I closed the front door, went through to the sitting-room and turned down the volume. My cassettes were in their usual state of disarray after Christina had been at them. When we had first begun to live together I had tried to keep the stereo equipment out of harm's—which meant Christina's—way, but she loved music as much as I and it was a lost battle. So I had become used to seeing my cassettes all mixed up, some put back in the wrong boxes, records in the wrong sleeves.

She must have registered the drop in the volume for she called, 'Is that you, darling?' Being Swedish she pronounced it 'dorling'.

'No,' I said, putting some of the cassettes back in their correct boxes.

'I'm in the bathroom.'

The bathroom and kitchen were at the far end of the flat, down a corridor long enough for cricket practice. She was sitting on the lavatory seat with a towel on her knees and on the towel was the pink, plump body of our six-months-old daughter, Elisabeth. I waded across the floor, stepping over wet towels and plastic ducks and kissed them both, thinking again that the only time babies smelled nice was after a bath.

'How was it?' she said.

'All right.'

'Let me feed her and then tell me.'

I went back into the sitting-room, poured myself a glass of wine and took it into my study. In her remorseless quest for unpretentiousness Fay would have called it a 'workroom' and I felt a kind of guilty delight in thinking of it as a study. I telephoned Victor Granville. He was impressed by the sum paid for the VC, as I had known he would be.

'Who bought it? Spink?'

'No, it wasn't a dealer. The public relations man wouldn't tell me, only that he was a foreigner.'

'That's unusual. I thought the regiment might have bought it. They usually try to buy in VCs that belong to them.'

'A couple of dealers went pretty high. One might have been bidding for the army.'

'What sort of foreigner was he?'

'Could have been Dutch. German, perhaps.'

'Did you find out who put it up?'

'The PR said that was classified information.'

'Well, we can probably get around that.'

'How?'

'Strings.' He paused. 'If you're interested, that is.'

'It's intriguing,' I said. 'That sort of money always is.'

'I hoped you'd feel that way. Will you do the book?'

'I'm going down to see the regimental historian tomorrow, I'll be clearer in my mind after that.'

We said our goodbyes and I went back to the sitting-room and put on another tape. The place still looked as though a bomb had hit it. Last night's wine bottle had rolled across the floor and was resting against a bookcase; one of my pipes had fallen and spilled ash on the coffee table; an open packet of paddi pads lay on the TV; the central heating radiators were covered by drying infant's clothing and there were old newspapers scattered over the furniture. It was the sort of set a movie director might have lingered on to suggest an orgy by a modern Jimmy Porter, yet all we had done the night before was listen to music and watch the box. Fay wouldn't have tolerated the room at all and, to be honest, it was something I didn't much care for either.

'Well, she's fed,' Christina said.

'Burped?'

'Ya.'

She was wearing a light blue cotton T-shirt with nothing underneath and there were damp patches where the milk from her nipples had spread.

Christina was thirty-two and at her absolute and ripest best. She was a big woman; everything about her was generous: her breasts and bottom, her thighs, her heavy blonde hair, her wide-spaced grey eyes, her smile; she was an Edwardian shape unfashionable at present, but one which gave me great pleasure not only to look at, but to feel. She was also, in spite of her sumptuous appearance, a cosy, tactile person. When we sat in a room she liked to share the sofa so that we were touching; in bed she liked to cuddle; now she came over and put her arms around me and kissed me again.

'You did not kiss me properly,' she said accusingly.

'I didn't want to corrupt the child,' I said, feeling the warmth of her saliva. 'Red or white?'

'White.'

I poured a glass of white wine and sat down next to her; immediately she moved towards me so that our bodies were touching in one or two places.

It is said that when two people who have been married split up they often subconsciously search for, and end up with, replicas of the originals. This was not so as far as I was concerned. No one could have been a greater contrast to Fay than Christina. Where Christina was large and fair, Fay had been small and dark; where Christina was careless and untidy, Fay had been precise and of a ferocious neatness; where Christina liked to share a double bed and to spend the night entwined around me like some fleshy vine, Fay had insisted on single beds which meant that any sexual contact had been on a visiting basis; with Christina it happened as naturally as breathing and almost as often. There was a vast difference, too, between them on the purely organic female level. Had Fay and I ever had children I am certain she would never have allowed herself to be seen without a feeding-bra and much less with milk stains on an old T-shirt; when Fay had had her period it often lasted for as much as seven days—though I realize now that this was a defence against me—and it was a tight-lipped affair of pain and aspirins; Christina on the other hand flowed like the Jordan and the flat was littered with Tampax boxes.

This naturalness, however, had another side. Where Fay had kept our home neat and my workroom inviolate, Christina spilled over from room to room and did not seem able to understand that what I needed was total silence when I worked. When she wanted to make love at eleven o'clock in the morning, or three o'clock in the afternoon, she wanted to do it *then*; when she wanted to tell me something, or if she needed something at one of the nearby shops—it was *now*. It wasn't that she did these things with malice aforethought, it was simply that there was no forethought.

So I had developed a kind of donjon within the bailey of our living quarters. I placed a radio, broadcasting Radio Three's non-stop music, between my desk and the door of my study and then put wax plugs in my ears. The music acted as a first filter and whatever sounds passed through it I hoped would not pass the ear-plugs. Where Fay had prided herself on her cooking, on how the meals were served and the regularity with which she served them, Christina could go for days on nothing more than whole-wheat bread, pickled herring and yoghurt. Then there would be occasional cook-ups of Beef à la Lindstrom, or Swedish meatballs and, on two memorable occasions, something called Janssen's Temptation. This irregularity and eccentricity had played havoc with my digestion.

Occasionally I felt overwhelmed by love for her, but these times were balanced by others when I lay wakeful in bed feeling a sense almost of despair, only supported by the knowledge that I did not have to marry her; that no one could make me marry her, that I was free to leave her whenever I wanted to in spite of the child. Not very noble, I know, but you cannot be married to someone, as I was to Fay for fifteen years, without taking on some of her coloration. I wondered whether I could ever loosen up to the point of finding Christina's lifestyle natural. Christina herself never put any pressure on me; not once in the two years we had been living together had she mentioned marriage. She seemed content with things as they were, seemed to believe that they would go on forever and ever. This made me feel worse.

I gave her another glass of wine and began to tell her about the sale.

She liked to hear things in detail, nothing was too insignificant and I suppose this was from being confined so much to the house. She made me describe the sale-room, what sort of man the auctioneer was, some of the other medals that had been sold. I told her about the woman in country tweeds and finally how the bidding had gone for the VC and the final bid for twenty-three thousand pounds. 'But who was this man?' she said, and I had to admit for the second time in less than a hour that I had been unable to find out. When I described the fracas in the passageway during which the woman had hurt her hand, I admitted again that I had not discovered who she was either, nor why she had done what she had. I seemed, for a onetime reporter, to have been singularly unthrustful in discovering basic facts.

'Will you do it?' she said.

'Do what?'

'Write the book.'

'Victor has just asked me that and I'm not sure. I was going to do the novel next.'

She got up, poured herself a glass of wine and came back to the sofa and curled up on one end, her bare feet touching my thigh.

'I think you should do the novel.'

'Victor says the VC book will do very well.'

'Ever since I know you you've been talking about your novel. I think you should do it next.'

The novel was a sort of talisman. I had wanted to

write a novel for years and never done it. Christina had a childlike faith in the project: it was going to be wonderful; we were going to sell the film rights and the paperback rights for a massive sum in America. But somehow I had never got round to it. Although Fay had not asked for alimony—she had a small private income—I was on a kind of treadmill, turning out articles for newspapers and magazines, and the occasional book, just to keep things going. Now there was a child I told myself I couldn't afford the time to write a novel and at the same time make enough money to pay the bills. This was something Christina did not understand. In her opinion, I could do anything. Instead of giving me confidence this had the reverse effect of making me irritable, for it showed a lack of understanding of the real world; on the other hand, Victor Granville had a very precise understanding of the real world and he did *not* want me to write a novel, which made me irritable too. Fay had been more subtle. She had steered me away by implying somehow that novels were trashy things. 'You're a historian, David, and a good one,' she had once said. At first I had interpreted this as meaning shoemaker stick to your last, but later I began to realize that it might have meant something entirely different; perhaps she had never wanted me to move into an area for which she had no feeling and over which she had no control. There is a story of Thurber's, *The Curb in the Sky,* I think, in which a wife so frequently corrects her husband's anecdotes that he takes refuge in recounting his dreams. Finally she follows him into this world, too, allowing him no privacy, no escape. Fay had a rather better degree than I and had worked closely with me on some of my books—the first one had been her idea—so closely, in fact, that whole chunks of them were really hers. She had influenced them enormously.

Privately, and only at times when I was being introspective, I wondered whether I had a novel inside me at all. Perhaps this fear had so far stopped me, for I knew that people who really were novelists wrote them at whatever cost to themselves or their families and I sometimes had the feeling that I might be like many other journalists I had worked with who were always *going* to write a novel.

'Do you think you *could* write this book?' Christina said, and there was something in the way she said it that caused me to swing round and look at her.

'What are you getting at?' I said.

'Well, it is about your father, isn't it?'

'That's what they want.'

'But you would need to look at him honestly.'

'I think I could do that.'

'Do you really?'

'Of course. Why not?'

'Because you hate him.'

'What?'

'You do, David.'

'I've never said that.'

'Of course you haven't, but it is there whenever you talk of him. And if you feel like that, how can you do the book?'

'I don't remember speaking to you about him.' It was unpleasantly said, implying she wasn't worthy of a confidence.

'You have, many times. Even in your sleep. Once I heard you talk of a body. And a blanket. And water on the floor of a room.'

Suddenly the picture was there. I had gone in with a cup of tea for the undertaker and he had been taking off the blanket and water mixed with blood must have collected inside it for as I came in it spilled out and ran along the top of the gate-legged table and dripped down on to the carpet.

'And once you said it out loud.'

'Said what?'

'That you hated him.'

'In my sleep?'

'You must have been dreaming.'

'Are you sure it was about him?'

'You talked of the medal. And a wall.'

Again the picture formed in my mind. This time of a boy in a room. But I knew it was not always the same occasion for I had spent long periods of punishment in that room. Was it the time I had borrowed a bicycle at school without permission? Or the time I had pretended to have a sore knee so that I would be excused from rugby? (A 'little funk' my mother had called me then.) Or perhaps the time I had been caught cheating in a geography test? I must have been ten or eleven and what had once been their bedroom had become father's shrine; a room dedicated to his memory where my mother slept and where I was sent to meditate on my transgressions. She once kept me there an entire weekend, only coming in to bring me food.

If Christina was right, that's when I had really grown to hate him. I'd been in that room with his medals and his uniforms, the photographs on the walls of himself and my mother. It was a pathetic shrine, really: a few mementoes of their honeymoon in Swanage, a couple of prize books, his dark bank suits still in the wardrobe, his shirts and ties, polished shoes in shoe-trees; his cap and swagger stick, sword, an old camera in its case, a tennis racquet twisted and warped out of shape and half a dozen other things I couldn't recall. On one wall, all alone, was the VC and the ribbon and below it the citation and the newspaper photograph of mother at the Palace receiving it from King George. It was a room filled with death and I can recall being very frightened of it; there was nothing comforting in my father's memory.

I wondered what had happened to the room, who lived there now, for my mother had died some years before and with her had perished the memorial. I had gone to see her shortly before her death. She had been living in an old people's home in Liss and had had a room to herself. She had made me promise to look after his things. I'd said yes, not thinking that their responsibility would devolve on me quite so soon, for she died in her sleep two months later.

I found myself sick of talking and thinking about my father. I had not been so concerned with him—or my mother—for a long time. Christina must have sensed my change of mood for she said, 'I'm sorry, I shouldn't have said that.'

'Let's forget it.' I got up and poured us another glass of wine each and put on a tape. 'That doesn't sound like Fischer-Dieskau,' I said. The tape cover had been marked *Winterreise* but the voice was Elly Ameling's, singing Bach's *Wedding Cantata.*

'Not unless he had a little accident,' she said. 'Leave it on.'

'Talking about little accidents,' I said, 'is she asleep?'

'Why?'

'I'd like to interfere with you.'

'On the ottoman?'

'On the linoleum if it makes you happy.'

She slid down the zip of my trousers and put her somewhat chilly fingers between my legs. 'How do they do it?' she said.

'Do what?'

'What happened to Fischer-Dieskau.'

'Don't even mention such a thing.'

'Does it put you off?'

'It's your hands, they're cold.'

'You never used to say things like that. You used to call me a . . . what was it? . . . a perambulating sex organ.'

'Sheer flattery. Dismiss it from your mind.'

She took off her T-shirt (that was the miraculous thing about Christina, she wore so little she could be naked in a second). 'Which part of the organ do you like best?'

I touched the side of her breast. 'There's the swell,' I said. 'And the piccolo,' I touched her nipple. 'Though it's more of a flute, really.'

'And you have the gemshorn. How big are they?'

'Eight feet usually.'

'Wow!'

'And then,' I said, slipping my hand downward, 'there is the box humana.'

'It's vox humana.'

'Not on this organ.'

'What do you supply?'
'The piston,' I said.

Colonel Jonathan Tinsdale Smithson, MC, lived near Stoner Barracks, the depot of the Royal Hampshire Fusiliers, on a hill to the west of Petersford. It was typical of him that although he had retired some years before, he could not bear to tear himself away from his old regiment. I interviewed him in a nice chintzy room with windows looking out over Petersford to the South Downs. He was not only the official historian of the RHF but also a writer of popular military histories and battles. The *Author's and Writer's Who's Who* had listed half a dozen works, among which were such diverse reconstructions as *Teutoburger Wood: The Turning Point* and *Isandlwhana: The Great Mistake*. He was dressed in a comfortable suit of brown Donegal, a Viyella shirt in a small tattersall check and the regimental tie. Even to his clipped grey moustache and carefully brushed hair he was the epitome of the officer in mufti, and the only jarring note was his carriage: he walked very slowly, and I guessed arthritis.

'This is a privilege,' he said, leaning on a stick as he crossed the room towards me. 'Sit down and we'll have a cup of tea. I'm on my own today so you'll have to put up with a soldier's brew.' There was a kettle and tea things on a tray in the corner so he would not have to walk to the kitchen. 'A great privilege,' he said. 'Our most famous soldier, you know. Never thought I'd meet his son.' The room was very cold and I assumed that the central heating had gone off at the end of March and probably wouldn't come on again until October. 'How do you like yours? Milk? Sugar? Have a piece of fruit cake. My wife made it.'

We chatted for a few moments about fruit cake and its permutations and agreed we both like lots of fruit and not too many nuts and then he said, 'You were at school here, weren't you? What happened to your mother? When did she leave?' We sorted this out and discussed what I had been doing since and where I lived and how Hampstead was being spoilt in the same way as Chelsea, and then he said, 'Were you at the sale?'

'Yes.'

'Damn shame. We had Renfrews acting for us but of course we never thought it would go nearly as high as it did. What do you suppose will happen to it now? Sit in a bank vault somewhere?' He was bitter, it was the only VC the RHF had ever won and now it had disappeared.

He had apparently tried to find out who the buyer was but had received the same dusty answer from Sotheby's as I had, dustier in fact. I thought of telling him the buyer was foreign but decided not to in case he had a seizure. He talked on for a while about why such things happened and as far as I could make out the reason was twofold: the decadence of Britain and the Socialists, although I was not clear how they came into it. He had set his heart on the medal. 'Tragic. Tragic. I won't see it again in my lifetime. Medals should come back to their rightful place.'

'You could have bought it when my mother sold,' I said.

'What are you implying?'

'Nothing. Only it went for a hundred and fifty then.'

'Absolute tragedy. I was in Germany. If I'd been here we'd have got it. I'd have gone to see your mother myself.'

He had a second cup of tea—it was too powerful for me—and then moved on to the reason for my visit. The moment I mentioned the word 'book' the atmosphere changed. 'Have you written military history before?' he asked.

'No.'

'Were you in the Army?'

'No.'

He stared at me and I wondered if this wasn't the territorial imperative in action.

'Have you read my book, *Theirs Were of Courage*?'

'No.'

This seemed to annoy him further and he said he didn't think there was any need for another book on World War II VCs. I told him I was only interested in one VC, my father's. I stressed the word *my* but one could sense that in his ethos being a person's father was secondary to being a member of the regiment.

'Well,' he said finally, 'what is it you want to know?'

I told him I wasn't sure whether to write the book or not. He said that was my decision, he couldn't make up my mind for me.

The trouble was, I said, there was so little detail. I'd been to the War Office and seen the citation and I'd read accounts in old newspapers and in official histories and wondered if there was anything in the regimental library.

'You'll have to do what any good historian does, go to the original papers.'

'But there are almost *no* original papers.'

Yes, he said, that was a bugger. He offered me another cup of tea and seemed to cheer up at the thought of the difficulties ahead of me. He said it was a unique medal. The evidence on which the award had been made all came from French civilians. There was no other medal quite like it.

'It's what's called a "good" VC, that's what made it so damned expensive. You can buy an Indian Mutiny medal for a few thousands, but try and buy Boy Cornwell's or one of the Rorke's Drift VCs and see what you'd have to pay.'

It was the timing of my father's medal, he went on, that had made it so important: the bad days after Dunkirk.

What about the officer who had taken the statements from the French civilians? Where was he, I asked?

There was a note of triumph in Smithson's voice when he told me the man had been killed in Italy in 1944.

I rose, it was pointless going on. 'You've been very kind.'

That must have brought a moment of guilt, for he said grudgingly that there was one man, someone my father was said to have helped. He had been wounded and my father had brought him into the village.

'Do you remember his name?

'Dolland. Sergeant Dolland. It's all in my book, you know.'

I wrote it down in my notebook. 'You wouldn't know where to find him, would you?'

He shook his head. 'I heard he had died a few years ago.'

There was a cold wind blowing across the plateau when I left Colonel Smithson and the afternoon had turned chilly. I looked at my watch and found that it was only four o'clock. If I left now I would be entering London at the height of the rush hour, so I decided to have a look around Petersford. I drove down the hill and could see through the trees the huge white buildings of Stoner Barracks. I remembered the soldiers in the streets of the town, sometimes at night one saw them rolling out of the pubs and often there would be fights between them and the Teds who came up from Portsmouth looking for action. I had wanted to be a soldier and so had most of my contemporaries at school; you forgot the fights and the drunkenness and you saw only the smartness of the uniforms and the look in the girls' eyes.

I drove through the town square. It was market day and there wasn't a parking place to be had, so I went over the main A3 and found a place in a small, tree-lined street. It was very familiar and I realized that it was next to the street in which we had lived. I felt a strong urge to see our old bungalow and so, instead of going back into the town, I walked to the corner and made my way along Wellington Close. It was a cul-de-sac and the house was at the far end. It looked much the same from a distance, red-tiled roof, bow windows on either side of the front door, a little veranda where my mother had sat on hot days; but when I reached the gate I realized there had been changes. A room had been added, the hydrangeas had been pulled out and a gravel path had been laid. What really hit me was the smallness of the place. It seemed to have shrunk, everything seemed to have shrunk—except the tree on the lawn. It was a beech and had only been a sapling when we had lived there. Now it was a fine spreading tree coming into young green leaf. It was under this tree that I had stood as a child and looked into the bay window of the parlour when they had worked on my father's body; it was still easy to see into the window and in my mind's eye I could visualize the figures of Dr March and the undertaker and my mother; I could see the hands moving in jerky stresses and the high murmur of voices raised in argument, and I wondered again what it had been all about.

I suppose it was talking to Colonel Smithson that had brought everything so much closer in my mind, for the scene certainly did not seem as though it had been acted out nearly forty years before. I had achieved singularly little with the Colonel, and if I was to do the book I would need to know a great deal more; my starting point might be right here. Why had they quarrelled? Why had Dr March been called? I tried to recapture his face, tried to estimate how old he might have been at the time, but I had been five and anyone over twenty would have seemed old to me. Say he had been in his forties. It would make him eighty something now. It was just possible he might be still alive.

I walked back the way I had driven and came to the post office in the square, got some change and dialled the cottage hospital. They had never heard of Dr March. Wasn't there anyone who might have worked with him during or after the war? Well, there was old Mrs Daniels. She had been a nursing sister then. She might know. Where could I find her? Right here, in the hospital. She did the library books for the patients, just to keep in touch.

You could tell she was very old by the thin, reedy quality of her voice. Dr March? What a pity I hadn't come last summer. He'd died in the winter, you see. Was there anything she could do? I was tempted to tell her of my quest and then thought to hell with it, I'd only waste my time in the stuffy telephone box, so I thanked her, said no, and rang off. I hadn't really expected much but I put the phone down with a sense of disappointment, some vestigial remnant of my journalistic career, I suppose.

It still wasn't much more than half past four and the pubs weren't open so I crossed the square, went into the Spinning Wheel to kill time and ordered a pot of tea. After Smithson's brew I drank it very weak with lemon. The place was much the same as it had always been, dark beams, leaded panes and smelling strongly of baking. It was one of the few buildings in the town that had not changed. The High Street was a ruin. Once it had been a place of small busy shops, but high rents and rates had created a desert of supermarkets, insurance companies and building societies. I had been brought by my mother to the Spinning Wheel for birthday treats—always the same, fried plaice and chips followed by Black Forest gâteau and ice-cream—and there I had brought my first girlfriends. A mood of uneasy nostalgia came down on me; I felt I should be pining for lost youth but instead could only feel a sense of unhappiness. I had the notebook which I had begun to use as a kind of diary of the VC project and I jotted down briefly the interview with Smithson—there wasn't much meat in it—then stared out of the window at the bustle of the square. Market day had always been the best time. I remembered the old chap who came up from Portsmouth with his fish stall. His prices had remained the same, they said, since the war. No one knew how he made any money but it was too good to miss and on market days the queue would begin to form at half past seven and by eight would be nearly fifty yards long. Now there was a new fish stall, clean, neat, hygienic, quite unlike the earlier one. There were a number of dark faces among the stall holders, something I could not remember. They all seemed to be Indians, selling jeans and cheese-cloth shirts. I let my eyes wander over the stalls and watched the greengrocers begin to pack up. It was time for me to go, too. I didn't want to do the book. I didn't want to rake up the past, I didn't want to see Petersford again. I thought, with a sense of relief, of Christina in the flat, and I thought of the novel. Why not the novel? There was sufficient in the bank to start it in peace and I might be able to sell enough articles to keep going while writing it. It was worth a try. But even as I made up my mind, my eyes were seeing something that was to change everything.

On the far side of the square was a sign which said *Pink and Blossom, Funeral Directors, Est. 1933.* The combination of names was such, one would have thought, as to make them unforgettable, yet I had managed to forget them. Seeing them now reminded me that it was old Mr Blossom who had laid out my father's body. As far as I could recall there had never been a Mr Pink. In a way it was annoying being confronted by those names when I had decided that I was not going to have anything more to do with Granville's idea. I knew I couldn't go back to London without having one more try. I paid my bill and picked my way across the square through the litter of old cabbage leaves and polystyrene packing.

I explained to a lady of somewhat advanced years in the front part of the funeral parlour that I came, not to bury someone, but to find out what I could about an earlier burial, and she said, 'You'll need to see young Mr Alec.' She pressed a buzzer and young Mr Alec, who was a few years older than myself, plump, balding and wearing a dark suit with a trendy yellow tie, came into the front office. Again I explained and he asked me to come through into his own room. One might have stepped back fifty years. It was panelled in mahogany and had two gas jets in porcelain shades, no longer functioning, I imagined, but lovingly restored. The window, looking out on to a small alleyway in which stood a large black hearse, was of engraved glass and I was able to read the same sign as the one above the door, only this time backwards from right to left.

'I'm afraid our records are private,' said young Mr Alec.

'My name is David Turner,' I said. 'My father was Geoffrey Baines Turner.'

He looked up with a flash of interest in his eyes. 'Do you mean the VC?'

'Yes. And it's really about him I've come to see you. You're Mr Blossom, I take it?'

'That's right.'

'Then your father would have made the funeral arrangements.'

'That's right,' he said again. 'He told me about it at the time. I was only a kid but I remember how proud he was. We'd never had a VC here you know. Your father's the only one in the history of the RHF.'

'I've been asked to do a book about him and I'm in something of a quandary. I was only five when he was killed and I can't remember much about him. My mother died some years ago. I've tried to find Dr March who looked after us but he's also dead. I was wondering if there was the slightest hope—'

'You mean that my father might still be alive?'

'Yes.'

'Well, he is. He's eighty-six, but he's still very much alive.'

'Do you think he'd talk to me?'

'I'm sure he would. He'd love it. The season hasn't really started yet so he's just mooning about the house. I can't think of anything he'd like better. I know he thought highly of your father.'

'What should I do? Write to him or ring him?'

'You don't live near here, do you?'

'No, I've come down from London.'

'You don't want to come all this way again. Why don't I give him a tinkle now?'

Ten minutes later I was driving up a road along a small sparkling stream to what had once been an old mill. It had been expensively and beautifully converted and stood overlooking a mill pond about a hundred yards long and perhaps fifty wide, narrowing to a mill-race and a rusty iron wheel. As I parked, the front door opened and a little old man, not more than five feet four in height and with a slightly crooked back, came down the steps to meet me. 'Well, this *is* a treat!' he said.

I assumed that this was Mr Blossom, senior, but there was not a single feature in his face that brought back a memory. In my mind I had created the stereotype of an undertaker, tall, dark, cadaverous, a caricature by Boz. Mr Blossom was gnomish, nut-brown, and wore a bright red wool shirt and a heavy brown cardigan. His right hand had a singularly firm grip for a man of his years. He led me through into one of the loveliest rooms I had ever seen. One wall was glass overlooking the mill pond. 'I can watch them rising from here,' he said. 'Do you fish?'

'I have done.'

'Not much doing yet,' he said. 'Weather's been too cold. Had a beat on the Test for twenty years after I retired.' He flicked a brown-mottled hand at a glass case on the wall which contained a large, angry-looking stuffed trout. 'Now I fish this when I want a bit of exercise, but mainly I like to watch them rising.'

He marched me across to an oak table which stood in the window where it got most light and indicated a small fly-tying vice which held a single barbed hook on which a tuft of bright orange feathers had been tied. There were several boxes on the table, full of highly coloured breast and hackle feathers from birds I could not recognize. 'Teal,' said Mr Blossom, pointing to one. 'Bantam. Jungle cock. Did you ever tie your own flies?'

'No.'

'Fascinating. But not much good for the eyes. Fiddly work. I have to use these now.' He pointed to a pair of magnifying spectacles. 'This is the way they tied them long ago,' he said. 'I'm using all the same feathers, even the same gut when I can get it.' He opened a tortoiseshell fly box and showed me flies lying snugly in coloured rows. His finger went out. 'Woodcock and yellow. Black spider. Green drake. I hardly ever use them now, but I can't stop tying them. Beautiful things.' He turned away, stood for a few moments at the window, but no fish were moving, then said, 'Alec said you'd want a cup of tea, but you don't want tea at this time, do you?'

'I've just had a cup at the Spinning Wheel.'

'What about a glass of claret?'

'That's sounds excellent.'

He left the room and was back in a moment with a decanter and two glasses. 'I decanted it at lunch,' he said, 'so it'll be just about right.'

It was round and smooth, and I knew it was one that I would never be able to afford.

'Do you like it?' he said.

'Very much.'

'I've got enough to see me out. Alec can have the rest, though I don't think he knows the difference between a first growth Margaux and British sherry.'

We settled ourselves in chairs by the window and drank in silence for a minute, enjoying the view over the river and the steely clouds behind the dark trees. 'Well, now,' he said, 'Alec tells me you want to talk about your father.'

I nodded and told him what I'd told his son. 'I think he deserves a book,' he said. 'Though you may have some difficulty getting the details now if, as you say, there's not much either in the official histories or up at the barracks.'

'The trouble is,' I said, 'I don't know whether I'm making up whole scenes in my mind or whether I can really remember them. My mother told me quite a bit but some things seem clear and some hazy. I have it in my mind I met you, and yet when I got here this afternoon nothing rang a bell at all.'

'Of course you met me. You brought me a cup of tea.'

'Wasn't he wrapped in a blanket and weren't you just opening it?'

'Yes, he was. He was wrapped in a blue blanket. He'd been sewn in, the way they do it at sea when someone dies. They sew them in canvas. He'd been sewn in with a heavy twine and the knots were very tight and I had to borrow a knife from the kitchen to cut the string.'

'And when you opened it water came out. Rusty water.'

He looked up sharply. 'I'd forgotten that, but it's true. I cut open the stitches and I pulled the blanket apart and the water must have been trapped in his boots because the moment I moved his legs it poured out on to the blanket—'

'And on to the table,' I said, 'and dripped down on to the carpet. That's when I came in with your tea.'

'You've got a better memory than I have.'

'That was just before the row, wasn't it?'

He was staring out over the water and he slowly nodded his small wizened head. 'Yes, that would have been just before the row.'

'Dr March must have come about then.'

'I suppose so. Where were you, listening at the door?'

'I was out in the garden standing on the lawn, but I could see everything from there and hear most of it. You seemed very angry,' I said, taking a plunge.

'It wasn't so much anger, I think your mother was the angry one; it was more, well, in our business we've got to do things very much by the book and when I saw what had happened to him . . . to your father, that is . . . I thought, hello, there's been some dirty work at the cross-roads. That's why I called in Dr March. But your mother will have told you all this.'

'Some of it,' I said, lying easily now, 'but you know how it is, she was getting old and her mind wasn't . . .' I broke off in embarrassment.

'You can say what you like,' said old Mr Blossom, smiling at my discomfiture. 'I'm past caring now. My mind will go, too, one day, but it hasn't gone yet.'

'Can you give it to me in sequence so that I'll be absolutely clear,' I said.

He sipped at his claret. 'It was a great honour, you know, laying out your father. He's the only VC I've ever met. And then I met him too late to shake his hand. But that's a hazard of the profession. We tend to meet people too late . . .'

'Mother called you in,' I prompted. 'It must have been late in the afternoon.'

'It was. I remember I'd just bought a new Hardy. Ten foot six. I wanted a chance to see what the movement was like and I'd arranged for an evening on the Itchen and then she came, I think it was on her bicycle.'

'It would have been.'

'She told me he had been brought home. Well, you

can't say not today thank you, I'm going fishing, not in my profession. He was in the parlour and he'd been wrapped in this blanket and as I say sewn in it like they do if you die at sea. When I got it open I could see he hadn't been long dead. Not more than a day. Probably died in the night, I should have thought. Stiff of course. Difficult to move the limbs. Difficult to get his clothes off. And there was a lot of this water mixed with blood. It was odd because I couldn't see where he'd been hit. He was lying on his back and I got his tunic off and his trousers and his other things and still it was just like looking at someone who'd died of a heart attack. Not a mark on him, and it was only when I turned him over that I saw the wound. A hole like a cricket ball.'

He broke off, looked at me and said, 'Do you want it in detail like this? I never know how much people can stand. We have to be euphemistic in our business but I dropped all that when I retired. Tried to forget about circumlocution, but some people still don't like to be told things as they are.'

'I'm not one of them,' I said. 'You can be as brutal as you like.'

'Oh, it's not brutality. It's telling things the way they are. I must say, turned over on his front your father wasn't a very nice sight. The hole had gone light blue and purple and dirt had got in. You could have put your fist into it. But there was something about the wound that didn't ring true, somehow. I'd seen one or two like it before. You can't live in a country community as an undertaker all your business life and not come across wounds like this.'

'How do you mean?'

'Accidents happen.'

'I still don't understand,' I said.

'When you're out after a hare or a couple of partridge. At times like that. It had been made with a shotgun.'

'*What?*'

'No doubt about it. You could see some of the pellets.'

'You're saying my father died of a shot-gun wound in the back?'

'That's what I thought. So I rang Dr March. The thing didn't sit right. The Germans didn't use shot-guns, so how was it he died of a shot-gun wound? I wanted another opinion. And that's what made your mother so angry. I used the telephone in the parlour and called Dr March and he came in and confirmed what I'd seen. We stood there over the body, none of us knowing what to do, all of us arguing. It seemed to me we should tell the authorities. But your mother wouldn't have it. She said he was up for a medal. It was Dr March who said it wasn't really our business; that the Army must know what they were doing. That's when you saw us arguing . . . I wasn't certain in my own mind, but I decided to do nothing. And a few weeks later there was the announcement of the VC and there wasn't anything more to be said.'

Coming up Haverstock Hill I could see our flat from about half a mile away; it was like some great brightly-lit liner sailing down towards Swiss Cottage; every light seemed to be on and as I went up the three flights of stairs I heard the familiar blast of music. The front door was ajar and the sitting-room was in its usual state of disarray. I switched off the equipment and took out the cassette: I noted that our neighbours and the north-eastern section of Belsize Park had been enjoying a Baroque evening. Christina was sprawled on the bed, still dressed but with a blanket pulled up over her. A piece of paper on her chest read, 'Do not touch.' I lifted it, wrote 'Don't flatter yourself,' replaced it, switched out the three blazing lights and closed the door. I went to check my typewriter. It is something I have done ever since working on a newspaper. There was a message rolled into the platen telling me that Victor Granville had telephoned and would I ring him back any time before midnight. It was then nearly ten o'clock and I was cold and tired and hungry. Mr Blossom had opened a second bottle of claret, but wine eventually demands food and this was something he seemed to do without.

I heard the baby moan in her sleep in the room next to mine and went through and immediately wished I hadn't: the smell told the story. Well, it wasn't my job. I went back to my study. I wondered how Fay would have coped with children. It was tragic that she had never had any. She would probably have made a very good mother. I remember her saying once that having babies was the easiest thing in the world, every shop-girl, every peasant woman, had them with ease, everyone except her.

We had tried everything we could think of or had been told to by at least three doctors: temperature-taking, pills, examinations, blown tubes, special diets, sperm counts; the only thing we had not done very well was the basic requirement. With Christina it had been somewhat different; I think she got pregnant the first time I kissed her. Fay would never have allowed her husband to change dirty nappies; at least I'd have been free of that. Christina's philosophy was that if the child was wet or dirty then she had to be changed—it didn't matter by whom. I tried without success to forget it but couldn't, and finally I went back, changed the child, cleaned her up, cleaned myself up and by then the last thing I wanted was food. I poured myself a whisky and phoned Granville. He lived in a penthouse suite at the top of Eccleston Towers, near Victoria, and had one of the best views of London. His wife had died five years before and he was said to have the odd lady friend of tender years but I'd never met any of them. I imagined him now coming across the white carpet to answer the telephone.

'I've got some names,' he said, as soon as he heard my voice.

'What names?'

'I know who sold the VC and I know who bought it.'

'How did you manage that?'

There was a slight purr as he said, 'I told you: strings.'

'What strings?'

'You remember Pearson, don't you? Billy Pearson?'

My mind was a blank for a moment and then I remembered a man who had come fishing with Victor and me in Wales. We had put in five days on the Dovey but Pearson hadn't touched a rod. He was a Detective Chief Superintendent at Scotland Yard, head of the porno squad. As far as I could determine he had spent the time with a married woman, an ex-colleague's wife, in Aberystwyth. In the evenings he would tell us all about her; kept on saying he'd been 'pleasuring' her. He had been an unpleasant bit of work and the reason Victor had brought him along was the possibility that he might do a book on the world of pornography for Granville and Baker. He had done it eventually, ghosted of course, but it had been a success and had enabled him to get out of the force—before he was tossed out, some said; he missed the bribes scandal by a matter of months. He was now, apparently, in private security work. Pearson was just the man to get the sort of information Victor wanted.

'Got a pencil?' he said.

'Go ahead.'

'Seller's name is Mrs Rose Crawley, 21 Guildford Street, SW1; buyer's name is M. Henri Mourass. M-o-u-r-a-s-s. "Le Tilleul," Route du Canadelle, Nord 59, France.'

'Any idea why he bought?'

'I thought I'd done well enough just to get the name. What happened with the regimental historian?'

'Not much help, really, but something else has come up that's kept my interest alive.'

'Oh?'

'It may turn out to be nothing at all. It may make a book.'

'This one?'

'Not perhaps the way you imagine it.'

'You intrigue me.'

'Leave it with me, Victor.'

'As you say.' His tone was slightly affronted. I put the telephone down and pulled the typewriter towards me. It was time to make a note of exactly what I'd got and where I stood. But Christina woke and came in.

'You didn't phone,' she said accusingly.

'I did,' I said, lying. 'You had the record player on full volume. No wonder you never hear the phone. The neighbours don't *all* like Couperin, you know. You'll get us kicked out.'

She was looking rumpled and sleepy, her heavy blonde hair swinging down in front of her face, half hiding it. 'Give us a kiss, then,' she said in a grotesque imitation of a Cockney accent. I burst out laughing. Swedes were supposed to be lugubrious, yet Christina had a kind of zany quality that defied definition or categorization. She had had a Brazilian grandmother, perhaps that explained it.

'Have you eaten?' she said.

'Yes.'

'Come to bed then, it's late.'

'That's all you ever think about.'

'Don't flatter *your*self,' she said.

Guildford Street is in Pimlico and lies in that maze of streets between Buckingham Palace Road and the river. The houses had all been built in the last century on land that had once supplied London with vegetables; all at much the same time, all to the same basic design. They formed street upon street of terraces, each house three storeys high and having a portico supported by two round pillars. The area had gone down badly after the war but since the early sixties many houses had been done up so there were some with smart black and white painted fronts, brass door knockers and elegant basement kitchens, and others with blistering paint, rotting woodwork and ulcerated plaster caused by the acid spewing out of Battersea power station just across the river. There were few trees and fewer amenities. It was not a pretty place. Overlooked as it was by Churchill Gardens, one of the largest post-war sub-economic housing schemes in Europe, it never would be.

It was mid-afternoon and spitting with rain as I walked up Guildford Street. I had decided not to try and get in touch with Mrs Crawley by phone since if she had insisted on no publicity she might refuse to see me. No. 21 was a house of the second category. At one time it might have been elegant, for the large top step had been set with mosaic tiles, and the railings were more ornate than I had seen around the basement areas of other houses in the street. It had once been painted white but Battersea and the London air had turned this the colour of porridge. Large areas of paint and plaster had dropped away, exposing the old brickwork. The portico seemed hardly attached to the front of the house, so deep were the cracks around it, and the pillars themselves had lost chunks of plaster. The window panes were so heavily covered with dust it was almost impossible to see the dirty net curtains hanging askew in the lower rooms. Some of the windows on the first and second floors were broken and open to the weather.

About a hundred pigeons stood in the light rain on the pavement in front of the door, stirring only slightly as I walked through them. At first I thought no one was living there. A couple of dusty milk bottles lay near the door and a notice had been stuck on one of the pillars which read: 'Why is this house allowed to stand empty?' Underneath was the address of a charitable housing organization. As I pressed the bell I saw a faded wartime sign on the wall: an arrow pointed towards the basement and the still-legible words said, 'To the air-raid shelter.'

I listened, but could hear no ring. I banged on the door. Paused. Banged. Paused. Banged again. All the time the pigeons shouldered each other and moved around my legs like big feathered insects. The door suddenly opened. I had heard no footsteps.

I was confronted by an elderly woman in a long flowing dress clutching a brown paper bag.

'Oh!' she said.

'I rang,' I said.

'I didn't hear you.'

'And knocked.'

'I was at the back.' She spoke in a soft, almost apologetic voice and there was a trace of a country accent. 'Have you come to feed the pigeons?' she said, taking corn from the paper bag and sprinkling it on the steps.

'No.'

'Don't you like pigeons?'

'Yes.'

'They kill them now. They shoot them and poison them.'

'They say they damage the buildings.'

'Come along . . . Come along . . .' she called, ignoring the statement and talking to the birds themselves. Pigeons began to sail down from the roof-tops opposite.

'It's the power station that damages the buildings,' she said.

She must have been in her seventies with a thin, lined face and faded blue thyroid eyes. 'Here.' She held out the bag. I took some corn and sprinkled it on the pavement.

'Did you want me?' she said.

'Mrs Crawley? Yes, I did.'

She looked up with sudden suspicion. 'You haven't come to complain about the pigeons, have you?'

'No.'

'People do, you know. From across the street. They say it's unhealthy. Is it about the rates?'

'No, it's not about the rates either. It's about the VC.'

She brightened. 'Have you brought the money?'

'I'm not from Sotheby's.'

'You're not a newspaper person, are you?'

'I'm the son of the man who won it.'

Her hand stopped, poised above the bag. 'You're Geoffrey's boy?'

'That's right.'

She took half a pace towards me and stared into my face. 'Then you're . . .'

'David.'

'Good gracious me! Come in.'

I followed her in and wished I hadn't. The house was completely devoid of furniture or carpets and was used as a roost for pigeons which had come in the upstairs windows. They perched on the stairs and banisters, they sat on every window sill, and their droppings were everywhere, staining the windows and walls. The floor was thick with the stuff and crunched underfoot. The bodies of several dead birds were lying in the hall. The top floors of the house were inhabited only by birds.

She led me along a dark passageway into what had been, in better days, a drawing-room that extended through double doors into a dining-room. There were windows at either end, one window overlooking the street, the other overlooking a backyard of indescribable filth where pigeons hovered and fluttered and roosted. Fortunately the two interlinked rooms were empty of birds. They were clearly the only habitable part of the house. She had turned them into a bed-sitter with the bed in one corner; the rest of the space was filled to capacity with furniture.

'I'm going to make a cup of tea,' she said, hovering over a small gas cooker. 'Would you like one?'

'Please.'

She moved slowly about the room, getting down cups and saucers from a Welsh dresser, filling a kettle from a tap in an adjoining room, which I guessed must be her bathroom, lighting the gas. She seemed, in her long dress, to float. She handed me a cup of tea and said, with a shy smile, 'I'm very pleased to meet you, David.'

We sat down in two Victorian spoon-back chairs and stared at each other. I looked away but could feel her eyes on me, searching my face. The silence extended to the point of embarrassment and to break it I said, somewhat fatuously, 'I didn't know you knew my father.'

'Oh, yes.'

'Well?'

'As well as two people can.'

'Really? As well as that?'

'Have you ever been in love?'

'Yes.'

'Was it a great love?'

'Is that what you're saying about yourself?'

'He was my lover. My master. My everything.'

'I see,' I said, thinking the woman mad and the sooner I was out of there the better.

'That's how I remember him,' she said, pointing to something I had not noticed in the clutter. It was a photograph in a metal frame and stood on her dressing-table. I picked it up. It had gone brown with age but was still clear. The photograph was of my father in his uniform with his cap on and his pips up. At the bottom I could make out the faded writing which said, 'To my darling Rose, with all my love, Geoff.' I knew the photograph well. It had been taken just after he had been made a lieutenant. My mother had been very proud. She had hung her copy on the wall of her bedroom with his other things. There was one difference between this copy and the one she had; on my mother's there were no endearments.

'You say he was your lover,' I said, to give myself a chance to arrange this new thought in my mind.

'Yes,' she said, 'for eight months and twelve days. Would you like a biscuit?'

I took a Rich Tea biscuit and said, 'When was this, exactly?'

'Just before war broke out. Then he was taken from me, you see.'

I began to feel uneasy. The phraseology she used came from wartime movies, but another thought was beginning to enter my mind, straight out of *East Lynne*.

'When you are part of a great love,' I said, going into her world for a moment, 'it is your destiny . . .' I paused, groping my way towards the end of the sentence, but could not find it, and instead blurted out, 'What I mean is . . . did you . . . have I any half brothers or sisters?'

Thank God she shook her head. 'No, fate decreed that we should never be blessed.' Then she looked up and said with a curious innocence, 'All great love stories are tragic. They have to be.'

'Can you tell me about it?'

'Why have you come to see me?'

I told her and she nodded slowly. 'I knew it would have to be. Your mother passed on, didn't she?'

'Yes, some years ago.'

'So I'm the only one left who knew him well.'

'That's right.'

'I don't want his memory sullied.'

'It would be giving him his due.'

Slowly at first and then with greater ease I drew from her the story of those eight months and twelve days. It was a story that had a kind of pathetic ordinariness about it and the only thing that gave it any interest at all was that one of the characters was my father; she gave me each trite detail as though it were part of some richly woven romantic tapestry, instead of a tawdry little account of infidelity, adultery and infatuation. That she'd had a grand passion for my father there was no doubt; it would have been interesting to hear what he had to say about her.

She had been a typist in the same bank and had had a room in a house just off the High Street. It was owned by a widower who worked in Havant, so was completely empty and quiet during the day, and it was to this house, a minute or two from the bank, that she and my father would go at lunchtime with their little packets of sandwiches.

One can imagine the furtive ambience, the two of them leaving the bank in different directions on their bicycles, a few minutes apart; the fear of meeting someone; the fear of being held up, for the time was so short; then the meeting in the room, the taking off of bicycle clips and suspenders, stockings and girdles; the coupling; the cheese-and-chutney sandwiches; the Thermos of tea; then back to the bank by different paths and the long afternoons, he with his cash drawer, she with her letters, and the semen still deep inside her. And only once did they go away and spend a whole night together. My father was in the army by this time and had a weekend's leave without telling my mother. It was the autumn of 1939 and they took a room in a small hotel in Portsmouth and went across by ferry to the Isle of Wight and spend the day at Bembridge. It was the only time she had left mainland Britain. And then he had gone away to war, as she told it, like some mailed knight on his destrier, to fight for his King and his Country, for God and the Right, for Rose—and had died. Only to be enshrined in her mind. Two women had worshipped the memory of a one-time bank clerk who had done something brave in war, yet how different that worship was: my mother gave expression to it in the physical memorial and the constant use of his memory as an example to hold up to me; Rose kept him fresh in her mind, gilding memory a little more each year until it may well have borne no relationship to fact at all.

I asked her what she had done after he was killed and it was simply and quickly told. She had married another bank employee, a sub-accountant who had clawed his way up the banking ladder and had finally ended his days as manager of the branch in Pimlico. The house had been an investment. But he had died eleven years ago leaving her nothing but the house, its furnishings and his pension. To keep inflation at bay she'd had to sell her belongings one by one and retreat through the house to her present accommodation. She had been unable to raise money to do up the house and convert it into flats, from whose rents she might have lived; nor did she wish to sell it, for she had nowhere else to go; she was caught in the classic dilemma of the aged. The VC was the last valuable object she possessed.

'I bought it with my own money that I'd saved,' she said. 'A hundred and fifty pounds. A fortune then. But I didn't care. My husband never knew; it was *my* money, you see. I kept it in a drawer with my clothes. I always thought it was part of Geoffrey. His heart. It broke my own to sell it.' But her eyes were suddenly bright with the thought of the money and I suppose one couldn't blame her. I wondered how much she really remembered of my father.

Christina wasn't in when I got home; nor was the child; nor the carry-cot. There was a note saying, 'You are *late*. Have gone to Birgitta's.' She often went to the Svenssons'—he was at the Swedish Embassy and his wife was Christina's closest friend in London—and I decided to drive over and pick them up later.

I ran a bath, gave myself a drink, and lay in the hot water luxuriating in the peace that came from knowing that the flat was empty, that nothing was on the verge of breaking, going out, going off, blowing up, or somehow needing my attention; and that the child could compete with the Cloacus Maximus if she chose and I wouldn't have to do a thing about it.

My mind went back over the afternoon, to the ghastly house and the woman who lived in a dream of the past. What was really intriguing was what I had learnt about my father: that he wasn't the Shining Example of Christian Virtue so often held up to me by my mother; but had been having it off in a rather grubby way with the nearest thing to hand. Perhaps Christina was right. Perhaps I did hate him, or at least his memory, for I couldn't help feeling a somewhat vindictive pleasure at finding him out. I think this more than anything else decided me. I finished my drink, got out of the bath and, still dripping, went to my study and phoned Victor. He sounded genuinely pleased.

After we'd made the usual noises about financial arrangements and discussions with my agent he said, 'What next?'

'France,' I said.

After I put down the phone I sat at my desk for a long time staring at the empty typewriter. Gradually it was replaced by other images: the corpse in the blanket lying on my mother's table, the rusty water dripping on to the floor. And then something I had never seen but only heard about: I saw my father's naked body lying face down on the table. My mind placed the hole just below his left shoulder blade. Light-blue and purple, Mr Blossom had said. Could have put your fist in it. I saw the pellets driven deep into the flesh, just visible like tiny black ants. Accidents happened when you went after hare or partridge, he'd said. But no one had gone after small game at Dunkirk. Then why a shotgun? And why in the back?

The warmth from my bath had left me and I shivered. What if I found the answers to these questions? What if I didn't like them?

It was then I began to experience the faint hint of the feeling that was to grow and grow as I went back into the past to search for answers: the feeling of fear.

France

St Claude-sur-Mer is one of those villages unfamiliar to the tourist in France unless he strays not only from the main roads but from the secondary roads as well. I had come across places like it before in the Auvergne and in the Massif des Maures, not physically similar, but evoking the same air of loneliness and cut-offness. It was difficult to imagine that a few kilometres behind me lay the bustling port of Calais and an equal number ahead was the largely rebuilt town of Dunkirk; less than fifty miles to the west Dover and the heavily populated south coast of England, and to the north, south and east, the whole Continent of Europe. Here, as I drove across a railway line and began to follow a narrow unmade road through a world of sandhills and wind-bent dune grass, I felt as alone as I had ever felt.

I had crossed on the ferry to Boulogne early that morning, hired a Renault, and driven up the coast towards Dunkirk. The ferry had been filled with holidaymakers searching for the sun, but the day was overcast with dark scudding clouds, and rain had begun to spot the windscreen by the time I reached Calais. Among the dunes, sand was blowing across the road and there seemed to be half a gale coming out of the southwest. Every now and then I could see, through a break in the hillocks, the grey-brown water of the Channel and I had the feeling that I was no longer in the twentieth century, but half expected to see a British three-decker under full sail on her way to blockade the French fleet at Brest. It was that sort of day. I crossed a canal and became even more hemmed in by the dunes. A farmhouse, half-ruined, loomed on my left; it had a mansard roof and would have pleased Charles Addams. A little farther on a road twisted away to the right, and a sign read, '*A la Fleuve*'. I kept to my own road and within a kilometre came to the village. It was a surprise. I had been expecting, because of my frame of mind, a few wind-bleached buildings with peeling plaster and a depressing hotel. Instead it gave an impression of being newly cleaned and painted, hallmarks of the strong French economy. It had a narrow main street that ended at the *plage,* which was small and cut off from neighbouring beaches by two headlands of dunes which stuck out on either side of it like the claws of a crab. Away to the right I could see the mud flats of the river estuary. The only thing I knew about the village was that it specialized in mussels and I assumed the mussel beds had to be somewhere in the estuary.

There were two signs on the outskirts. One told the traveller the times of Mass, the other read: '*Bienvenue au village de la Croix de Guerre.*' I stopped at the Garage de la Croix de Guerre and filled up with petrol. A mechanic with a half-smoked Gitane in his mouth came out from beneath a Citroën Pallas and began to fill the tank.

He was unprepossessing to look at, thin, dark, with an Algerian cast to his face and the pores of his skin filled with the black grease of his occupation, but friendly enough.

'On holiday?' he said, the half-cigarette bobbing in his mouth.

I nodded. 'I hoped for some swimming.'

He looked up at the dark windy sky. 'Farther south, perhaps.'

'Is there a hotel in the village?'

'Two.'

'Which is the best?'

He smiled. 'I come from the next village, m'sieu. We think our hotels are better.'

I heard a step on the other side of the car and saw a large red-faced man come around the bonnet. 'I heard you ask for a hotel, m'sieu.' He nodded to the mechanic. 'All right, I'll take it.' The mechanic handed him the petrol hose and returned to the Citroën.

'How long will you be staying?'

'A few days.'

'There are two hotels, both on the beach. The Miramar and the Relais Croix de Guerre. Both are good. The first is big, TV in the rooms, the second smaller.'

'I don't care about TV,' I said. 'Which would you choose?'

He patted his belly; it was big and bulged over the expensive snake-skin belt. 'For me, there is only one choice: the table. The table at the Miramar is good, at the Relais excellent. It has one rosette in the Michelin. But it is more expensive.'

Victor Granville was paying, I thought, so why not spoil myself? 'The Relais it is, then.'

He took my money and went to the office. When he brought the change he gave me a small plastic key-ring holder.

'Good holiday, m'sieu. Good eating.'

'Thank you,' I said, aware of a welcome I had rarely experienced in France.

Coming through the dunes my unease had been heightened by a fact which I had half expected but for which I had remained unprepared: the presence of my father. For so many years I had tried to stamp him out of my mind that now I had entered his territory—that is how I saw it—he seemed to join me in the car and more than once I found myself fighting off the desire to look back to the rear seat as though afraid his *doppelgänger* might be sitting there staring at me in silence. Was this the road he had walked? Was this a dune he had climbed? The landscape could not have changed very much in forty years and this was the only road to the village; he would have had to come along it.

The cheerfulness of the Relais caused my spirits to rise. It was nearly noon and I had been passing locals with newly baked *baguettes* strapped to the carriers of their bicycles. I had not eaten since the ferry and the hotel smelled of good cooking. I was shown up to a room with a view of the *plage* by the wife—I assumed—of the proprietor. She was middle-aged and good looking, short, rather plump, but with an efficient and friendly air.

'Are you on holiday?' she asked.

Driving up from Boulogne I'd had a schoolboy fantasy of coming into the village, letting the inhabitants know who I was and being treated as some kind of proxy hero: kissed on both cheeks by the mayor; the freedom of the village; a magnificent banquet; champagne. But now I found I could say nothing more than, 'Yes.'

'How long will you be staying?'

'Three or four days.'

'Will you be eating in the hotel?'

'Of course.'

She seemed to relax. I have noticed that the extent of one's welcome in France often depends on whether one eats in the hotel or not. Having established that I would, she smiled and said, 'The weather is not too good for you.'

'I'm more interested in food. You're famous for your mussels.'

'They are on the menu for lunch. Does m'sieu know this part of the coast?'

'I've never been here before. But my father was one of those who fought here during the war.'

'Those were bad days.' She handed me a *fiche*. 'At your leisure, m'sieu.'

'I'll bring it down.'

She smiled again. 'Lunch in a few minutes.'

I made a good lunch at a table in a glassed-in veranda. The hotel seemed only half full, mainly of Belgians. I began to feel cosy, being able to look out at the dark clouds and the cold sea, yet protected and well fed. After lunch I went up to my room on the pretext of going through the notes of newspaper articles, and passages from military documents and official histories which I had spent the past fortnight collecting, but I was unused to drinking a whole bottle of wine at lunch and soon fell asleep.

I woke about four and lay in a half daze staring

across the room through the window to the headland beyond. The dark clouds were beginning to break up and I saw an occasional patch of blue, though the wind, from the sound of it, had increased. I lay there unwilling to get up. It was a typical bedroom in a small French hotel: a strange floral wallpaper, a bentwood chair, a table, a bidet and washbasin in one corner, and in a sort of cupboard, which had no window except a fanlight, a shower and lavatory. It was like so many French hotel rooms that I had occupied, mostly with Fay, and I was reminded of the first one in that long line, the one in which we had spent our honeymoon, near the Boulevard St Michel in Paris.

We had corssed in the ferry from Dover to Calais on a Monday morning. I had had an open sports car then, a Triumph Roadster bought eighth or ninth hand when I came down from Cambridge. It had once been a pseudo-opulent looking vehicle but by the time it reached me it was dented and rusty and had a craven engine. Driving down from London we had begun to boil long before we arrived at Dover, but the nightmare really began when we reached France. I thought that the addition of some water to the cooling system would be all that was needed, but this was not so. There was something basically wrong with the engine and it took us the entire afternoon and half the evening of a hot and sultry July day to reach the outskirts of Paris. Every few miles we had to stop to allow the engine to cool. It was early evening and very close when we came to Paris and somehow I missed my way, for we came into the centre of the city on a road that grew progressively narrower until it passed through a choked area of street markets and small bars where we could only just squeeze between the cars parked on either pavement.

We were in a long, slow-moving stream of cars when a man came out of a nearby bar and stood, swaying slightly. He staggered towards us, looked for a long moment at the car, then said, 'Where did you get this bit of shit?'

The traffic had temporarily come to a halt.

'Ignore him,' Fay said, and I nodded.

'I said, where did you get this bit of shit? This piece of English crap?'

The car ahead of us moved on and thankfully I put down my foot. Steam began to come out of the radiator. We stopped again. He came up to the side of the car and leant on the door with his elbows. He was very drunk and I could smell pastis. He thrust his head towards Fay and said, 'English girls . . .' He made an obscene motion with his thumb between his first and second fingers and then reached in and, before either of us knew it, had slipped his hand into her blouse and was fondling her breast. It was a grotesque moment. The traffic had moved ahead of us and someone was hooting behind. I knew I should get out and hit him but the street seemed suddenly to have filled with grinning faces, waiting for me to make a fool of myself.

I have often wondered what Christina might have done in the same circumstances. Taken his hand away; smiled; said something unprovocative; perhaps even tried to make a joke of it. Fay was different. She turned very deliberately and spat in his face, the saliva landing over one eye and dripping down towards his mouth. He stepped back and I put my foot down. He came after us, lurching across the road, but we steamed quickly away and found a corner and I lost him, and us, in a maze of narrow streets and it was nearly ten o'clock by the time we reached our hotel.

We had a late meal and I drank too much wine too quickly. I felt euphoric, perhaps as a reaction to the ghastliness of the day. We had arrived, we had a room, we were in Paris and that seemed enough for the moment. I knew I would have to do something about the car but nothing could be done that night. We must have got back to the room about eleven. It was much like the one in which I now lay, rather small, rather dark, with a double bed that sagged in the middle, only it didn't have a cupboard with a shower and lavatory, only a washbasin in one corner with a bidet next to it; nor did it have a view. The long narrow windows opened out on to a small airwell and the backs of buildings similar to our own. I remember feeling nervous on top of everything else, for apart from one or two unsatisfactory sexual encounters in the back of cars, Fay and I had never spent a night together nor even a few comfortable hours in bed; I had never seen her naked. We were both sticky and hot and rather dirty and she said she would use the bidet first and would I turn my back. I went to the lavatory down the corridor and then out into the street and walked to the river only one block away and I remember looking out over the water and feeling excited.

She was in bed when I got back. I undressed, washed myself and got in beside her. I put my arms around her to draw her closer but she felt stiff and unyielding. She had been angry in the car and the hostility had lasted for some time but I had put it down to the natural consequence of what had happened.

'I don't feel like it,' she said.

'Ladies are supposed to be nervous on the first night.'

'Don't you understand?' she said, shifting away. 'I don't want to.'

'It's supposed to be very good for the skin.' I took refuge in the wrong sort of humour.

I put my hand on her breast—a mistake—and she pushed it away violently. 'For God's sake, leave me alone!'

'All right,' I said, dropping the light tone, 'but would you mind telling me why?'

'I've already told you. I don't feel like it.'

'Do you think you might feel like it some time in the future; It's partly what we got married for.'

'You may have got married for that reason. I didn't.'

'It must have been my money, then.'

'Don't be so stupid.'

We lay there in the dark, radiating hostility at each other and I thought, My God, here we were, if not quite in the springtime, the pretty bloody ringtime, at least in Paris. Wasn't it supposed to be the place for young lovers? It had been a hell of a day. She was tired. I was tired. And I said so, trying to make up. 'You'll feel better in the morning,' I said.

She was not to be mollified. 'Don't patronize me.'

'Look, this is our honeymoon. People are supposed to be friendly, if not actually conjugal, on their honeymoons. Why don't we kiss and make up?' She pushed herself into a sitting position and I could feel her body begin to shake and suddenly I knew what was wrong. The words came spitting between her teeth. "You just sat there!' she said.

'I'm sorry,' I said, 'it was a bloody awful thing to happen.'

'You didn't do a thing!'

'What could I have done?' I said, remembering the traffic and the hooting and the grinning faces, but equally ashamed at my lack of courage.

'If you don't know,' she said, 'there's not much point in discussing it.'

There were thunderstorms in the night and the following morning was grey and cool and I was woken by the clack of shutters being flung open. In the grey light the room looked more depressing than it had even by the light of the weak electric bulb. All the furnishings were green, a dark, plush-green that seemed to absorb the light coming in from the airwell and deaden it. We had to have the electric light on during the day.

We spent a week in that room; that is how long it took a garage on the far side of Paris to mend the car. With Christina it would have been a week of unbridled lust, a week to remember, but with Fay it was a disaster. We had planned to stay in Paris for only two nights before leaving for the Mediterranean and now we saved our money by eating bread and cheese in our room twice a day, by spending hours in the Louvre, by allowing ourselves only one drink in the evening at a sidewalk cafe. We went to the movies once and there was an embarrassing scene when I failed to tip the usherette. The final blow was the bill for the car. It took all our money expect for a few pounds and instead of going south we had to return to London a week early. During that stay in Paris we made love only once and I don't think either of us enjoyed it much, we were too strung up. It was not a very good start to married life.

I forced myself off the bed and dug around in my briefcase for the notes I had brought with me. I glanced at them rapidly but decided they didn't make much sense unless I knew the ground so I picked up my camera and went downstairs. As I passed through the small lobby Madame came out of her office and asked me if I had filled the *fiche*.

'Not yet, I'm afraid.'

'It makes no matter, later.'

From what I could make out the village was much the same in size as it had been in 1940. Its means of access to the main coast road was still the single unmade road on which I had entered; its major industry remained mussels and, I suppose, tourism. I walked down the main street and out among the sand-dunes. I climbed the highest dune I could find and tried to get a bird's eye view of the area. To my left was the village, to my right was the road among the dunes winding away until it came to the canal and the railway line, ahead of me was the river, behind me more dunes. I tried to carry myself back in time but the village was the anachronism, it seemed too new, too bright. Of course it had had to be largely rebuilt but even so it did not seem to fit into its surroundings. Mentally I took off the paint and replaced it by peeling walls, broken stucco, bleached window frames, wind-torn posters and the old chipped enamel signs for St Raphael and *pneus* Michelin, and tried to imagine it that day in June 1940 when my father came in.

In the river, small boats, the 'little ships' of Dunkirk, would have been evacuating the wounded. On the canal or perhaps the railway line the Germans would have had their guns. I tried to imagine the noise, the Spitfires and Hurricanes screaming over the village on their way to give air cover to the troops on the Dunkirk beaches; I tried to imagine the horizon dotted with big and little ships; the ack-ack puffs in the sky; the tracers tearing the sea into white fountains. And slowly I did begin to see these things. Standing there on the dune in the chilly wind I felt myself back in those times, on a sunny June morning along with thousands of men pouring into the Dunkirk perimeter, many, like my father, cut off from their units, a mixture of frightened humanity, all seeking to get back to England. Old newsreels came into my mind: Frenchmen hiding in ditches, pushing their belongings in prams, diving off the roads as Messerschmitts came down to machine-gun them; I saw shrapnel hissing into the shallow waves and I heard the constant drone of aircraft engines.

And down through the centre of this picture came the figure of my father and the man he was helping, Sergeant Dolland. He would have had his arm around the sergeant's shoulder, easing his weight. I wondered how this bank clerk had managed, speaking little French, to organize the villagers. I imagined a machine-gun in that building, a mortar over there, a forward position at the mansard-roofed farmhouse which dominated the road intersection. Twice my father had left the village to rescue French civilians. I wondered who they were, if they were still alive, if I could meet them.

I slithered down the dune and fitted a 135mm telephoto to my camera. I liked to photograph scenes when I was doing research, so that I could look at them back in England and regain the flavour and physical characteristics of a place. I photographed the farmhouse, the road, climbed another dune and took some long shots of the village, then came down again and walked towards the river where I took several pictures of the small jetty and the fishing boats at anchor.

The wind, the dark racing clouds, the moving sand, the loneliness, had all combined to give me a sense of desolation. I was in an empty wasteland, yet I had a feeling that I was not alone, that somewhere, perhaps behind the next dune or the one after that, someone was waiting and watching. Was it my father's ghost again? I took what photographs I wanted and made my way back to the ruined farmhouse at the intersection of the two dirt roads. Again I had the feeling, strong this time. I stopped and turned, quickly. The farmhouse was on my left, with its broken walls and boarded windows. But nothing moved, only the shadows of the clouds passing across the stone walls. I shivered and hurried on through the wind to the village.

Halfway down the main street opposite the Crédit Lyonnais was a small square consisting of two lines of plane trees, lopped off about twenty feet from the ground, a *boule* pitch and several benches. At this time in the afternoon one might have expected the only activity to be a few pensioners playing *boule*, instead it was the centre of bustling industry. A Renault van and a Berliet lorry were parked on the pitch and half a dozen men in blue overalls were putting up decorations. There were strings of coloured lights hanging between the trees. Some wreaths and two crossed tricolors had been placed on the obelisk at the end of the square, and the men were now erecting a triumphal arch of red, white and blue papier mâché. My path took me past the obelisk and I stopped to look at the decorations and photograph it. It was made of reddish marble and the lettering on it was in gilt. 'To the fallen,' it said. '1 June 1940', and underneath that the phrase, 'Murdered by the Nazi hordes'. I didn't count the names but there seemed to be about ten, quite a lot for a small village like this one. These were men who must have helped my father. Something jogged my memory. The first four names looked familiar. They were all Mourass. Then I remembered. Mourass was the name of the man who had bought my father's VC. I opened my notebook and found his address. 'Le Tilleul,' Route du Canadelle, Nord 59. St Claude was also Nord 59. He was closer than I had imagined. I walked over to a bar on the far side and ordered a beer. The barman was about my own age but limped as he moved behind the zinc. His hair was white.

"What's happening?' I asked him, nodding out towards the decorations.

'For the celebrations.'

'What celebrations?'

'Tomorrow is the first of June.'

Then it all fell into place. These were the French celebrations to mark the Dunkirk evacuation. Somehow it had never occurred to me that the French would honour it; it was such an intensely British anniversary. 'But why this year?' I said. 'This is the thirty-ninth anniversary. Wouldn't next year be better?'

It was his turn to look puzzled. 'But we celebrate every year, m'sieu. We are the Croix de Guerre village.' He went to the far end of the zinc where there was a small pile of booklets, took one from the top and gave it to me. I glanced at the cover, which read, *'St Claude-sur-Mer. Village de la Croix de Guerre. 1 juin 1940.'* I flicked through the pages and realized it was the story of the village at that time. 'How much?' I asked. He shook his head.

'Thank you, I shall read it later.'

'A pleasure.'

'What do you do at the celebrations?'

'Will you be staying?'

'Yes.'

'Then you will see.'

I sipped my beer and watched the men finishing off the decorations.

'I'm looking for the Route du Canadelle,' I said. 'Do you know where it is?'

'You've just come from it. It's the main street. Canadelle is the next village.'

'A house called . . .' I flipped open my notebook. ' "Le Tilleul." '

His eyes seemed to widen. 'M. Mourass?'

'Yes.'

'You can't miss it. Go up the road and cross the railway line and the canal. Turn left as though you were going to Dunkirk. About a kilometre along you'll see the gates, and two lines of lime trees up to the house.'

'He must be well known,' I said.

'He is.' There was the slightest trace of acid in his voice.

I went back to the Relais, had a shower and a couple of whiskies from the tooth glass, filled in the *fiche* and by that time it was half past seven, when Frenchmen all over the world sit down to dinner. I went downstairs, gave the *fiche* to Madame and was shown to the same table I'd had at lunch. There seemed fewer people in the glassed-in dining-room but it was just as cosy, if not more so, for each little table had an orange light, the table cloths were orange and white and there were orange wallhangings which gave the room warmth and colour.

The Relais deserved its one rosette in the Guide. The meal began with pâté en croûte and I was well into my turbot when Madame came up to the table and said, 'Excuse me, please, m'sieu, but I cannot read your hand-writing. What is this name?' She put the *fiche* down and pointed to the entry marked *'Prénoms'*.

'Baines,' I said. 'My middle name. David Baines Turner.'

'Thank you.' She turned and walked quickly away. She had seemed less friendly and her tone had been cold.

After dinner I fetched a coat from my room and went out to stroll along the front. Madame was telephoning as I passed through the lobby. She turned her back to me and cupped the receiver in her hands as though I was trying to eavesdrop. It was puzzling. The wind had died and the sea was much calmer. The evening was bright, if chilly. This was the worst time of day to be alone in foreign parts—or anywhere, for that matter. I began to miss Christina. It was odd, but I had not thought either of her or the child since leaving London, instead my thoughts had been haunted by Fay. Now it was Christina I wanted. I wanted some brightness, some humour and I wanted Christina in the place that she and I like her best and that was in bed. I walked down on to the sand, feeling it crunch under my shoes, right to the water's edge and watched the shellfish burrow down as each wave receded. The village looked very pretty. It was rather like the beach at Estoril, where Christina and I had really begun whatever it was we *had* begun.

I had gone to Lisbon to do some research for a book on the Portuguese banknote swindle of the 1920s which damaged the economy of the country and had been a major factor in bringing the economist Salazar to power, with a resultant dictatorship lasting more than forty years. I had gone out on a week's package deal at the end of March to get the feel of Lisbon and such places as Sintra, Estoril and the Avenida Palace Hotel where the conspirators had met. Christina was our tour guide: the meeting was as simple as that.

She had stood beyond the customs barrier at Lisbon airport with a little handwritten sign which said, 'Hemisphere Holidays Over Here', and I remember thinking what an astonishingly attractive girl the holiday firm had managed to recruit after the pedestrian hostesses of the flight out. There were not more than half a dozen of us to be cared for—it was early spring and the season had not started—but she had managed to lose an elderly gentleman from Romford, two suitcases and my portable typewriter before we reached the coach that was to take us into the city. It had been an unpleasantly bumpy flight and once or twice I had considered reaching for the paper bag in front of me. That had been preceded by a long wait at London's Heathrow Airport. We had been called on time but then had to stand in the sparsely furnished departure lounge for nearly an hour without anyone telling us why. So when we stood milling about on the pavement at Lisbon Airport waiting to board the coach and Christina said, 'We have lost Mr Phillips,' I had replied, before I could stop myself, '*You* have lost Mr Phillips.' There was a kind of shuffle of support for me from the other tour members and another voice said, in tones of richest Lancastrian, 'And my two cases!'

It was a warm day and Christina was flushed with effort and confusion. 'I am very sorry, ladies and gentlemen,' she said. 'You must excuse me, please. It is my first day.'

Regretting my outburst, I said, 'Let me see if I can find Mr Phillips.' She smiled tentatively and I noticed that beads of perspiration had broken out on her brow.

I found Mr Phillips in the lavatory. His shirt-tail had become caught in the zip of his fly and he was standing in the middle of the floor making ineffectual tugs. 'It would never have happened with buttons,' he said.

He was well into his seventies and his old wattled hands were never going to close the gap.

'Can I help you?' I said.

He took his hands away and stood like a child waiting for me to fix it. As I wrestled with the zip I thought with some nervousness that if a member of the Portuguese Airline Police came through the door at that time I might well spend my holiday in prison for attempted buggery. Victor Granville would never forgive me.

I led Mr Phillips back to the group and noticed that the typewriter and the two suitcases had arrived. Christina smiled again in relief and this time I smiled in return as we got aboard.

It was the duty of the tour guide to be in the foyer of the hotel every day from noon to one o'clock so that we could discuss with her any one of a dozen sight-seeing trips which were advertised. I became her best customer. I would wait for Mr Phillips or whoever it was requesting information on how to get to the Belem monument or a *folklorique* tour of the *fado* nightspots, and then I would sit down with her on the big couch and take out my notebook and cross-question her about Lisbon. She knew the city and its environs backwards. Her family had lived there for many years; her father was Swedish and had been a charcoal buyer. Her mother was English and Christina had gone to school in Geneva and then to art school in Stockholm. None of this emerged from out little tête-à-têtes in the hotel lobby, but by the second day I had invited her for an evening drink at the Avenida Palace Hotel and there, in the first floor bar which could not have changed by one chandelier or one piece of polished mahogany since the Portuguese banknote swindle had been planned there fifty years before, I drew her out about herself. She seemed willing to talk and it became clearer that we both needed someone to talk to, for Fay and I had separated the previous autumn and I had spent a wretched winter of loneliness and too much liquor in a furnished flat in Highgate. When Christina finished with art school she had travelled for a time in South America before returning to Lisbon. She met and married a

Swedish commercial pilot and made her home in Sweden. She had been happy for a while and then her life seemed to fly off at a tangent. In the space of two years she had a miscarriage, her father died of a stroke and her husband was killed in a skiing accident at Garmisch. That had been twelve months ago. She had sold her house in Stockholm and had gone to England to live in Godalming with her mother, but they had not got on and after nearly a year she had joined Hemisphere Holidays as their Lisbon representative.

By the second night we had extended our evening drink to two and then three and had gone on to a restaurant off Black Horse Square which she said served the best grilled chicken in the city.

The following day I hired a car and we drove out to Estoril along the coast road in the last of the evening light, to our left the Atlantic rode in on small breakers that foamed white on the rocky littoral, to our right the occasional suburban train, coaches glowing with light, wound its way to Cascais. We parked at the railway station and walked through the subway under the line to the beach. There was a restaurant almost at the water's edge and it was to this that Christina guided me. We were the only diners except for an elderly man with short iron-grey hair at the far end. The seaward side of the restaurant was glassed-in and it was almost as though we were dining on a ship, on one side were the twinkling lights of Cascais, on the other the silhouette of the strange pseudo-Gothic castle on Estoril beach. It should have been rather *triste* since there were only two tables occupied but the muzak was loud enough to make talking tolerable and we began to spin fantasies about the elderly man. Could he, we wondered, be the last of the war criminals still living along this part of the coast, or was he perhaps an ex-king in exile? The food was simple and good and we drank two bottles of Dao. After we'd had our coffee I bought a cigar and we walked down to the water's edge and Christina took off her shoes and tights—a memorable moment, that, as I watched her flesh appear—and we walked along the wet sands. Occasionally she would jump away from an encroaching wave. We were like two children, talking and laughing, and it seemed natural when the wave caught her unexpectedly around the ankles, for me to grab her and help her to jump away, and just as natural to keep my arm around her shoulders.

We walked up to the subway, which smelled of urine and dampness and I kissed her. I had not had another woman in my arms since Fay, and that was a long time ago. What little sexual activity we had enjoyed in the past few years had dwindled to almost nothing by the time the marriage broke up, but it was Fay's kisses and Fay's body which were imprinted on my subconscious, her rather cold chaste lips, her thin boyish body. Kissing Christina was a different experience entirely: her mouth was large, her lips full, her saliva warm and sweetish and her body round, soft and feminine.

I cannot remember ever being quite as happy as when we drove back to Lisbon for I knew and she knew and we both knew that we knew that she was coming back to the hotel with me and that any other arrangement would have been unthinkable.

The next few days we spent in each other's company whenever we could. We went to Sintra and the market at Sao Pedro; to Coimbra and back to the restaurant on the beach at Estoril. And then the time was over and we were at Lisbon Airport and I shook hands with her and said goodbye like any other member of the tour, but in my mind was the picture of us in bed early that morning as light had crept over the city, when we had spoken of the future and how she would come to England and how we would live together there. But as I boarded the aircraft I had a sense of utter desolation: I knew she would never come. This was one of those holiday things that seem so right and permanent at the time and so wrong and impermanent once one reaches one's own surroundings. But she did come. About three weeks later on a grey drizzly morning the telephone rang and her voice was like a warm wind from the south. 'When are you coming?' I said, imagining her in the sunshine of Lisbon.

'I am here.'

'Where?'

'In the call box at the end of your road.'

I couldn't believe it. I ran out of the house. It was true. She was standing on the corner, with three large suitcases at her feet, paying off a taxi. I had never been so pleased to see anyone. But things were different now. I told myself that no relationship stood still, that change was necessary, yet I felt that something had gone.

The wind had died; away to the west the sun was sinking in a mass of flame-coloured clouds, a beautiful northern sunset, and a mist full of ozone was beginning to settle on the beach. It had turned cold for the end of May. Thinking of Christina had unsettled me. I could go and have a cognac and coffee, but that's what the two of us always did when we were in France and I had no wish to do alone what we enjoyed together. The night stretched out balefully and I decided to meet it with physical tiredness, which meant a walk. I started off at a brisk pace along the beach and then climbed the semi-cliffs at the southern end and on to a headland that ran out to sea for perhaps a quarter of a mile. Once again I was in dunes and the going was heavy.

I had not walked far before I came upon traces of World War II; rusty barbed wire, concrete platforms, a single decaying pole that might once have been part of a radio mast. This had all once formed part of Hitler's sea wall to keep the Allies out of Europe and I thought of Rommel who had been in charge of it coming down here to inspect the huge bunkers and gun caves, the only part of the Third Reich that *would* last a thousand years, and then going home to be murdered by Hitler. All this, of course, was long after my father had been killed.

As I neared the end of the headland I passed massive emplacements and deep underground bunkers, which must have once held great guns that could have sunk a battleship, and anti-aircraft guns and machine-guns. Shot-guns seemed to have no place in a German army as professional as this one had been, in spite of what old Mr Blossom, the undertaker, had said. I had looked up the official records and found that my father had died of shrapnel wounds; perhaps Mr Blossom had mistaken small pieces of shrapnel for shot-gun pellets. He had seemed so certain, yet how often had one found absolute certainty based upon absolute error; and he was in his eighties. The same feeling of unease that I had experienced that afternoon descended on me once more.

I threaded my way between pieces of torn barbed wire where wind-blown picnic papers had caught, and stood out at the very tip of the headland. It was a bleak, exposed place and in the last rays of the sun gave one a feeling of standing on the rim of the world. After a few moments I turned and was beginning to walk back when I saw some steps half covered by sand disappearing into the ground, and I knew they led into a bunker where once soldiers had lived and brewed coffee and written letters home and been afraid, as they waited for the Allied invasion fleet.

On an impulse, I went down. There was just enough light to see by. People had used it as a lavatory and the smell was damp and unpleasant. The walls were covered with aerosoled names, hearts and arrows. It was like being in a cave system. The floor was sand, where it had blown in over the years, and one had to avoid the little piles of faeces. Each bunker was linked with another and I walked through several, taking particular care to remember which way I turned, for I was reminded of Knossos and the Maze and had no wish to meet the Minotauros without knowing my way of escape. The place was dank and dead, filled with ghosts of the past and I was about to turn back towards the staircase when I looked through into yet another chamber and saw something which made my heart stop. It was lit by a single slit window through which the last of the evening light was slanting. On the far side of this shaft was the figure of a man. I stood and stared. I was looking at a German officer in a peaked cap and boots.

At that moment the dying rays of the sun must have

been abruptly killed as it slid beneath the western sea, for the shaft of light was cut like a spotlight on the stage, and for a few seconds the bunkers were plunged into darkness. Then the grey light seeped back. I flicked my lighter. The bunker was empty. I stood there, unwilling to move, in case whatever it was I had seen had somehow got behind me. Then I turned slowly, holding the light high. But all I saw were the scrawls on the walls, the hanks of human dung, the tins and the empty wine bottles, and around me was the damp sea smell.

I pulled myself together. Some configuration of light and shadow must have created the image in my mind—already susceptible to *doppelgängers*. I told myself that my imagination was overheating, and made for the staircase that rose out of the bunker. Then I stopped again. A little trickle of sand was coming down the stairs. There was no wind to start such a movement, nor had it been started by me. I ran lightly up the stairs and came out into the fresh evening air. But there was no one, the headland with its detritus from World War II was as lonely and lifeless as it had been a few moments before. I walked back to the hotel. There *had* been someone there. But a German officer? That was imagination tricking the mind. The person I had seen could have been wearing a Beatle's cap and knee-length leather boots. That would explain the phenomenon; but it did not explain what he was doing there or, and this came with a sudden prickling of the skin, why he had been following me; for I had no doubt now that it was the watcher's presence and not my imagination which had brought down the feeling of unease on me.

When I got back to the Relais Madame was waiting for me at the desk.

'It's clearing well,' I said.

'A moment, m'sieu. I regret there has been an error in your booking. We do not have a room after tonight.'

'But you asked me how long I was staying. Why didn't you tell me then?'

There were reddish tints on either cheekbone and she spoke as though I had offended her. 'I regret it was a mistake. The hotel is full.' Her lips compressed into a line and her eyes challenged me to make a scene. I felt the familiar anger one has for foreigners when something has gone wrong in their countries, but there wasn't much I could do. I couldn't force her to throw other people out. At that moment there was a movement in the doorway of the office and I saw a middle-aged man with a sallow skin dressed in chef's trousers and jacket, with a white kerchief tied around his neck. I assumed he was Madame's husband. He, too, stared at me, but without the same hostility. He seemed only a pale shadow of his wife and I had little doubt that it was she who ran the place.

'Will you please try the Miramar?' I said coldly.

'I regret that, too, is full, m'sieu.'

'Will you please try?'

'It is as I say.'

Again there was not much I could do. I couldn't take the telephone and ram it down her throat, much as I might have liked to.

'Please prepare my bill for the morning,' I said.

'Certainly.'

I turned and went out of the hotel, walked fifty yards along the front and entered the heavy double-glazed doors of the Miramar. It was an altogether plusher affair, with a doorman and a clerk in a black jacket. He watched me come across the flowered carpet towards the desk with a look of expectancy and faint apprehension as though he already knew who I was and why I was there. I had hardly finished my sentence when he shook his head. 'I regret, m'sieu, that the hotel is full.'

I was still angry when I went upstairs to my room in the Relais; I poured myself a large whisky and drank it and thought what the hell, there were other towns along the coast. It was just that the food had been so good. I got into bed and opened E. F. Benson, my panacea for all upheavals, and was about to try and lose myself in the saga of *Mapp and Lucia* for the fourth time, when I remembered the booklet from the bar. It was lying on the floor. I retrieved it and began to read. It was only eight pages long, an extravagant and heroic résumé of the part St Claude had played in the Dunkirk evacuation and how the villagers had held the Germans off with a few machine-guns and some mortars left behind by the British Expeditionary Force. The overblown phrases reminded me of a speech by General de Gaulle. It recounted the entry of the German troops and the execution of more than a dozen heads of household because of the village's resistance which had allowed hundreds of Allied soldiers and wounded to be evacuated. All through the booklet it described this action as The Victory. It was xenophobic to the degree one would expect of such patriotic writing and left a rather unpleasant taste in my mouth: after this length of time one had tired of propaganda from either side. But that was not the main thing about it. The importance to me was in something it left out completely. The writer had managed to give a detailed account of the fighting of 1 June 1940 without a single mention of my father.

The following morning I paid my bill in chilly silence and drove out of St Claude, over the canal and the railway line and turned left, as the barman had directed, towards Dunkirk. Soon I came to a high stone wall with a pair of iron gates set into it and an avenue of lime trees. This was greener country and the dunes had been left behind. The house, had it been in England, would have been described as a small manor; it looked very grand. The gates were open and I went up the gravelled drive.

A maid opened the door to me. I asked for M. Mourass and waited on the front steps. A moment later a woman of about Christina's age, hair pulled sleekly back over her head and dressed by Chanel, at a guess, came to the door and said that M. Mourass was engaged at that moment but that she was Madame Mourass and was there anything she could do?

I said it was very kind of her but that it was rather complicated and difficult to explain. She looked at me with that cool stare which seems to come naturally to wealthy Frenchwomen and said she was sorry but her husband could not be disturbed.

A voice from one of the front rooms called out, 'Who is it, *chérie*?'

'Someone who wishes to see you,' she said.

'Tell him I'm busy.'

'He knows.'

'Tell him to make an appointment.'

She turned to me. 'If you cannot tell me what it is, you must make an appointment.'

'What about this afternoon?'

The voice said, 'I'm busy this afternoon.'

His wife said, 'My husband is busy this afternoon.'

'Perhaps tomorrow.'

'Tomorrow is impossible,' the voice said.

'I'm afraid my husband is busy tomorrow,' said Madame Mourass. It was like a game.

'Next week?' I said.

'My husband will be away next week.'

'Next month?'

We stared at each other with some irritation and then a man appeared at a doorway in the hall.

'What do you want, m'sieu?'

'I'd like to talk to you about the medal you bought in London two weeks ago.'

I don't think I would have recognized him. He was older than I had thought, in the middle fifties and powerfully built, almost squat, with thick fingers and hands. He was very fair, too fair. The skin was lacking in melanin. One knew he could never go out in the sun. His eyes were a purplish-blue, his hair, what was left of it, almost ginger. He did not have the pink-eyed look of the true albino mutation but even so his face in close-up was a forbidding sight. His clothes were as well cut and expensive as his wife's, but more casual; his cardigan was a soft peach-coloured cashmere, his shirt silk, his trousers dark blue linen, and on his feet were a pair of white buckskins obviously hand-made. He must have been at his desk when disturbed. In one hand he held a pair of heavy tinted spectacles and in the other a gold Schaeffer pen. His face showed a sudden flash of anger. 'So this is how your famous Sotheby's respect a confidence! I told them no publicity.'

'I didn't get your name from Sotheby's,' I said.

'Who then?'

'I'm afraid I can't disclose that.'

'You wish me to answer your questions but you cannot answer mine?'

'I'm sorry.'

'I, too, am sorry.'

'It isn't just idle curiosity.'

'Why do you wish to talk about this? You are in the business? If you have a client, then tell him the medal is not for sale.'

'I'm writing a book about the Dunkirk evacuation and—'

'You English amaze me! You are always writing about your defeats. Is that something to celebrate?'

'We don't look upon it as a defeat. We think of it as a great achievement.'

'How so?'

'That we managed to get hundreds of thousands of men off the beaches and back to England.'

'Perhaps if they had stayed and fought a little better you may have had some reason to call it a victory.'

I was about to remark on the collapse of France, but I checked myself. It would do no good to get into a fight with him as well. I said quietly. 'My father did stay and fight—and died.'

He shrugged. 'I am sorry, but there were many such.'

'Not like my father.'

'How is that?'

'He was shot in the back by someone with a shotgun.'

They stood staring at me for a moment, then he said, 'I have nothing to say to you,' and closed the door.

I found a motel on the coast road about eight kilometres from St Claude. It was in the worst French taste but comfortable. It owed its genesis to the colonial period and was styled after an African village. The restaurant and reception area was a large square thatched building, the rooms were individual thatched huts, grouped like a village. On a cool day at the beginning of June on the Channel coast, it seemed a long way from French Equatorial Africa. My hut was on the outskirts of the village.

I had lunch in the main building: fish soup, sweetbreads and cheese. After my coffee I found I had run out of cigars so decided to drive to St Claude. One of the front tyres had gone down a bit and I stopped at the Garage de la Croix de Guerre. The Algerian mechanic was working on a GS Club and I smiled and held up the air line. He stared back blankly and I checked the four tyres. While I was putting back the valve caps I saw him walk across to the office. A moment later he came over to me.

'Thank you,' I said, getting back into the car.

'That will be five francs.'

'What for?'

'The air.'

'What?'

He gazed at me impassively, the half-smoked Gitane—it might even have been yesterday's—in the corner of his mouth.

'You cannot just take what you want,' he said.

'I asked you. I held up the air line.'

'When you buy petrol the air is free.'

'I've never heard of a garage charging for air,' I said.

He shrugged. 'I cannot help that.'

'I filled her up yesterday,' I said. 'Don't you remember?'

'That was yesterday.'

It occurred to me that I might have space for a gallon or two in the tank which would meet the crazy requirements of the garage but I was so angry by then that I felt in my pocket and took out a five franc piece and handed it to him. He accepted it with the same impassivity with which he had conducted the dialogue. As I drove off I looked in the rear-view mirror and saw that the fat, red-faced owner had come out of the office and the two of them were standing together looking after me.

I was still angry when I arrived at the bar on the square. It was the dead time of early afternoon and I was the only customer. The barman was sitting in one of his own cubicles reading a newspaper and he looked up as I came in. He came round behind the bar. I noticed that he shuffled as he walked, dragging one foot. I ordered a brandy and a packet of Dutch cigars. There was no hint in his behaviour that we had spoken the day before or that he had given me a copy of the booklet on the bar.

'Do French garages usually charge for air?' I said.

He put his head to one side in a half-shrug and said, 'Not for air, not for water.'

'Well, your garage has. They charged me five francs to put air in my tyres.'

'Perhaps it was a charge for service.'

'I put it in myself.'

'Perhaps you owed something from a previous time.'

'It had nothing to do with any other time.'

We looked at each other in silence. There was the same feeling I'd had about the garage mechanic; the same impassivity, the same non-involvement, almost as though he were acting a part.

'Perhaps you misunderstood,' he said.

I drank the cognac and ordered another. 'Yes,' I said, 'perhaps.'

He filled my glass and placed the bottle back on the shelf. 'Tell me,' I said. 'Who is this M. Mourass who lives at "Le Tilleul"?'

'How do you mean?'

'I mean, what does he do? He seems very wealthy. Where does his money come from? Is he from an old-established family? Does he farm?'

'He does a lot of things.'

'For instance?'

He raised his eyebrows. 'For instance, he owns this bar. And . . .' He pointed across the square to the block of buildings of which the Crédit Lyonnais was part, 'And all those.'

'What about the hotels?'

'The Miramar.'

'The Relais?'

'The Miramar.'

I took out a handful of notes to pay him and as I did so I saw the plastic key-ring holder which the garage had given me the previous day. While the barman shuffled towards the till to get me change I looked at the inscription. On one side it said, *1 Juin 1940* and on the other, *Garage de la Croix de Guerre* and underneath that, *Prop: H Mourass.*

When I returned to the motel I found that someone had been in my room. My suitcase had been opened and some of my clothes were on my bed. The papers had clearly been taken from my briefcase, for they had been pushed back carelessly and some of them had been crumpled. Whoever had broken in had made little effort to hide the fact. I found myself experiencing a mixture of fear and revulsion. I sat down, for the moment unwilling to touch anything that might have been touched by the intruder.

Was this part of the pattern which had begun with someone following me? That there was a pattern I was now certain. Madame's behaviour at the Relais was part of it, so was the clerk's at the Miramar, the boorish treatment at the garage. Why? Had I trangressed in some way? Had I been insensitive to local custom in particular, or *la belle France* in general?

I had walked across the dunes, I had taken photographs, I had gone down a bunker, had lunch, dinner, lain on a bed, drunk a beer or two—there seemed to be nothing heinous in any of these. Or was it simply because I was me, David Baines Turner? But that didn't make sense either.

Whatever the explanation it was clear that I was not wanted. In which case I would leave. I'd seen enough of the village to be able to project myself back in imagination to its physical condition in 1940 and, as far as Mourass was concerned, he had made it clear that I would not get much from him.

I decided not to wait. I went through my things, found nothing missing and began to repack. For a moment I thought of going to the police, but dismissed it.

What was I to tell them? That the hotels were full? That a garage mechanic had been unpleasant? Someone had broken into my room and stolen nothing? I tidied up until the room was as neat and impersonal as when I had arrived a few hours before.

The only thing left was the *fiche*, which I had not filled in and now would not need to. And then a thought came to me. I remembered Madame entering the restaurant at the Relais with the *fiche* and questioning me about my middle name. After that she had seemed abruptly colder. Was that the watershed? Had things changed then? I kept telling myself that it could not be that because I'd never been in St Claude before. *But my father had*. Could what was happening to me now have its roots in events which had taken place almost forty years ago? I thought of the booklet which had been given me in the bar. It described the action for which my father had been awarded the VC and never mentioned him once. Yet according to Colonel Smithson, the historian of the Royal Hampshire Fusiliers, the award had been based solely on evidence by French civilians. I sat down again and lit a cigar.

Darkness came early that night. Banks of heavy cloud had begun to build up from about five o'clock and the wind had freshened. By nine o'clock the plane trees in the square were lashing their branches and causing the coloured lights to swing and dip, throwing gigantic leaping shadows on the buildings opposite. I had spent the afternoon in my room and had found out from the desk clerk that the celebrations were to begin around nine-thirty or ten. I reached St Claude about nine and the streets were deserted. I parked in an alleyway off the square and waited and watched the shadows and the wind in the trees and the occasional cat's paw of rain that blew in off the sea. It was an eerie, deserted place, and I wanted to be out of it, yet I knew I had to see whatever was coming, for the beginnings of a different type of book were growing in my mind. What had started off as a fairly clear-cut commission had now entered an area where things were not as they had seemed and I realized that there was no use trying to squeeze the unfolding story into the strait-jacket of my original concept; the concept itself must alter.

I sat in the car until twenty to ten and I began to think that the weather might have had a decisive effect on the proceedings and that the word had gone out that they had been postponed. Then I heard a noise which caused the hairs on my neck to rise. It came from across the dunes on the wind, very faint, but gradually growing in volume. It was a wailing, almost an ululation; as it became stronger, I realized that it was an air-raid siren. The volume grew and grew until the sound was in the village itself. Moments later a small Peugeot with the siren on its roof drove slowly down the main street, past the square and on towards the *plage*. It was clearly a signal, for people began to arrive immediately. They came out of the buildings opposite, from the main street and from the alleys letting on to the square. They passed my car in a steady stream. Soon there were perhaps three to four hundred in the square, the entire population of the village, I imagined. I joined them.

I felt uncomfortable and exposed. People were turning to look at me and I thought I could read anger in some faces. Was it because this was a private celebration, only for the village? But the barman had given no hint of that the day before, and surely there were other tourists from the hotels present. It was then that I saw the Algerian mechanic. He was standing a little apart from the crowd staring at me. There was a movement forward, and I went with it, my height enabling me to see over the heads of most spectators. A procession of sorts was coming up the main street and was turning into the square.

It was a small procession, consisting of one car and a dozen men, some walking at the back, some at the sides and one in front. Each carried a *flambeau* and the flames and the smoke reminded me of a *semana santa* procession I had once seen in Arcos de la Frontera. In

Spain, the centre-piece was the swaying platform holding an effigy of the Virgin Mary surrounded by burning candles, here it was the car. As it turned into the square and began a circuit flanked by the twelve men I began to understand why. It was a pre-war *traction avant* Citroën of the sort one sees now in old French *crimis*. But there was something odd about it. A sort of drainpipe rose from the back. As it drew closer, I realized it was not a drainpipe, but a chimney. I had read enough to realize that this was one of the cars adapted for burning coke when petrol was short druing the war. I looked more closely at the men who marched with it. They were dressed alike: black berets, macintoshes, black armbands, and each had slung around his shoulder a Thompson sub-machine gun which dated from Chicago's palmy days and which I knew the French had used in the Resistance. The car was clearly a symbol.

As it went around the square the crowd turned with it and watched in total silence. The men were all middle-aged, I suppose the youngest would have been in his late forties. When they drew level with me I noticed that the one who walked along in front of the Citroën was the man I had spoken to earlier that morning, M. Henri Mourass. I saw other faces: the garage proprietor, Madame's husband, the barman from the café. As I watched now on this damp and windy night, with the flames and the lights casting wild shadows on the buildings, and the curious bubbling sound of the car, I felt both moved and disorientated.

The strange cortége completed a circuit and came to a halt opposite the obelisk. We all moved across under the dripping plane trees to get a view. As I moved with them, I saw the Algerian a few paces away to my right and I was conscious of his stare. Mourass left his position and opened the door of the car and that was the first time I realized it had been occupied. I did not have a clear view, but was able to see enough. Whoever it was got out and placed a single bunch of small flowers loose at the foot of the obelisk. I could not see what they were, they may have been violets or poppies, but there were few of them. Everyone stood in silence for two minutes, then the person who had placed the flowers got back into the car and the procession completed a half-circuit of the square before moving off down the main street.

The crowd began to break up and people drifted slowly away. I said to a woman, 'Is that all?'

'It is the weather,' she said. 'We usually have a sheep roast and a dance. If it is fine tomorrow we will have it then. But we always have the flowers on June the first no matter what the weather.'

The rain was beginning to come down in earnest now and I hurried to the car. When I reached it I found one of the tyres was flat. It was the one which had caused me trouble before. I looked in the boot and found the jack and the spare wheel. It was only when I got down on my haunches to take off the wheel nuts that I saw it was no slow puncture or faulty valve. The alley was lit by a single wall-light but even so I could clearly see the cut in the tyre-wall which could only have been made by a knife.

In a curious way I took a sort of savage delight in this discovery for the way my book was reshaping itself in my mind meant that each such incident was now good copy, and as I hunched down in the rain looking at the destroyed tyre by the dim light cast by the wall-lamp I thought that this would make an effective paragraph. I pulled the wheel spanner out of the tool box and began to wrestle with the nuts. They had been put on by machine and were very tight. I worked until I was drenched with rain and sweat before I got all four nuts started and I must have been pulling at them for five or ten minutes, oblivious to everything else, before I realized I was no longer alone. Until then the alley had been deserted and I had been working in silence, now some sense of being watched caused me to look up and I saw three men at one end. I turned and looked the other way and I could make out two more shapes against the darkness of the square. I began to feel afraid; I had no doubt that they had come for me. I thought of the car. I could travel on a flat tyre and perhaps batter my way through, but the wheel nuts were off and the tyre itself could come away from the axle in the first few revolutions. The figures began to move towards me from both ends of the alley. One or two had bicycle chains in their hands. I stood up and gripped the tyre lever. I was very frightened, but it gave me a little confidence. Even if it was taken away from me at least I would get in a couple of blows. Then the single light in the alley went out and a voice, almost in my ear, said, 'This way, m'sieu.'

A door had opened in the wall just behind the car. A hand came out of the darkness, gripped my elbow and drew me back into the building. Outside there was the sound of running footsteps. The door closed. I heard the scrape of lighter flint, then came the flame, and I found myself looking into the face of the Algerian mechanic.

'You are lucky,' he said.

We were in a musty corridor that smelled of dust and disuse. I followed him through a doorway that led into what looked like a store-room, then down some steps, along another corridor of raw stone which had a strong feeling of damp. It seemed we went on for an inordinately long time yet it couldn't have been more than a minute. We had taken several twists and I thought we must be walking along the backs or sides of buildings for none in the village was big enough to maintain this length of corridor. Finally we stopped and he motioned me ahead of him into a small room. It was a lavatory, an old-fashioned one with a cistern up on the wall and a hanging chain. He squeezed past me and gripped the lavatory bowl in one hand and the pipe from the cistern in the other and pulled. With a grating noise the lavatory bowl moved forward exposing a narrow aperture in the wall. A light shone through. 'Go on,' he said. I moved forward cautiously and stood in the narrow cleft blinking to try and accustom my eyes to the light. A voice, which I knew, said, 'Please come in, Mr Turner.'

The wall closed behind me, shutting the Algerian out and I found myself in a small, well-lit room about the size of an ordinary bedroom. M. Mourass was standing next to a bare deal table, at which Madame of the Relais was seated.

'My sister and I are sorry to inconvenience you,' Mourass said, 'but it was necessary after what was said this morning. And it was fortunate for you we were able to step in when we did.' Mourass's skin looked phosphorescent in the artificial light.

Part of my mind was confused from the events in the alley, another part seemed to stand aside taking notes. Mourass was still dressed in his macintosh and beret, and the sub-machine gun he had been carrying lay on the table. He stood with his legs apart, hands thrust deep into his coat pockets. Madame, too, was dressed as a man, in similar clothing to the others and as I had not seen her among those walking next to the car I realized it must have been she who had been inside the car and who had placed the flowers on the obelisk. So she was his sister. My mind began to fit that piece of information into the picture.

Mourass said, 'We have something to say to you which I am sure will clear up the confusion you must be feeling.'

'That would be a help.'

'You must be wondering why we are dressed like this and why we are here; believe me it is not so sinister as it looks, nor is there very much of a mystery.'

'I saw the parade,' I said.

'Yes, I know.'

'The mechanic?'

'We asked him to look after you.'

'Look after?'

'I didn't mean to make it sound as though he was looking after a child, Mr Turner, but there are elements in the village who might like to make things uncomfortable for you. This, too, will be explained.'

I thought of the men with the bicycle chains in the alley and then the use of the words 'elements' and 'uncomfortable'. But I turned to Madame instead and said, 'Are you one of the elements?'

She had the grace to look embarrassed. 'I'm sorry,

m'sieur,' she said, 'but when you hear what we have to say, perhaps you will understand.'

While we had been speaking my eyes had been taking in the room. Coming through the artificial doorway had been like going back forty years. The furnishings were of the simplest. There were two narrow cots with khaki blankets on opposite sides of the room; a couple of Morris chairs, the pillows of which were worn and torn and from which some of the stuffing was emerging. The table was scarred with cigarette burns. There were half a dozen bentwood chairs. In one corner was a smaller table on which stood a suitcase. The lid was open and I could see that the case was filled with an old radio transmitter. Around the walls were notices in German. '*Bekanntmachung-Avis*' one said. Then below, in German and French, 'The following have been condemned to death for giving aid to the enemy. 1. Roger-Henry Dupont of Abbevile. 2. Alfred Jollivet of Calais. 3. Raymond Henriot of Canadelle. 4. Henri Jean Mourass of St Claude-sur-Mer.'

Mourass followed my eyes. 'Yes,' he said, 'it is our shrine. My family's, the whole village's. This was the centre of our organization during the war. But you have guessed that.'

'It fits in with the procession.'

'Of course.' He indicated the room and said, 'It is part of an old mill. This room was built specially. You see it has no window.'

He walked around, pointing to the posters and then to smaller pieces of paper tacked to the walls and said, 'Identity card, draft card, labour card, ration card—there were seven kinds of ration cards, for meat, wine, butter, bread, conserve, textiles, tobacco. Sometimes a man would need a marriage certificate—like that one—and we could print them all here in the village.'

'For Resistance members?'

'Resistance members, RAF pilots, American pilots, escapees from German prisoner-of-war camps. We hid them, sometimes for months. Then we tried to get them across the water in fishing boats. Here is something nice. Do you know what it is?'

It was a small black box from which several wires protruded. At the end of each wire was a metal disc. I shook my head.

He tapped the pieces of metal. 'These are electrodes. The Gestapo used to put them on various parts of our bodies.' He pointed to his scrotum. 'Thank God it never happened to me, but I can tell you it was terrible. The room is untouched since May 1945. It is just as it was when it was our headquarters.'

'My brother was leader of the Resistance here in St Claude when he was seventeen,' Madame said. 'When he was nineteen, of the whole coast.'

He pointed to the wall behind me. 'Do you see the list?' It was the same list, as far as I could make out, as was on the obelisk, but here it was framed and lettered in gold on vellum. 'To the Fallen', it said, and then came the names. There were more than I had thought. Perhaps nearer a dozen and, as on the obelisk, the first few were all Mourass. Next to it was a kind of display box with little purple curtains covering the front, which reminded me of the small niche-shrines in the Spanish mountains containing effigies of the Virgin Mary.

'Show him the medals,' Madame said.

'You know we are the Croix de Guerre village?' Mourass said.

'Yes. One can hardly miss it.'

'Do you know what it was for?' I nodded. 'Do you know that we were also given the Belgian *Medaille du Roi Albert* and the American Medal of Honour, Special Category?'

'And from Britain?' I said, knowing the answer.

'Nothing.'

'And so you went to buy one.'

'That is true.'

He pulled a tassel on a cord at one side of the display box and the little purple curtains parted. The medals were behind glass on black velvet and my father's VC was in the middle.

'I can understand how you feel,' I said. 'I can even understand you buying my father's medal, what I cannot understand is the booklet which describes the action, the one that was given to me in the bar.'

'I wrote that,' he said.

'You don't mention my father at all.'

'That is what we have to explain,' he said.

The explanation took more than an hour and long before it was done Madame and I had joined Mourass at the table and I had smoked a cigar. It was painful, not only for me, but for them as well, especially Madame. They took it in turns, each telling what they knew best from personal experience. This is their story, and to understand it one has to translate oneself back to that other First of June nearly forty years ago when the guns were roaring and the planes were bombing and hundreds of thousands of frightened, disorientated soldiers were struggling towards the Dunkirk perimeter and the hope of salvation. In St Claude the war was at its height. The Allied wounded were being taken off by the little ships in the estuary and the village itself was being flattened by Stuka dive-bombers, the roads were being machine-gunned by Messerschmitts. Most of the inhabitants had taken to the dunes for safety. It was into this holocaust that two men came. One was my father, the other was his prisoner, a German captain from one of the armoured regiments. My father had tied the German's hands behind his back with wire and walked him along the road at the point of his pistol. The villagers who remained had already begun their heroic fight against the German attack, using any weapon they could find, when my father and his prisoner came through the first line of the French defences.

According to Mourass they stopped at what was now the ruined farmhouse, which then had been in good repair and was owned by the Mourass family. My father brought the German into the stable-yard and Mourass's older brother told him to put the prisoner in the barn. My father stayed with him. It is at this stage that Madame, then a young girl of fourteen, Louise Mourass, enters the picture.

My father had asked for water and she had taken some into the barn. They had talked for a little while and then Louise had asked if he would not like some bread and cheese. She went back to the house to fetch it. When she returned my father closed the door behind her and placed a wooden bar across it. The first thing she saw was the German prisoner. He had been shot in the back of the head and was lying face down in the dirt of the floor, his hands still wired behind him. According to Madame, who told the story in halting and nervous sentences, my father had then raped her. He told her that if she screamed he would cut her throat. At least that is what she thought he said, for his French was bad and he had mimed the actions.

She had not struggled nor had she screamed, but had lain still under him. He was just getting off her when her own father entered the barn from the rear and saw what had happened. My father apparently turned to reach for his pistol. Mourass was armed with the only weapon he owned, his shot-gun, and he fired at my father's back.

At about the same time a British platoon had broken through the German line and soldiers were already at the farmhouse, searching the buildings for snipers. If they were to find my father, unconscious and mortally wounded by shot-gun pellets, there was no knowing what retribution might be exacted. The French villagers had already witnessed acts of extreme violence and brutality perpetrated not only by the enemy but by their own soldiers and even by French civilians on one another as they fled to safety. It was quite possible that if the British saw one of their own dying from a shot-gun wound in the back they might wipe out everyone at the farmhouse. So my father was recast as a hero, organizer of the perimeter defences, saviour of lives in the face of the enemy, now wounded by shrapnel. The commanding officer had taken hurried notes—why should he doubt?—and then he had done what the Mourass family hoped he would do: ordered my father to be taken to the boats. What happened there no one knows. He would have been one wounded man among hundreds. There was probably not even a doctor in his boat. Some time on the voyage home he died. They had sewn his body in a blanket and brought him to Newhaven. Had they been planning to bury him at sea when the white cliffs rose above them? Or were heroes brought home for burial? I would never know now.

I sat in silence—we all sat in silence—when the two of them had finished speaking. It had been vivid in my mind for I knew the farmhouse, I could see the rooms, the broken roof, the surrounding dunes. I could see my father coming down that road, I could see the ripe, youthful girl's body spread-eagled. It explained a lot of things, but not all. I could understand why the Mourass family might loathe the name David Baines Turner, but not the whole village. Nor could I understand why nothing had been said to me. I put this last point to Mourass.

'It was something you said this morning,' he said. 'You see, for all these years nothing has been said of your father's wound. The last time we saw him was when he was being carried to the river. We knew he had died, we knew he had been awarded the Victoria Cross. And there the matter had ended, or so we thought. But then you spoke of a shot-gun and I knew we had to tell you.'

'I accept that. What I don't understand is why the whole village is against me.'

'When the Germans finally broke through they found the body of the dead German. His hands were still tied behind his back. Now do you see?'

'You mean they . . . ?'

He pointed to the list of names on the wall. 'They executed the men from four village families. They shot my father and two of my uncles and also my brother.'

It was after midnight when I returned to the motel. The village was deserted and the tyre on my car miraculously restored. I drove back slowly, still apprehensive that something might suddenly happen to me. I did not try to sleep but instead took the whisky bottle out and sat drinking and smoking until well after three o'clock. Emotionally I felt as though I had gone through a mangle.

All my life, as far back as I could remember, I had disliked my father. I was going to say loathed, but that is too strong a word, for it was not so much as an individual that I disliked him—in my first memory of him he was already dead, only a body wrapped in a blanket—but the image which I was expected to live up to. He was the standard against which I was judged, the yardstick by which I was measured, his memory the shrine at which my mother worshipped: he was the only hero of a small country town, the pride of his regiment. For all I knew the bank he had worked for was proud of him. I know that old Mr Blossom the undertaker had been proud of his share in putting him under the ground. He had been held up as that classic example of English manhood, a man who came not from a wealthy or aristocratic background but who, when a job for his King and Country needed to be done, had done it. Over the long sweep of English history one might have seen him as a bowman at Agincourt; one of the thin red line at Balaclava; grimly hanging on in the Flanders mud.

Yet how fragile it all was. The very moment I had begun seriously to probe this image I had come across Rose Crawley, the little bit he'd had on the side at the bank. And I think that discovery more than anything else caused me to accept what Mourass and his sister Louise told me. The knowledge of his adultery had made it possible to accept the horror of what had happened in the French farmhouse that day nearly forty years ago. Not that I wished to accept it, not even then, for the image of his rectitude had been driven deep into me; and in any case no one wants to believe that they come from a family which contains a murderer and a rapist. But the circumstances seemed to point to the truth. Why, in any case, would Mourass or his sister lie?

I could understand now why Mourass wanted the medal; why the villagers so hated the name Turner. I sat in the chair for a long time, the pictures of the farmhouse, of the girl, the German, my father vivid in my mind. I thought of him firing into the back of the man's head; I thought of the girl with her dress up to her waist, limp under my father on the dirty floor. I thought of the execution later when the French heads of family were shot. It all added up. But the picture was too neat, too perfect. In real life there were always loose ends. And then I remembered the wounded man. According to Smithson, he had been a sergeant called Dolland, but neither Mourass nor his sister had mentioned this. According to *their* story, it had been a German prisoner. Who was right? Had they deliberately left Dolland out of it, or had he played so insignificant a part that he had faded from their memories? If it was deliberate, then why? Other questions crowded into my mind. Who had searched my room, and for what reason? And how had Mourass snatched me away from the alley before the villagers' hatred had spilled into violence? Could he even have orchestrated the whole thing?

Morning brought no answers. I had coffee and croissants in the restaurant, picked up a couple of *jetons* at the bar and telephoned Mourass. I recognized Madame Mourass's voice and asked to speak to her husband. 'Who is it?' she said, though my accent must have given me away.

'David Turner. We met yesterday.'

'I regret that my husband is not here.' Her voice was polite, but chilly.

'What time will he be back? I'll phone later.'

There was an almost imperceptible pause and then she said, 'He has gone to Paris. He will be away four days, perhaps five.' I recalled the conversation of the day before. She had said then that he would be away the following week.

'Isn't that rather sudden?'

'Yes.'

I thanked her, and rang off. I decided to phone Madame at the Relais, but then I thought it was too easy on the telephone to say that someone was away, so I paid my bill and drove into the village. I remembered the way she had told her story the previous night: everything very graphic, everything quite clear. It was probably the most traumatic thing that had ever happened to her and all the details were etched on her memory. She would certainly remember Dolland.

It was well after ten o'clock, yet the Garage Croix de Guerre had a *fermé* notice at the pumps. I drove on through the square, remembering the *flambeaux* and the marching men of the night before and even though the sun was out, I shivered. I parked outside the Relais and was getting out of the car when Madame's husband came out of the front door. He saw me, paused, then turned and went back. When I entered he was behind the desk and the office door was closed. I asked for his wife. He regretted that she was not there. She had gone into Dunkirk and would not return until later. No, he did not know when.

I wandered back into the square, unsure now of what to do. I crossed to the bar but several men looked up as I reached the doorway. Had any of them been in the alley last night? Their faces seemed hostile; their eyes full of hate. I turned away and walked under the plane trees. The old men playing *boule* stopped and stared at me. Or at least they seemed to. Everyone seemed to be staring.

I paused irresolutely outside the Crédit Lyonnais. Part of me wanted to stay at least until Madame came back, but another part wanted to leave. I tried to tell myself that my reason for wanting the latter was that I might more easily be able to check the Dolland story in England than in France, but that was pure pretence. The underlying motive was fear. What if she did not return until evening? I thought of darkness coming on. What would I do once I had seen her? Return to the motel and stay in my room? Go into the bar and lay myself open for another round of hostilities? I finally compromised. I decided I would spend the morning inspecting the canal, the railway line, the dunes, but more particularly the ruined farmhouse now that it had moved so far into the forefront of the story. I would give Madame until mid-afternoon to return and if she had not arrived by then I would set off for one of the Channel ports and a ferry home.

By now my imagination was so overheated that not even a pale and intermittent sunshine could soften the atmosphere of the dunes. They still seemed sinister. The south-wester had come up again, bending the grass along their flanks and whipping eddies of sand across in front of the car.

Soon I came to the farmhouse lying in its ruined isolation. Forty years ago it would have presented a very different sight. Then it would have had a roof of pantiles, or perhaps of reeds, its windows would have been framed by heavy wooden shutters; there would have been fences, windbreaks, much more grass, sheep. Even the shape of the dunes would have been different. Now the roofs of both the house and the barn were gone and the windows were eyeless sockets in the broken walls. I drove past the house and turned off on to a little track that must once have been used by bullock carts. I parked beside the barn. Apart from the soughing of the wind I was surrounded by a desolate silence.

The death of the house must have been started by a salvo from a German tank or perhaps a self-propelled gun, for the walls which faced towards the canal and railway had been reduced to rubble. What Man had begun, Nature had capitalized on with storms and gales of nearly half a century. Unlike the gigantic walls of the bunkers these walls bore no graffiti for there were no flat areas to write on. It was not possible to walk through the house for the floorboards had long since gone and the walls had crumbled in and weeds had grown up. I could see the old hearths but even they would soon be covered by weeds and sand. I wandered round to the barn. This was in slightly better repair. The roof had gone, but the four walls were intact and through the yawning doorway I could see a bank of drift-sand. I went in cautiously but the floor was solid and in parts not so thickly covered. I scraped with my shoe until I saw the original cobblestones.

I tried to visualize it as it must have been, with farm machinery hanging from the posts, stalls for horses, perhaps a half-floor above for hay. Is that where he had raped her? Is that where he had shot the German? It seemed as though I *wanted* to believe.

I'm not sure how long I stood in the barn, perhaps five or ten minutes, lost in thoughts of forty years before, when I began to get a feeling that I was no longer alone. Perhaps it had been caused by a noise which had filtered into my mind. I glanced around, but even the darkest corners were devoid of any living thing. I turned and looked down at the farmhouse. The barn was on slightly higher ground. I could see right through the broken windows and doorways to the low dunes on the far side, and it was there on the top of a dune, outlined against the sky, that I saw the figure of a woman. She was about fifty or sixty yards away and I could make out her big square body and what looked like a tweed jacket and skirt and heavy walking shoes. Incongruously, she held a handbag in her right hand. She seemed to be staring down at the farmhouse. Then there was a movement closer at hand, in the house itself. I found myself staring down at a man. He was wearing a grey windcheater and a peaked cap and was crouched at one of the window openings. In his right hand he held a pair of binoculars.

The woman began to walk slowly down the dune towards the house, swinging her handbag like a weapon. The man crouched lower so that she would not see him. She reached the road, paused as though uncertain of what to do, then turned to her right and walked in the direction of the village. After a minute or two the man slipped out and went in the same direction.

I stood, hardly daring to breathe. It was a curious and at the same time menacing little scene. I went to the car and drove a short way back along the road but the man and woman, whoever they were, had vanished and the dunes were empty again. I stopped. All my old fears had crystallized and I knew I couldn't face the village. I drove to the motel and had an early snack and then I phoned the Relais. No, Madame had not returned. I had not really expected her to. I felt a sense of relief. At least I had tried. I paid my bill and drove to Boulogne. I had just missed a ferry and there wasn't another until six o'clock. I spent the afternoon wandering around the shops and the docks and all the time I was haunted by the scene at the farmhouse. There had been something familiar about both the actors. I had not seen the man's face and yet I felt I had met him before. The feeling was even stronger in the case of the woman, but it wasn't until I was on the ferry that I realized who she was. It was the handbag that gave me the clue: the way she had swung it in her right hand. She was the woman I had met at the sale of medals in Sotheby's, the one who had smashed the glass case.

London

I reached Dover about seven-thirty and caught a fast train to London. It was dark by the time I reached Haverstock Hill. Instead of a beacon in the Hampstead night the flat was in darkness and I assumed Christina had gone to the Svenssons'. The lift was out of action as usual and I switched on the light at the bottom and went up the stairs. My footsteps were loud on the stone treads. The stairwell, being made entirely of brick, concrete and plaster, was an echo chamber, but even so the noise I was making seemed louder than usual. Then I realized that it was not an echo, but other feet.

The staircase itself wound around the lift shaft and it was impossible to see anyone coming. And then suddenly the light was switched off and the whole stairwell was plunged into darkness. I was between light-switches. I stopped. The other footsteps came on down towards me.

'Hello,' I said. 'There's a light-switch on the wall.'

As my eyes began to get used to the dark I saw a black shape ahead of me. I thought for a moment that it was going to attack me and I raised my hands to my face, but whoever it was brushed past me and I felt something hairy on my cheek and I got a whiff of a subtle after-shave. Then the person was past me and down the stairs and in a moment I heard hurrying feet on the gravel outside. I groped my way farther up the staircase until I found the switch. The door of the flat was open and I began to run. As I reached our landing I shouted, 'Christina! Christina!' No one answered. I pushed the door fully open and put the light on in the long passage. 'Christina! It's me! Where are you?'

I heard a voice reply from the far end of the flat. 'I'm coming,' I shouted, and ran towards her.

She was in the bathroom with Elisabeth. She had been crying and her face was blotchy. I had never seen her like that.

'What happened?'

'Someone came into the flat.'

My arrival and the consequent release of tension caused her to begin weeping again, a low uncontrolled sobbing. I had never seen her so vulnerable, had hardly imagined that she could ever be. I knelt down and took her in my arms. She was sitting on the lavatory clutching Elisabeth and we must have made a curious sight.

After a while I managed to calm her down and took her into the sitting-room. She sat on the sofa, still holding the baby tightly in her arms and I gave her a large whisky and found out what had happened.

She had been to the Svenssons', but had come back about four, had put Elisabeth down and then she had gone into our bedroom and dozed. When she awoke it was dark and she heard noises. The whole flat was dark except for a light in my study. She'd been on the point of calling out to me, thinking I had returned, but through the partially open door she had seen someone in a camel's hair overcoat. She had been terrified and gone into Elisabeth's room, picked her out of her cot and retreated into the farthest part of the flat, the bathroom, where she had locked herself in in the dark.

All this had happened about half an hour before and I realized that the noise of my footsteps on the stone stairs must have disturbed the intruder and that he had cleverly used the lights to pass me in the dark. I telephoned the police and two young men arrived in a panda car within fifteen minutes. One of them was hardly discernible behind rampant whiskers, the other was foxy-looking, and began to question Christina. She repeated what she had told me.

'Are you saying, madam,' said Foxy, 'that you don't know whether you closed the front door or not?'

'Yoh,' Christina said. 'It is what I cannot tell.' In the crisis her English was beginning to desert her.

'Hang on a second,' I said. 'There's no need to upset her further.'

'I don't want to upset anyone, sir, but your wife said she can't remember whether she closed the door or not. Does it happen often?'

'What?' I said, being purposely obtuse. 'That she can't remember?'

'That she leaves the door open.'

'Sometimes,' I said, thinking of all the times I had come home to find the flat blazing with light, front door ajar, and the volume of the stereo turned up; under those circumstances it would have been possible for burglars to empty the entire contents of the flat into a large pantechnicon in the street and drive away without Christina being any the wiser.

'Well, sir, that doesn't give us much of a chance, does it?'

Later, when I managed to prise Elisabeth out of Christina's arms and put her to bed and get ourselves another drink, I went into the chaos of my study. It had been gone over very roughly: my papers were in a heap on the floor, my camera bag opened, my books piled in one corner, the contents of my desk spread out on the rug. He must have got a fright at hearing my steps, for nothing seemed to be missing. I sat down at my desk and felt panic sweep over me once more.

I started to tidy up my things and Christina came and stood in the doorway. Clearly she did not want to be alone.

'I must have scared him off,' I said. 'You can hear footsteps on our stairs a mile away.'

'What has he taken?'

'Nothing. Probably would have bagged the camera if I hadn't had it with me. There's nothing valuable here anyway. Most burglars already own more pinchable stuff than we have.'

'You think he came off the street, just like that?'

'Probably. Typical sneak thief. Sees a door open and in he comes.'

'I'm sorry.'

'What for?'

'For leaving it open.'

She went off and came back a minute or two later with a basin of water and a rag and a bottle of pine disinfectant and began to wash my room: the woodwork, the door, the window ledges, my desk, everywhere the thief might have touched. I knew how she felt, it was as though someone had dirtied our home just by being in it. I decided then not to tell her much about France.

She came to wipe down my typewriter and said, 'You found the note?'

'What note?'

'The one I put in here.' She touched the platen.

'No. Who was it from?'

'Mr Smithson.'

'Colonel Smithson?'

'Look among your papers.'

I went through them again but there was no note. 'What did it say?'

'It was about a man. Someone who is alive.'

'Who?'

'I forget the name. I wrote it down for you.'

'Dolland?' I said. 'Would that be the name?'

'That is it. Dolland.'

I heard little warning bells go off in my brain. 'Can you remember exactly what Colonel Smithson said? No, better still, exactly what you wrote down. Can you remember that? Here, take a pencil. As exactly as you can remember.'

She leant on the desk deep in thought, then wrote: 'S. phoned. He made a mistake. Dolland is alive. He wants you to phone him.'

'That's it?' I said.

'I think exactly.'

I dialled Colonel Smithson's number, but there was no reply. Half an hour later, I tried again. Still no answer. He was either out or asleep and I decided to leave it until the next morning.

As we lay in bed that night I kept telling myself that there was no need to worry. The note was somewhere among my papers. No sneak thief would have been bothered to take it out of the typewriter unless . . . unless he was going to steal the typewriter itself. Say he'd been about to take it. He might have stuffed the note into his pocket, picked up the machine (it was a good one, an Adler electric, and would fetch a couple of hundred pounds) but stopped when he heard me. That would explain it.

I phoned Colonel Smithson early in the morning. This time he answered.

'David Turner,' I said.

'I've got some news,' he said. 'I thought it might help with your book. Do you remember I told you about Sergeant Dolland? The man your father saved.'

'Yes.'

'I said he was dead. He's not. Apparently there were two Dollands in the RHF. It was his brother who died. *Your* Sergeant Dolland is still alive.'

'Where?'

'Oddly enough, not very far from you. At the Royal Hospital in Chelsea.'

'I'm just getting a pencil,' I said. 'What's his first name?'

'Herbert. Sergeant Herbert Dolland. I hadn't been accurate,' Smithson continued in a frosty voice. 'I don't like inaccuracy. Thought I'd set the record straight.'

'I'm grateful.' And I meant it, for my interview with him had hardly encouraged me to think he might give any further help.

'How's it going?'

'So, so.' And then, before I could stop myself, I went on, 'I've been to France.'

'Did you find out anything new?'

'I'm not sure. Look, may I come down and see you again?'

There was a pause. 'If you think I can be of help.'

'I'll try see Dolland first.'

I rang the Royal Hospital, found that indeed Sergeant Herbert Dolland lived there and fixed a time to see him the following day.

I sat at my desk trying to sort out my thoughts but they simply went round and round and I achieved nothing. Too much had happened: Mourass's story, the villagers' hatred, my return to the burglary-that-was-not-a-burglary. Because I could find no answers, I became irritable and short-tempered. I drank too much at lunch, slept too heavily in the afternoon and woke feeling woozy. I spent an hour going through my records and tapes, placing each tape in its proper plastic box, each record in its correct sleeve, then I walked up to the Whitestone Pond and down the Heath for a pint at the Magdala. When I got home I found several tapes on the sitting-room floor where the child had been having a game. One of the Fauré piano quartets had been used as a teething ring. I ran through the flat.

'Look what that bloody child's done!'

Christina was in the kitchen and Elisabeth was sitting on the floor in her play-pen chewing a Marie biscuit, her face smeared in goo. Christina did not believe in washing up as she went along so the day's accumulated dishes were stacked wherever a clear surface could be found; it was an unpleasant sight.

'What?' Christina said.

'That!' I said, shaking the cassette at her.

She put down her wooden spoon, wiped her hands on her jeans and took the cassette.

'It's broken,' she said.

'Of course it's broken!' I said, hearing my voice spiral upwards. 'She chewed it. She's chewed the tape.'

'What is it?' She looked at the label. 'Oh, David!'

'You've got no right to leave her like that among my things.'

The word 'my' hung in the air like an ugly mark, but I was too far gone to register it.

'You'll record it again, they'll play it.'

'When? It could be next year. Or the year after. Can't you keep her out of the sitting-room?'

She bent forward and picked the child out of the play-pen; her heavy blonde hair swung forward as she did so and so did the front of her shirt, exposing the tops of her breasts. 'Yes, of course, David. And out of your study. And out of our bedroom, and the passage, and the bathroom and the kitchen. We could keep her in her own room. Always. Every day. And lock it.'

'A good idea.'

'And then you wouldn't have to see her at all, except just before she goes to sleep when she's nice and clean after her bath.'

It was on the tip of my tongue to say that I didn't want to see the kid even then; to blame Christina for having her at all, but I managed to stop myself; there are some things said that can never be taken back. I threw the cassette into the rubbish bin—though threw is not quite the right word: I pressed it down on the top of the rubbish that threatened to overflow on to the floor, and went back to check on the rest of my tapes.

Later I apologized and we made it up over a couple of bottles of hock but I could see she was . . . not so much offended as bewildered. She had every right to be. *I* knew what was causing the tension in me but I couldn't explain it without frightening her and I didn't want that.

But it was not only the tension that was colouring my behaviour; I was worried about the book itself. My difficulty in approaching the story now was that I *did* partly believe Mourass's story. What nagged at me was this: was I believing because I wanted to believe? In other words, was the dislike I had for my father clouding my judgement?

It was ten to eleven when I parked the car in Franklin's Row just off the King's Road in Chelsea and walked to the Royal Hospital. In some ways it was like entering a private world. In the distance I could hear the traffic on the Embankment but, surrounded as it was by Ranelagh Gardens and its own park, it was cut off from the bustle of London. Wren had built it nearly 300 years before and it had a monastic quality. I gave my name at the gate and walked on down the private road in the sunshine and the monastic feeling was heightened by the fact that everywhere one looked bowed figures were shuffling along, the famous Chelsea Pensioners, old soldiers who had fought in God knows how many forgotten wars and were now living out their last years still in the Army's care. Some were dressed in navy blue, some in their long red going-out coats. Sergeant Dolland was sitting on a bench in one of the cloisters. He was pointed out to me by a member of the office staff and I was able to look him over before he saw me. He sat staring into nothing and it seemed that unless I disturbed him he would sit there all day, not deep in thought, but in a kind of geriatric limbo.

There was a constant to-ing and fro-ing of old men as they plodded about their business but he did not look up and even when I addressed him by name it took some seconds to penetrate.

'Sergeant Dolland?' I said again.

This time he swung his head slowly to face me and I recoiled for where his right eye should have been was only an empty socket, and where his cheekbone should have been, there was a depressed area as if it had been stove in by an iron fist.

'My name's Turner,' I said.

'Turner?'

'I made an appointment to see you.'

'You made an appointment to see me.'

I wondered how long it had been since anyone had made an appointment to see Sergeant Dolland.

He got quite smartly to his feet and said, 'Good morning, Sir! Sar'nt Dolland.'

I could see that my name, and the fact that we had spoken on the telephone, meant nothing to him. He was of middle height and, I suppose, in his seventies. He had long arms and bow legs and this gave him a simian appearance. Suddenly he said with an almost childlike eagerness, 'Are we going out?'

That hadn't occurred to me. I had assumed we would either sit in a room or on a bench and do our talking there, but I said, 'Would you like to go out?

'Yes.'

'Where would you like to go? A pub?'

He smiled and again there was that childlike quality. 'Guess!'

'I'm not very good at guessing.'

'Come on.'

'You'll have to tell me.'

'The swing park.'

'Swing park?'

He pointed to Battersea Park across the river. 'All right,' I said, still not really understanding.

We drove across the bridge and parked where once the fun fair had been. Suddenly he darted off at great speed, his short legs going like pistons, arms swinging. He made a curious figure in his long red coat and Peninsular cap. I followed him along a twisting path until we came out into a small children's play area. There were swings, a roundabout, a slide and a sandpit. He climbed aboard one of the swings and sat waiting. 'Push,' he said.

The play area was deserted, thank God, as I began to push him gently to and fro.

'Harder,' he said. I thought, if I go on like this I'll be here all day. He'll be wanting to go on the roundabout and the slide and back on the swings and we'll end up making castles in the sandpit. So I said, 'I'll make a bargain with you, you tell me what I want to know and I'll push you harder. And I'll push you on the roundabout. Then I'll give you an ice-cream. How's that?'

'A penny lick?'

The phrase was fifty years out of date. 'Yes,' I said. 'A penny lick.'

He looked doubtful for a moment, then said, 'All right.'

I came round in front of him and squatted down and said, 'Does the name Geoffrey Baines Turner mean anything to you?'

The doubtful look became one of incomprehension that gradually gave way to the sly look and he said, '*You're* Turner.'

'I'm *David* Baines Turner. *Geoffrey* Baines Turner saved your life in the war.' His one watery blue eye which had been blank, almost out of focus, seemed to clear, and he nodded. 'I remember,' he said. 'He was given the Victoria Cross.'

'Right,' I said. 'That's exactly what he was given and that's what I want to talk to you about. I want you to try and remember something for me.'

'You promised me an ice-cream.'

'And you'll get it, but first you'll do some remembering and then I'll give you a swing and then I'll give you an ice-cream. All right?' He nodded.

'I want you to try and remember the last day you were in France. When you were wounded.'

He pointed to the hole where his eye should have been. 'I lost my eye there,' he said.

'Yes. It must have been a terrible day.'

'A mortar.'

'That was before you came into St Claude,' I said. He looked lost. 'The village. Never mind the name now. Geoffrey Baines Turner, who was my father, brought you into the village. Can you remember if you went into a farmhouse?'

He shook his head. 'I was hit by a mortar. That's what did this.'

'Yes. My father brought you into a village. Was there another man with you? A German?'

'I don't remember.'

He sat on the swing in the sunshine, moving his feet like a child and I thought, oh dear, oh dear!

Then he said, 'I remember something falling.'

'What was that?'

He shook his head. 'Trees and something falling. And *it*. Your father brought me in.'

'I know that.'

'And put me in the shade of some trees. It was hot.'

'And you saw something falling?'

'And there was shooting,' he said. 'And *it*.'

'There must have been a great deal. And bombs. What's "it"?'

'Yes. Bombs. The shooting was close. It seemed right in my head.'

'What sort of shooting?' I said. 'Rifles? Machine-guns? Cannon?'

'No. It didn't sound like shooting.'

'It was shooting, but it didn't sound like shooting?'

'That's right.'

'What happened then? And what's "it"?'

'You said you'd give me a swing.'

I stood up and began to push as one pushes a small child.

'Higher.'

I moved to one side and swung him higher.

Then he said, 'Somebody took photographs.'

'Who?'

'An officer. And a body. Your father's body. And then the officer robbed him.'

'What?'

'Robbed him. And then he ran. I could hear his boots.'

'Ran where?'

'I don't know. Can I have my ice-cream now?'

'Just one minute and then we'll get it,' I said. 'Let me be clear about this. My father brought you into the village . . .'

'I don't want to talk about it. You promised me an ice-cream.'

'All right,' I said wearily. 'Let's go and get the ice-cream.'

'It? It?' Colonel Smithson said. 'What do you make of that?'

I shook my head. 'He just kept on saying, "And *it*." I asked him a dozen times.'

It was a few days after I had seen Sergeant Dolland and we were in Colonel Smithson's conservatory. It was built on the south-facing wall of his house and had the same lovely views over the Hampshire countryside to the Downs. There were half a dozen garden chairs and vines in pots and some pink geraniums and he was using another part of it as a greenhouse with seed trays on staging.

He kept on glancing at the seedlings while we talked, as though afraid they might all suddenly die on him. Much of the frost had gone out of his manner and he dealt with me now as he might have done with a junior officer. We had been talking for about half an hour when his unease caused him to rise. 'Do you mind?' he said. 'I was just thinning out some winter cabbages.'

'Please,' I said. 'We can talk while you work. Always a pleasant arrangement for me.'

He smiled and his whole face changed. There was a look of relief. He walked rather painfully to the far side of the staging, facing me. 'I always feel a brute when I do this,' he said, pulling out a couple of undernourished cabbages. "They struggle so hard and then one comes along and kills the little beggars with a pinch of the fingers.'

'The law of the jungle.'

'I suppose so. They say they feel it, you know.'

'Do you talk to them?'

He looked embarrassed for a moment. 'As a matter of fact, I do. My wife started talking to the begonias and then I had the odd chat to the young tomato plants. Don't know if it made much difference.' Then he pulled himself together and said, "Well, go on.'

'I bought him the ice-cream,' I said, 'and we talked a little more in the car. Nothing new, but the picture got clearer. As far as I can make out my father brought Dolland into the square all right. In other words, he did save Dolland.'

'We know that.'

'It's complicated,' I said. 'He remembers my father putting him down on the ground and leaving him. He remembers seeing something falling. After that there's a bit of a blank. Then he heard the shooting which he describes as unfamiliar. And soon after that my father must have been hit because Dolland says he saw his body not more than twenty feet away. But God knows if it's in the correct time sequence. He was badly injured.'

'Then we get to the officer,' Smithson said.

'That's right. The officer who takes the photographs. Again, I'm not sure of the sequence. As far as I can make out he had seen the officer in the square taking the photographs before my father was killed. Then he saw my father's body. And then . . .'

'It's the next bit that sticks in the throat,' Smithson said.

'What, seeing him rob my father?'

'That's what he said, isn't it?'

'Yes.'

'Just don't understand it,' he said, shaking his head. 'I mean, use your logic. Why would one British officer rob another? What would he have of value? Especially at a time like that? I suppose he definitely *was* a British officer?'

'I was particular about that. He remembers the uniform.'

Smithson continued murdering seedlings for a few minutes longer and then came back to his chair and lit a pipe. 'Anyway,' he said, 'it doesn't change things, does it? It's basically what the official accounts give.'

I had not yet told him what I had learnt in France and I said, 'There is another story. But first of all can you tell me a little about the VC? I mean generally . . . how it's awarded and can it ever be taken away?' His head shot up. 'I'll explain what I mean,' I said, 'but tell me about the VC. You're the expert.'

'In detail? It would take us all day.'

'Just the outline.'

'Well, it was started in the middle of the last century as a sort of Order to Merit to be bestowed on persons in the Army and Navy, to *honour* them for gallantry. That was the point. And it was the first decoration for which all ranks were eligible although it was kept away from the higher ranks by a kind of unspoken law until 1917, I think, when it was won by a Brigadier General. I think I can remember part of the original warrant: ". . . the Cross shall only be awarded for most conspicuous bravery or some daring or pre-eminent act of valour or self-sacrifice or extreme devotion to duty in the presence of the enemy." There have been changes, of course. The Air Force wasn't in existence when the VC was first awarded and so there have been changes in the Warrant to take them in.' He went on for a few minutes, filling details about the award, some of which

I had come across in my research, some of which I hadn't.

'What about the medal itself,' I said. 'Can it ever be taken away having once been awarded?'

'Something *is* bothering you.'

'Don't worry. I'll tell you about it.'

'There was some cases in the early days and there was a provision for withdrawal in the Warrant itself. Hang on a second.' He went into the house and returned a few moments later with a book, found the place he wanted, and said, 'Yes, here it is. Now this is from the Warrant instituting the VC in 1856. The Fifteenth section reads, ". . . any person on whom such distinction, (in other words, the VC), "shall be conferred be convicted of treason, cowardice, felony or any infamous crime . . . etc, etc . . . his name shall forthwith be erased from the Registry of Individuals upon whom the said decoration shall have been conferred." And the pension of ten pounds a year went west too.' He flicked over the pages, but did not seem able to find what he wanted, and said, 'I think there have been eight cases altogether in which the VC has been forfeited and they've been mostly for drunkenness, theft, forgery . . . there was one Irishman who stole a cow after he had been given the award but when they investigated they found he was a rather simple man and the cow was owed to him as part of a debt and he'd simply gone along and taken the cow and considered the act within his own rights. So they gave him back his VC. Bigamy was another cause. And desertion. But that doesn't apply any longer. They can only take it back now for treason, mutiny, sedition—things like that. It was King George V who started the process of gentler treatment for offenders. He once said that no one who won the Cross should ever be forced to give it up. Even a murderer should be allowed to wear his on the gallows.'

'What if the act of gallantry for which the award was made had never taken place?' I asked.

'You're being very mysterious, Turner.'

I told him about France. I told him the whole thing

at length exactly as it happened from the time I reached St Claude to the time I left. When I finished he sat sucking a cold pipe for some moments before removing it from his mouth and saying, 'I've never heard such a pack of bloody lies in my life! That's just the sort of thing the French *would* say.'

'Look, there's no point in us getting het-up about that. Just for argument's sake and between ourselves let's say their story is the correct one.'

'Whatever for?'

'Well, Dolland's practically incoherent. He was so badly wounded his story's almost worthless. And I've checked with the French authorities. A German *was* found murdered with his hands tied behind his back and the heads of families *were* executed. Anyway, humour me for a few minutes.'

He was about to protest again, then shrugged and said, 'All right. What now?'

'What I want to know is this: how does the evidence get presented? Who makes the decision whether to award the VC or not?'

'It's supposed to be quite simple,' he said. 'There's a joint Services committee which hears the evidence.' He turned over some pages of the book, found what he was looking for, and went on: 'Here it is, Clause Eight of the Warrant: "The officer commanding the force in the field shall call for such description and attestation of the act as he may think requisite." '

'And the officer commanding in the field would have been the platoon commander in this case?'

'I suppose he would. Yes.'

'And they did collect evidence from the people in the farmhouse?'

'That is correct.'

'Does it make any difference that they were French, and not British soldiers?' I asked.

'Not at all. There have been several stranger cases. In 1943 Flying Officer Trigg attacked and sank a U-boat but his aircraft was shot down while he was attacking it and there were no survivors of his own crew to give evidence. But there *were* survivors of the crew of the U-boat. It was on their evidence that he was awarded the VC. And there was a case in the King's African Rifles when a VC was awarded on statements made in Swahili. So it is perfectly in order that the French evidence would be accepted.'

'The award was made quite quickly,' I said. 'According to my research some take a long time.'

'That's true,' he said. 'But I think in this case it is understandable. It was something to cheer up the country when we were at a very low ebb.'

'So even if my father hadn't done what he was supposed to have done, his VC performed a sort of national tonic function?'

'You could say that. But even if you believed the French story, which I don't, how do you explain Dolland? If your father didn't organize the perimeter defences of the village and if he didn't on more than one occasion go out and save French civilians he *did* save Dolland.'

'But that wasn't what he was given the VC for,' I said.

'No,' he agreed unwillingly.

'The only question I forgot to ask Dolland,' I said, 'was why he didn't give evidence at the time. Then we might not have had the two stories.'

'I can tell you that,' Colonel Smithson said. 'He was in hospital for nearly a year. It was months before he was able to speak again. No, I think you're making too much of the story by what's his name? The fellow who likes to dress up in berets and carry sub-machine guns around with him?'

'Mourass.'

'Have you any evidence he *was* in the Resistance? I've never met a Frenchman who wasn't—according to his own version. It seems perfectly possible to me that your father could have brought Dolland in, organized the defences, performed his acts of gallantry and then perhaps when the German pressure became too great, moved back into the village itself to see what further delaying tactics he could employ. That sounds to me plausible.'

'What about the German?' I said.

'What about him? Who's to say your father shot him?'

'And the officer taking photographs? The one who Dolland said robbed my father's body? He was firm on that. He never varied and I questioned him about it several times. That and the odd sound of shooting, and something falling and "it", whatever "it" was. He even remembered the camera, said it was small and flat. And the noise of the officer's boots as he ran.'

We sat in silence for a few moments then he relit his pipe and said from behind a cloud of smoke: 'Turner, I don't know what to say to you. If you're proposing to do this book you'll have to check your facts damned thoroughly.'

'That's the point,' I said. 'Where does one check?'

'What one wants, of course, is to find the photographer,' he said. 'He'd be the one to tell you what happened.'

I went back to London, taking the road through Odiham and then on to the M3. I had made certain of leaving early enough to reach Hampstead in daylight. As I walked into the flat the telephone began to ring. It was Smithson. 'Is that you, Turner?' he said. 'I've had an idea, something I thought of after you'd gone. May give you a line.'

'Good. Fire away.'

'It's about the officer Dolland said he saw. The one taking the photographs.'

'Yes.'

'He was certain that he was an officer and in British uniform?'

'Absolutely. One of the few things he *was* certain about.'

'War correspondents wore uniforms. They were honorary officers. So were the accredited photographers. This chap could have been a newspaper or news agency photographer. I mean, it wasn't the time or place for the ordinary odds and sods to be taking snaps, was it?

Not with the Jerries bombing and strafing and generally creating hell.'

'No,' I said. 'Not really.'

'But if he'd been a real photographer, he would just have been doing his job.'

After he had rung off I sat at my desk for a long while. My main feeling was one of irritation at myself: I had once been a newspaper reporter, I had worked with photographers countless times. Why hadn't I thought of it? Why had it been Smithson who put it together? Down in the marrow of my bones I knew he had to be right. As he had said, it had not been the time for snapshots.

It has been said that if it does nothing else a university education teaches you how to search for information; something of the same could be said for newspaper journalism. First I telephoned the Imperial War Museum and asked for Miss Kendal, who had helped me on several occasions when I had been researching the Victoria Cross. We had struck a rapport.

'It's me again, David Turner,' I said.

'How's the book going?' Her voice was warm and interested and in marked contrast to many other voices which had answered my questions in the past.

'Not too badly, but something's come up and I need your advice. I'm trying to trace a newspaper or news agency photographer who was accredited to the British forces at the time of Dunkirk.'

'There must have been dozens,' she said.

'Yes, that's what I thought.'

'Is he still alive?'

'I don't know.'

'The War Office should be able to tell you, they'll have a list.'

'The trouble is, I don't know his name.'

'That does make it difficult.'

'I know where he was seen, though.'

'That wouldn't help.'

'Not even if he had been killed?'

'I doubt it. You could check that quickly enough if you knew his name, but without it the only way would be to get a list of all newspaper correspondents in the area at the time and track down each one.'

'That could take months.'

'Of course, if he was dead or missing the International Red Cross might have some record of him. If he had been captured his name would have been on the POW exchange lists and if he had been killed there would be a record of the place.'

'So what I must do is find a place and a name and put them together.'

'Except that entries are filed by names and not by places. You might try the Roll of Honour.'

'Where's that?'

'Army Record Centre at Hayes.'

I rang the Centre and spoke to an Army clerk. 'You must have a name, sir,' he said. 'Can't do anything without a name.'

'I thought there might have been an extrapolation—'

'A what, sir?'

'You know, an extract of names into special categories.'

'No. No extracts, sir. The Roll's made out into Regiments and Corps, sir.'

'All right,' I said. 'Thank you.'

Then I did what I had been reluctant to do: I went to the newspaper files, but not in Fleet Street. I remembered that the Westminster Library in the Charing Cross Road had a *Times* index with every copy of *The Times* dating back to the nineteenth century on microfilm. I booked the reading machine and took a tube into town. Once again I hit a snag. I couldn't look up anything in the Index itself as I had no name, so I started going through each column of every newspage for the whole of June 1940. At that time newsprint was not so severely rationed as it was to become later in the war and there was a great deal to read in each issue. It took me nearly three days before I was done and by that time my eyes were sore from staring through the enlarger and my arm was tired from cranking the microfilm in the machine. And at the end of it I had nothing.

I finished the month late in the afternoon and there was a general stir among the girls behind the desk as though it was now time for me to leave. There was nothing I wanted to do more. I wanted to go home and I wanted a drink. But I thought I'd have one last try and I asked for the microfilm for the three months beginning July.

'We're closing up this department,' one of the girls said, doing her nails with an emery board.

'I'll only be a few minutes.'

'We're not supposed to.'

'I'm sure you're not supposed to do a lot of things.'

She smiled then, a nice smile for six-fifteen, and went off to fetch the microfilm.

I found what I was looking for almost immediately. It was a small paragraph at the bottom of the second Home News page. The single column heading said, PHOTOGRAPHER MISSING. I began to take down the story.

> Mr. Stefan Granek, 30, a Polish-news photographer, has been posted as missing, presumed dead. He was one of several photographers working for International Press, the London-based photographic agency, and was last seen covering the evacuation of wounded from the Canadelle River near Dunkirk on June 1. Mr Leopold Finer, Managing Director of International Press, said that Mr Granek had been working for them since last year. Before that he had worked in Warsaw and had brought out some of the last pictures of the German *blitzkrieg* on Poland. Mr Granek was married with a family but it is not known whether they survive.

That was all, but it was enough. There it was, all these years later, mixed up with stories on how to conserve coal, how to make pies without meat, how to redesign an old coat to make it chic. *Missing, presumed dead.*

Within twenty-four hours I had managed to establish one basic fact: Mr Stefan Granek did not appear on any official list of the dead of World War II.

That discovery changed everything. Until then my search for this ghostly photographer had been more in the nature of flexing disused journalistic muscles, now I had to decide whether I was going on. The search for Granek would take time and money and quite likely lead me nowhere. If he had been thirty in 1940 it was probable that he was now dead, or even if he was alive he might be back in Poland or in some geriatric ward. The more I thought about it the more I cringed at the time and effort that would be involved. And yet my father haunted me now more than he had ever done before: who *was* this man who had been held up to me as the epitome of Christian virtue, a man who was supposed to have saved a French village, who was said to have murdered a German officer, raped a child, who was supposed to have been a gentil parfit knight, and at the same time an adulterer; and above all a man who had given his country hope in one of its darkest periods? If I ever wanted to find the truth it looked as though I would have to find Stefan Granek. And even if the truth were unpalatable it could hardly be worse than the story I had already heard. I was certain now of only one thing: it was not the only story.

'You say he was born in Poland?' Mr Schuman said. 'I was born there too.'

'You surprise me,' I said. 'You have no accent at all. And your name sounds more Austrian.'

'I can hear my own accent, especially on a tape recorder. As for the name, my own was unpronounceable outside Poland; too many Ss and Zs and Ms and Ns and not enough vowels for you English.'

We were in the offices of the British Red Cross just off Belgrave Square; Mr Schuman was Assistant Head of Tracing. He rose from his desk, walked to the long, elegant window and looked out over the traffic. He was a tall man wearing a silver grey suit, white shirt, silver tie; his immense head of hair was white; he gave an impression of a successful business man from Middle Europe. Still with his back to me he said, 'We must have come out of Poland about the same time, your Mr Granek and I. But I was somewhat younger; in my eighteenth year.'

'May I ask why you chose Schuman?' I said. 'Was it the musical association?'

He turned back and smiled. 'That is right,' he said, 'but I spell it with only one N."

"Why not Chopin? That's a good Polish name and easily pronounceable. And only one N.'

'I was at the Conservatoire in Warsaw,' he said. 'I was to give a concert. My first public recital. The *Davidsbundlertanze*. You know them?'

'Yes.'

'Then the Germans came over and bombed us.'

'So you never played them?'

'Not then nor any other time.' He stepped forward and struck the desk in front of me with his left hand. I thought the blow would split the wood, then I realized the hand was made of pink coloured metal. 'I lost my hand in the bombing. Schumann was the last composer I ever played so I thought—why not?'

He sat down and said, 'But that doesn't help you.' He pulled a pad and pencil towards him. 'You know, it's a thousand to one that you will ever find your Mr Granek.'

'I have a compelling reason.'

He waved at a pile of letters on his desk. 'Everyone has a compelling reason.'

For a moment I did not understand and then I said, somewhat surprised: 'Are these requests to find missing people?'

'Just today's post. There will be more tomorrow and the next day and every day.'

'I thought that problem was over.'

'Most people think so. About forty-five per cent of our work in London is still trying to trace and reunite people who were separated by World War II. There are two hundred thousand refugees in Britain alone.'

'In the early sixties, just after World Refugee Year, the *Guardian* asked me to do a series of articles on what had happened to the World War II refugees,' I said.

'Oh, you wrote those articles,' he said. 'I remember them. We have them on file, with all the others that were written. Of course, very few are published now. You know about Arolsen?'

'The town? It has something to do with refugees, hasn't it?'

'It's the tracing centre in Germany. Forty million names are on file there. If your Mr Granek was captured by the Germans at Dunkirk it would not have taken them long to establish that he was a Pole, which means he would have ended up in a work camp or a concentration camp and not a POW camp.'

'Is there no chance of doing anything from this end?'

He smiled without much mirth and said, 'Do you mean with my help?'

'Well, is there any way I can do it?'

He leant back in his chair and tapped his pencil on the surface of his desk. 'Can you think how much work I'd get done if all these . . .' He flipped his hand at the letters again '. . . came in and asked me to make personal searches for them?'

We looked at each other and the old feeling of antagonism, of unwillingness to ask favours, that had made my career in newspaper journalism unprofitable, surfaced, and I stood up and said, 'I'm sorry to have taken up your time.'

He raised his pink metal hand. 'Now Mr Turner . . . please . . . let us not part bad friends. Your Mr Granek interests me if only because there but for the grace of God . . . let me make a few phone calls. Why don't you go and see about this photographic agency? Perhaps it does still exist. I will be in touch with you.' I gave him my telephone number and he took me to the door. 'One tells oneself one must never really become involved with the lost people, but sometimes it is very difficult. I was also in France at the time of Dunkirk; in a French prison camp. I had been trying to get to England. I might easily have been picked up by the Germans and like Mr Granek would simply have disappeared. It would be nice to think that someone would bother to search.'

It was not difficult to find out what had happened to the agency for which Stefan Granek had worked. International Press had gone bankrupt in the middle 1950s when newspapers began to die in Fleet Street. The goodwill had been bought by Universal Press Photos which themselves had been taken over by a firm called Photo Peel of Lambeth in 1966. There was no Photo Peel of Lambeth in the telephone directory but there was one listing an address in Bayswater. I made an appointment.

It was mid-morning of a grey day when I parked the car in Sussex Gardens. Photo Peel's studio was in Bathurst Street about a hundred yards away but I was at least fifteen minutes early so I strolled across the Bayswater Road into Kensington Gardens. There were a lot of tourists walking about aimlessly. Some were wearing French tartan tammies on their heads and carrying orange rucksacks on their backs. I walked down to the Italian gardens and stood at the low railings watching the fountains. A party of shrill-voiced school children were being led towards the Peter Pan statue.

The house was on the north side of the street and the door was opened to me by a woman of perhaps forty with a beautiful, coal-black face, wearing a flowing mammy-cloth of sludgy browns, yellows and blacks.

'Good morning,' she said.

'Good morning, my name's Turner. I have an appointment to see Mr Peel.'

'Yes, of course, Mr Turner, do come in.' Her voice bore almost no trace of accent.

We were in a narrow house with big, high-ceilinged rooms that had been chopped up into smaller rooms; it reminded me of a dentist's suite. She led me into what looked like a waiting-room furnished with a low G-Plan suite covered in purple uncut moquette, and walls papered in dark green hessian. On the floor, what I could see of it, was a gold Wilton wall-to-wall. There were cardboard cartons everywhere. Some contained photographic chemicals, but most seemed to contain magazines of the naked lady variety.

'I'm Mrs Peel,' said the black lady, leading me between the cartons and seting me on the uncut moquette. 'My husband will be finished in a moment.' She removed a black bra from the sofa and placed it on one of the cartons. 'Would you like some coffee?' I noticed a glass beaker of Cona on a machine in the corner and said, 'Please.'

'Jesus H Christ!' a man's voice suddenly roared, seemingly in my ear. 'Get yer bleedin' head and shoulders back!' It came from behind a thin partition.

'Milk?' said Mrs Peel.

'Yes, please.'

The telephone rang in the next room and the same male voice said, ' 'Ullo!'

'Have you come far?' Mrs Peel said.

'From Hampstead.'

'That's not too far. The traffic's been . . .'

'Tits?' said the loud voice. ' 'Course I can give you more tits. Haven't I always? No . . . it was *you* said—'

'The traffic's been rather bad this summer,' Mrs Peel said. 'So many foreigners.'

'Yes,' I said. 'They're becoming too much for London.'

'Hair?' the voice said. 'What you want? Pubic? Underarm?'

'It just seems to get worse and worse,' she said.

'Listen, darlin', she's got nipples that'd put your eyes out. I'm telling you! All right. I'll put her in a blouse and spray it.'

'Much cooler today,' said Mrs Peel.

Her black face was calm, her eyes interested in me, the weather, the tourists, her voice gracious, soft. I could have been taking coffee with the head of a charm school in Bryanston Square.

'All right,' the voice said. 'And the same to you, with

rubber connections.' He put the phone down. A moment later the adjoining door opened.

'Here's Mr Peel now,' said the lady in the mammy cloth. 'Mr Turner, dear.'

A large man entered the room. He was wearing denim trousers, white high-heeled boots, a denim safari jacket which was unbuttoned and showed a fat hairy stomach. Around his neck hung a medallion on a gold chain. His head was bald except for a tonsure of grey hair; in his right hand he carried a Hasselblad. He was about fifty and dressed to represent someone twenty-five years younger. He reminded me of a trendy movie director I had once known.

'Wotcher, mate,' he said. 'What's it all about? Talk or pictures?'

'Talk.'

'Can't talk without a drink.' His breath was already adding a tang to the air.

'I've just had some coffee, thanks.'

He disregarded that. 'Come on, we'll go upstairs.'

A voice called from inside the studio, 'Do you still want me?'

'No,' he shouted. 'You can get dressed now.'

The studio door opened again and a young woman came into the room. She was one of the most beautiful things I'd seen. She must have been about seventeen years old and was dressed only in a pair of the briefest black pants, nothing more than a wisp of material. Her skin was the colour of Mexican honey. I understood what Mr Peel had meant on the telephone about eyes being put out. She came past me and seemed to be searching for something. Then she saw the bra, reached for it and put it on.

'This is Victoria,' said Mrs Peel. 'Our eldest.'

'How do you do,' I said.

'Hi.'

We shook hands and then she went out of the room and up the stairs, her bottom jigging from side to side in a jaunty manner. As though reminded of something, Mr Peel turned to his wife and said, 'That was Julius on the blower. They want more of the old busty substances.'

'Oh, yes,' said Mrs Peel.

He turned to me. 'Come on, let's get that drink.'

I followed him upstairs to their sitting-room, which was all yellow awnings and cane furniture and a bar in one corner; the whole thing reminded me of a veranda lounge on a cruise liner. He threw himself down on a lounger and indicated another with his hand.

'Haven't we met?' he said.

'I don't think so.'

'I've never taken your picture, have I?'

I shook my head.

'I could have sworn . . . You ever work in Fleet Street?'

'For a while.'

'That's it then. Never forget the old dial.'

'You were there, were you?'

'Thirteen sodding years.'

I felt something go off inside me like a small warning bell and I realized why I had been reluctant to go back to Fleet Street for information: some vestigial scoop syndrome still remained. I had a good story and I didn't want anyone else to get on to it.

'Mr Peel worked for the *Daily Sketch*,' Mrs Peel said, as though it had been *Paris Match*.

'And the *Daily Graphic*, and the *Empire News* and the *Sunday Dispatch*,' he said, reeling off the names on several tombstones.

'What about that drink!' He turned to his wife. 'Me wantum drink. Savvy?'

She rose and glided beautifully to the bar. 'How about you, Mr Turner?'

I wondered what would follow coffee this early in the day and said, 'Vermouth.'

She poured me a vermouth on the rocks, a large Scotch for her husband and one of the same size for herself. 'That's the girl,' he said, taking the glass from her hand. As she turned away he casually reached out and gave her bottom a friendly squeeze.

'Cheers,' she said, holding up her glass.

'I like something I can get a grip on,' Mr Peel said thoughtfully. 'White women are too bloody thin. It's all this Twiggy nonsense. Men like something they can get their teeth into. Don't they, love?' He swallowed half his drink and said, 'You wanna see what they're like where she comes from, mate. Backsides on them like mares.'

I felt obliged to say something. 'Where do you come from, Mrs Peel?'

She sipped her Scotch and stared over the glass without answering, and he said, 'Lagos. We met in romantic circumstances, didn't we love? I was out there covering some darky revolution in sixty-five. I said to the doorman at the hotel, can't you find me a decent woman in this dump, and half an hour later she turned up. Miss Tiger Lady, 1960.'

Mrs Peel sipped her whisky and nodded. Mr Peel drained his glass, looked at mine and saw with some surprise that it was hardly touched. He gave her his glass and she poured him another. 'Remember that night?' he said to her. 'My God, that was a time. Remember the song we used to sing? "D'ye ken John Peel with his prick of steel and his balls of brass . . ." ' He gave a roar of laughter and she smiled gently. ' ". . . and a carrot up his arse" . . . That was a hell of a time. "Oh, he fucked all day and he fucked all night and he couldn't get the horn in the morrrrr-ning . . ." Remember?' He laughed and sat down again. 'And when I came back to Blighty she came too.'

'We were married at Caxton Hall,' she said proudly.

'I made her famous,' he said. 'D'you remember the Ebony Look? Jewellery against a black skin? I was one of the first. Ve-ery sexy.' He reached behind his neck and pulled off the gold chain and medallion and threw it over to her. 'Show him, love. Show him how you used to look.'

She put the medallion over her head and suddenly unfolded her robe, slipped her arms out of the sleeves and let it drop to her waist. The gold chain against her black satin skin and the medallion nestling between her two beautifully shaped breasts, was a magnificent sight. She was Victoria's mother all right.

'What did I tell you?' he said. 'Still as good as new.'

Modestly she closed her gown and handed him his medallion.

'All right,' he said. 'Talk.'

'Tell me,' I said. 'Do you still work for Fleet Street?'

He cocked an eyebrow at me and said, 'Why?'

'I just wondered.'

'Look, mate, I still sell them the occasional picture, but I can't stand the place. And the sort of money they'd pay for a tip-off on a story wouldn't buy me a lens filter.'

I told him as much as I thought he should know, which wasn't very much, just the bare bones of the thing: that I had been asked to do a book about my father, that there was some question now of what had actually happened in France and that the one person who might be able to help was the photographer called Granek who had once worked for a company whose name now only existed as part of Mr Peel's little dead empire.

He listened quietly, only once handing his glass to his wife who poured him another drink. I began to get over his vulgarity. Perhaps he was the sort of man who liked to shock initially, to see what the reaction was. When I had finished he said, 'Jesus, mate, you're going back a bit.'

'Nineteen fifty-five,' I said. 'That was when Universal took over International Press, which was the outfit Granek had worked for. Then you bought Universal.'

'Universal.' He tasted the word. 'Sounds pretty grand, doesn't it? But it was only two rooms in St Bride's Lane, and all I wanted was the dark-room equipment.' He scratched his bald head and said, 'What is it exactly you want?'

'Anything,' I said. 'I'm trying to trace him. There may be something, some record, if you've still got the company files.'

'I don't know what I've got, all I know is she says I never throw anything away. Let's have a shufty.'

He led me downstairs again through the studio with its white umbrellas, its cameras, its batteries of lights, the fake backdrops, showing seascapes, sand and beach balls, into a different part of the house. There were three rooms off a corridor.

The first was a dark-room, everything neat and professionally laid out, prints drying, huge enlarger, sinks, taps, safelight; in contrast the other two rooms were piled high with junk. In the first I saw an enormous amount of camera and dark-room equipment. I noticed a couple of old Gnome enlargers of the sort I had once used; a Speed-Graphic he must have used twenty years before, a Rolleiflex and an old battered Linhof, and in the corner of one room a beautiful wood-and-brass tripod camera. He paused and looked down at it and said 'That was my father's.' He picked up a card which had fallen to the floor, blew the dust off it and handed it to me. It said, 'G Peel, 84 Crescent Road, Lambeth. Passport photographs. Bar-mitzvahs. Weddings a speciality.' He took the card from me and tossed it back on to the floor. 'Don't think the old man would approve of me nowadays,' he said. 'He never took a nude in his life. Still . . . times change. Anyway, it's not as bloody marvellous as they say. Like being in a chocolate factory. They put up notices for the workers: eat as much as you like. Management knows they'll be sick of chocolates in a couple of days. With me it's flesh. Nothing in here. Let's look in the next one.'

More cartons in the third room. Girlie magazines. 'That's where they'll be if they're anywhere,' he said, pointing to a pile of soap cartons in the far corner. We picked our way past a maze of stop baths and developing tanks and old glazers and began to manhandle the cartons. They were stuffed with papers, letters, contracts.

'Nineteen-sixty-six,' he said. 'This is the Universal stuff. If there's anything it'll be in the last boxes.'

The telephone rang and he said, 'Bloody thing.'

I heard his wife's voice calling, 'John, it's for you. Julius.'

'Oh, Christ, all right.' Turning to me, he said, 'Go ahead. You'll get dirty, though.'

I switched on the light and began to go through the boxes that had been at the bottom of the pile. Again there were letters, bills, receipts for dark-room equipment, bills for film. There were the financial books and then a file which was labelled EXPENSES. I flipped through it. These were on International Press paper and were for the early 1950s. One man had gone out on a job and claimed eightpence for bus fares and three-and-six for lunch. It was a different age. I went further back until I came to the 1940s and suddenly it was there, in a file marked WAR OFFICE INFORMATION.

The file on Granek consisted of a single sheet of yellowing foolscap on which a short biography had been typed. There was little more than appeared in *The Times*. I noted that he had been born in 1910 in Lodz and that he had been married in 1934 and that he had picture credits on material he had brought out from Poland with *Life* and *Look* magazines in America and *Picture Post* in Britain. He had worked for several periodicals in Warsaw—I could not tell from their names whether they were newspapers or magazines—and had joined International Press in January 1940. The document did not give a home address in London. It wasn't much from which to build up a picture of a man. To have been married in 1934, one year before I was born, made him seem very old and very remote, yet I suppose he would have been about the same age as my father had they both lived. But I didn't have to conjure up a picture because stapled to the top of the page was a passport photograph on the back of which was written, 'Stefan Granek, c/o International Press, Bouverie Street, London EC4.'

It was odd looking down at him in a musty photographer's store-room in London so many years later. The picture showed a man with a long, narrow face, close-fitting wavy hair and a straight parting on the left side. Although he wasn't smiling his mouth was slightly open. He had protruding teeth and one of them was chipped as though from a fall or a blow and I wondered if it had happened on his escape from Poland. His eyes were pouched and there was an expression of sadness in them as befitted someone who had left his wife and children behind and didn't know whether they were still alive. I stared at the picture for a long time. He would look completely different now, so it would be of no help at all, yet it fleshed him out for me; it gave me an image, albeit more than thirty years out of date, of the man I wanted to talk to.

Mr Peel returned and I showed him what I'd found.

'Mournful-looking bugger, isn't he?'

'You never came across him, I suppose?'

'Before my time.'

'Would you mind if I kept this for a bit?'

'Help yourself.'

By the time I reached home the day had improved and there was a warm sun striking through the sitting-room windows on to the couch. I sat down and Christina brought a bottle of cold wine from the fridge and gave me a glass. She threw a cushion on to the floor and sat in the sun sipping the wine. I had the file on Granek and showed it to her.

'How sad he looks,' she said.

'He'd left a wife and children in Poland.'

'Does it help?'

'Not much. At least I know what he looks like.'

We talked about Granek and I went back over some of the things we had discussed at other times. Then I told her about the Peels and she laughed and said, 'Better than mine?'

'Not better. Different.'

We drank the wine in the sun and the bottle didn't last long. Perhaps it was the warmth and the lassitude but the wine seemed so agreeable that she said, 'Should I fetch another bottle?'

'You randy old thing!' I said.

'What about you? Voyeur!'

She came back a few moments later with the bottle, but she had also changed her clothing. She was wearing a pair of black tights and nothing else except a necklace comprising a copper disc on a thin leather strap.

'Choose,' she said, standing in the middle of the floor. 'Mrs Peel or me.'

'What are you trying to do? Turn me into a racialist?'

The telephone rang and she turned and walked to the door. She had an extremely nice bottom; one you could get your teeth into, as Mr Peel would have said. 'You're jigging,' I said.

At the door she stopped and turned and in that manic un-Scandinavian way, said, 'I'll do the jiggery, and you do the pokery.'

I put on Pink Floyd's 'Wish you were Here', which she had once described as 'good for frownication', and sat back sipping the wine, feeling slightly high.

'Who is it?' I said. Dressed as she was and holding the bottle in her hand she evoked a piratical air.

'Someone from the Red Cross. A Mr Schuman.'

I didn't want to talk to Mr Schuman just then. 'Tell him I'm about to have carnal knowledge of a consenting adult and I'll ring him this afternoon.'

When she returned I said, 'What did you tell him?'

'What you told me.' She sat down on the cushion in the sun and the faint bloom of hairs on her breasts turned golden.

'And what did he say to that?'

'How lucky you were.'

I kissed her bare shoulder. 'Don't flatter yourself.'

In the afternoon I went to the old War Office library in Whitehall to see if there were any other journals or diaries which might contain something on the battle of St Claude-sur-Mer, but there was nothing. I came out into hot sunlight about half past three. Whitehall was full of tourists, most of them on the opposite side of the road to me photographing or just staring at the mounted guards in front of Horse Guards, who must have been sweating heavily in their burnished cuirasses and helmets. I had never seen so many cameras. There were instant cameras and polaroid cameras and box cameras and expensive single lens reflexes with telephoto lenses and wide-angle lenses and zoom lenses. A great number were carried by small Japanese men who photographed anything that moved and I gave a mental genuflection in the direction of Eastman Kodak. Then

I realized that someone in a light grey jacket was photographing me. I was looking directly into the eye of a telephoto lens in the crowd across the street. Then the man moved and I saw that it was not a camera, but binoculars. The second lens had been blocked from my view by someone's shoulder. For the past few hours I had managed to forget what had happened in France, but now apprehension came flooding back. Whoever it was looking at me must have realized I had spotted him for he disappeared into the crowd. I told myself that nothing could happen to me in the middle of Whitehall on a sunny afternoon in the middle of summer. But I remembered the man in the ruined farmhouse in France. He too had had binoculars. I crossed the road, dodging through a line of No. 11 buses. I wanted to know who it was. I was frightened, yet more afraid of not knowing. I had been followed into that ghostly bunker in France by some faceless person, now I was being followed again. I pushed into the crowd in front of the horse-guards. I could hear a dozen languages and not even the noise of the traffic could blot out the sounds of the camera shutters. And then I saw him, or at least his jacket, the light grey jacket that I'd seen from across the street. He was moving through the crowd up towards Trafalgar Square and I pushed after him.

Fear often causes shame and shame causes anger and as I pushed after him I became angry. I drew up with him and grabbed his sleeve and pulled him around to face me and said, 'What the hell do you want?'

He came round very quickly, like a cat, and how he did it I don't know, but I was no longer holding his sleeve, he was holding my hand and had twisted it so that I felt a pain shoot up to my elbow. 'What's that to you, mac?' he said. He spoke in a nasal American accent. He was a man of about my own height but more solidly built, and under his grey brushed-denim jacket he was wearing a T-shirt emblazoned with the words JUDO KWAI.

'I'm sorry,' I said. 'I thought you were looking at me.'

His binoculars hung on a leather strap around his neck.

'The trouble with all you fuckin' limeys,' he said, 'is you're all a bunch of fuckin' faggots.'

'I'm sorry,' I said.

He gave me back my hand and said more cheerfully, 'Forget it. No harm done.' He moved on up towards Trafalgar Square. I watched him for a few moments. He was much broader than I had thought, with heavy shoulders and a thick neck and he rolled slightly as he walked. I had thought the man with the binoculars was taller and thinner. I crossed back to the car and turned suddenly. Out of the corner of my eye I saw another grey jacket, just a blur this time, as it moved into the archway. Was this the man who had been watching me? If I ran across now would he be an Argentinian or a Bulgarian who would be even more offended than the American? Was my imagination over-heating as it had done in France? I got into the car.

Whitehall was solid with traffic going north so I went around by Chelsea, planning to cut through Hyde Park. But when I got to the bottom of Lower Sloane Street I realized I was within a stone's throw of the Royal Hospital. I decided to give Dolland one more try. If he wanted half a dozen ice-creams he could have them. He could go on the swings and the roundabouts to his heart's content.

I went to the offices on the left just before the main building and spoke to a woman who could have been the actress who always played vicars' wives in post-war British movies. She had a reddish, scoured complexion, eager and earnest eyes and faint traces of a moustache. One knew that the words 'sacrifice' and 'service' would never be far from her lips. I told her who I was and that I had seen Dolland before and asked if I could see him again. She said, 'Well, really, Mr Turner, this is *most* exciting, isn't it?'

'In what way?' I said.

'It's not often one of our in—one of our gentlemen has a chance of becoming famous at his time of life.'

'I'd hardly say famous.'

'Oh, but he will.'

'That's very flattering, but I'm afraid my books don't sell in those quantities.'

'What about TV?' she said.

'What TV?'

'He's going to appear on television.'

'Really?'

'A man came to see him today. You've just missed him.'

'What television?'

'It's a joint Anglo-French programme about Dunkirk.'

'I didn't know about that.'

'He's going to be the star. He was in a village. And they're going to make the film in the village. It was awarded a special medal for bravery. Isn't that fine?'

'Yes, I know the village.'

'They're going to pay him. He was wounded there, you see.'

'Yes, he told me that. And he's in one or two books as it is.'

'That's not quite the same as being on TV,' she said. 'Oh, I didn't mean that to sound . . .'

'You're quite right. It isn't the same as being on TV. You say he's gone out?'

'He's with one of the TV men now. One of the French team.'

'You didn't catch his name.'

'No. He phoned this morning.'

Again I felt that slight sickening clench of the stomach. 'Do you know where they've gone?'

'No, but not far. Sergeant Dolland wasn't dressed for going out. He'll be back for supper. You can wait if you like.'

'I'll leave it until tomorrow,' I said.

But I wasn't going to leave it until tomorrow. I had a good idea where they'd be. I drove over Chelsea Bridge and into Battersea Park. Occasionally I saw a Chelsea Pensioner in his red walking-out coat, but whenever I caught up with him he turned out, like the man in Whitehall, not to be the person I was looking for. I searched for half an hour and then I thought of the swings. I walked as fast as I could; soon I was running towards the secluded play area where I had taken him before. Even before I saw the small crowd I knew what I would find. I had known it instinctively since I had spoken to the woman at the Royal Hospital.

He was lying near the swings stretched out on his face in the dust, arms spread out, legs bent under him. A policeman was there, and a woman with a baby was telling him what had happened. Her voice was shrill with hysteria.

'. . . higher and higher,' she said. 'He was laughing. The man was pushing him higher and higher. Then suddenly he seemed to let go and he flew through the air. He began to fall. He fell and he never got up. It was awful. Horrible.' She turned to the crowd and said, 'I saw it all. I was over there. He wanted to go higher, see. Higher and higher. "Higher," he kept shouting. And the man kept pushing. And suddenly he let go.'

'Where's the man now?' the policeman said.

'I don't know. I had to put my baby in the pram.' Then she began to cry. A middle-aged woman put her arm around her and said, 'It's all right, dear, he wouldn't have felt nothing.'

'Has anyone sent for an ambulance?' another voice said.

The policeman turned from his notebook. 'It's all been taken care of, sir,' he said. 'Thank you very much.'

I stood at the front of the circle while the policeman questioned other mothers who'd had their children in the play area. Dolland must have come down on his head, for his neck was twisted as though it was broken and there was a huge bruise down the front of his face. His nose had almost entirely disappeared. Bits of gravel had been smashed into his skin. He was a pitiful sight sprawled out on the hot dusty earth but there was nothing one could do for him. I turned and went back to the car.

* * *

As I walked into the flat the telephone began to ring. It was Mr Schuman's secretary. I had forgotten all about him. They had been in touch with Arolsen, she said. Stefan Granek had been captured by the German army at a small French village called St Claude-sur-Mer in June 1940. He was not a British subject and so he had been separated from the other British prisoners at the time. He had been sent to a foreign labour camp and later to Mauthausen concentration camp in Austria. At the end of the war he had been moved to a DP camp in the Vienna suburb of Simmering. That was all. For further information she said I would have to apply to the relevant authority. I asked who it was. She said the High Commissioner for Refugees in Vienna.

I sat at my desk for a while. The name Simmering brought back memories. I saw it again in my mind's eye, the huddle of single-storey wooden building standing forlorn in the driving rain. I realized I could have been there at the same time as Granek was.

Christina was playing with the child in the kitchen. 'What now?' she said.

'Nothing,' I said. 'Absolutely nothing. Fini. The end.' I thought of taking a photograph of the two of them. Mother and child. Cartier-Bresson. A 'Family of Man' study. I thought of Dolland's broken body.

'What are you talking about?' She got to her feet.

'This bloody search.'

'What have you found out?'

'What does it matter? It's never-ending.'

'Of course it has an end! Tell me!'

'They have traced him to Vienna.'

'Then you must go to Vienna.'

'For Christ's sake, what happens if I get there and they say he went to Brazil?'

'Then you must go to Brazil.'

'Great. And what do we eat?'

'Granville will pay.'

'You must be joking.'

'You can't give up now. You've said over and over what a good book this will make. Even if you don't find Granek you can use all the search material.'

'I'm not going,' I said angrily. 'That's *it*!'

I was nervous and sweaty and knew that if we went on talking I would begin to yell at her as I had a day or so before. I went and lay in a bath and held my hands out in front of me. They were shaking. I kept on seeing the woman with the child saying: 'Higher and higher!' I saw Dolland's body flying off the swing, arcing through the air, falling, crashing. I hoped he was so demented with pleasure by then that he had not known what was happening; had not seen the ground race up to meet him; had not felt the crunching blow as it crashed into his face. I could see it all clearly, except for the figure behind him. Who had been pushing him? Mourass? One of the men from the alley in St Claude? Why not? Mourass seemed to own the town's buildings; why not its flesh and blood? But why had they killed Dolland? Or perhaps they hadn't; perhaps it had been an accident. The man who had taken him out had probably wanted information, just as I had. Had he demanded an ice-cream? Wasn't that part of his fee? And had he promised the same information that I had sought? Everywhere I turned there were questions, but no answers.

Vienna

The Vienna suburb of Simmering lies in the south-eastern sector of the city and to reach it one has to drive along the Rennweg, a dreary road of small shops and apartments. It's the road that takes one to the airport at Schwechat and the huge Central Cemetery where Mozart lies; roads that lead to airports or cemeteries always have a grim quality.

I drove out to Simmering in a little hired VW on a dull close morning, remembering the last time I had been this way. Then, in 1962, I had been taken to see Simmering camp by a middle-aged lady who wore a Tyrolean hat with a feather and carried a loden cloak. She worked for *Caritas*, the Catholic voluntary agency, and we travelled in a Mercedes.

I turned left off Simmeringhauptstrasse and drove down towards the Donau Canal. Simmering camp had been thrown up after the war on an area flattened by Russian shelling. It had been a dreadful place: wooden barracks, tarred-felt roofs, weeds, pools of stagnant water, paper blown against the chainlink fence. I remembered the smell of cabbages and drains and the alleys lined with empty shell cases to try and give the place an ordered look.

Now, as I drove down the mean little streets, I half expected to come on it again, but of course it had vanished years ago and in its place was a vast housing estate for workers; the blocks of wooden barracks had given way to concrete apartment houses surrounded by exhausted grass. I stopped the car and sat there helplessly, not knowing where to begin.

I had first come to Vienna between leaving school

and going up to Cambridge as part of the European Youth Movement to help rebuild the city after the war. I had arrived soon after Russia had agreed to Austria's neutrality and had pulled her troops out of Vienna. There was a wonderful feeling in the air that communicated itself from person to person and it was the best time to be there. Years later, when I landed my first important freelance commission, it had seemed only right it should take me to Vienna.

After Cambridge I had worked for *The Scotsman*, the *News Chronicle* and the *New York Times* before resigning to operate as a freelance. At that time Fay was working as research assistant to Professor L. V. Drake, the medieval historian, which was just as well, for in the first six months of freelancing I earned less than two hundred pounds, so we existed on her salary.

Then, typically, out of the blue had come the commission from the features editor of the *Guardian* who asked me to go to Europe to see what was happening to the refugees of World War II. Two years earlier, in World Refugee Year, there had been a flock of articles about the scandalous treatment they were still receiving and he wanted to know if the position had improved. We decided to concentrate on Austria because there had been a number of camps at Linz, one very bad one at Salzburg, and several others round Vienna itself. The day before I was due to leave the photographer who was to accompany me went down with hepatitis so I was asked to take the pictures as well for a higher overall fee. Fay took leave from her job and came with me. It was a mistake.

I left the VW and walked through the housing estate until I came to the office of the housing manager. His quarters were in the basement of one of the blocks and as I knocked and went in he was hastily removing the debris of second-breakfast.

'Gruss Gott,' I said. 'Herr Brainin?' The label on his desk gave his name.

He wiped away some crumbs. The room was pungent with the smell of smoked sausage.

'Bitte?'

I had already made up my mind which approach to take and now in a mixture of English and execrable German I began on a complicated story about having come from Australia to see if I could trace part of my family born in Austria. An uncle, I said, had once been in a DP camp which I understood was in this area.

Herr Brainin was a short man with a plump face and square rimless glasses. He had worn an expression of mild irritation at being disturbed, now it changed to one of bewilderment as he tried to penetrate my monologue. He let me ramble on as he lit one of those long and vicious cheroots with the straw mouthpiece. Suddenly he said, 'Bludger!'

I had once worked with an Australian and had become familiar with some of the slang he constantly used. As far as I could recall 'bludger' meant something like 'idle sponger' and, coming as it did from this serious face behind its rimless glasses, it carried the impact of an insult.

'No hoper,' said Herr Brainin. 'Bludger. Fair dinkum. You beaut. Sheila.' He smiled an innocent smile. 'You know of Bondi Beach?'

I began to grasp what was happening and nodded.

'There are many sharks?'

'Some.'

Herr Brainin's brother had migrated to Australia twenty years earlier and Herr Brainin, through the letters he received from Sydney, had developed a passion for the country and would have migrated himself had his wife not been unwilling to leave Vienna. 'My brother went to work on the Snowy River scheme,' he said. 'Do you know of it?'

'Yes,' I lied.

'Now he has a patisserie in Sydney. Brainin's. You know of it?'

'I'm afraid not.'

He looked mildly disappointed. He talked about his family for ten minutes before coming back to my problem. Yes, there had been a camp here, he said, but it had been torn down in the middle sixties and had been replaced by this estate. As far as he knew all the records were with the High Commissioner for Refugees in the First District. That's where I should begin. I told him I had already made an appointment with them for the following day—this was true—but had wanted to see where my uncle had lived. After all his sister was my mother who herself had migrated to Australia before the war and Herr Brainin knew what old people were like; she would want every detail. He nodded; yes, he knew what old people were like. His mother, God bless her, had been like that before she died. He himself had never seen the camp. Was there no one else, I asked? He paused and thought for a moment then clicked his fingers. 'Frau Nissel!'

'Who is Frau Nissel?'

'She lived in the camp. She was the very last person in the camp. When they built the estate they gave Frau Nissel an apartment. She has been here in this place since the camp was built more than thirty years ago.'

'Could I see her?'

'Perhaps.'

'Now?'

He picked up a ring of keys. 'Come.'

I followed him across an expanse of wet grass and into one of the concrete blocks. Frau Nissel's apartment was on the ground floor. He rang, got no answer, and opened the door with one of the keys. We went into a small bachelor flat. On the right was a bathroom, on the left a kitchenette, and beyond that a large single room with a double-glazed window looking out onto misty grass and dwarfish trees. The place was spotless. A table under a heavy green plush cloth stood against one wall. Opposite was a bed covered in the same green plush and next to it was a heavy glass-fronted bookcase. Everywhere were potted plants, mainly ferns. The room was of another age and so was the person sitting in the chair by the window. She was the oldest living being I had ever seen and made Mr Blossom, the undertaker, seem almost boyish by comparison. She sat very still, her hands folded in her lap, looking out at the bleak urban landscape. She was so old and her skin was so lined she appeared to be made of stitched leather patches; and so small and thin and wasted I felt I could have picked her up with one hand.

'Frau Nissel,' Herr Brainin said in the sing-song voice one uses for children. 'I have here a guest for you.' If she heard she did not react. 'All the way from Australia.' He turned to me. 'She hears, you know, but sometimes she plays these little games. Come now, Frau Nissel, a gentleman caller.' She ignored us. 'Frau Nissel has a story. Won't you tell the gentleman your story?' He turned to me again. 'Sometimes the newspapers send a reporter and he makes a story. Where are your stories, Frau Nissel?' He went to the bookcase and opened it with the air of someone who had done it often before. 'Ah, here are the stories.'

He pulled out a large buff-coloured envelope and emptied out a dozen or more cuttings on to the table. They were all in German and French. 'You see Frau Nissel is a famous lady. Isn't it, Frau Nissel? Look at this: from *Die Welt* and here from *Frankfurter Allgemeine Zeitung*, even *Der Stern*.' I began to read one from *Le Figaro*. It was a story of collapsed countries and erased borders, of people moving across the face of Europe seeking refuge but finding only guns and bombs and camps. Through this tapestry, like a gold thread, moved Frau Nissel. Names came from the text: Russia, Poland, Czechoslovakia; Danzig, Baku, Odessa. She had been travelling since the Russian revolution and had finally washed up like some piece of Danube flotsam, in Vienna. By that time she had a daughter with her. She had seen a granddaughter born in Simmering camp, and her daughter die there. She had lived in the camp until it closed; she had nowhere else to go. While I was reading I heard a noise near the window, a dry, rustling sound. Frau Nissel was talking.

'Ah, she welcomes her gentleman caller,' said Herr Brainin.

I went across and squatted near her chair. She was speaking French. 'Do you really come from Australia?' she said.

'Yes.' I felt ashamed of lying to her but there was no other way now.

'What is it you want?'

'I told her.

'Granek?' she said, and shook her head. 'There were so many. They came and came and some left. The lucky ones.'

'He had been a photographer.'

'Photographers, butchers, chemists, professors, railway workers . . . everyone was here.'

'He was Polish.'

'There were many Poles. But also Rumanians and Serbians, Slovenes, Ukrainians, Latts . . .' It was like a faint bugle call for lost millions.

'I have a picture of him.' I gave her the one I had disinterred from Mr Peel's dusty store-room.

She took a pair of small wire spectacles and placed them on her nose. Her eyes were violet. She stared for a long time and then gave a shrug. 'It may be.' she said. 'There is something about the face, the teeth perhaps. There was a photographer once. He used to take pictures of the children. Sometimes he took them of my granddaughter when she was a child. Sometimes he sold them and made a little money. When he did he would give the children sweets. It may be, I cannot say.'

'Is there any chance of seeing your granddaughter?'

'Perhaps.'

'Where does she live? Here on the estate?'

She shook her head. 'She got out, thank God. She lives in the Cottāge.' She gave a slight inclination of the head in the direction of Herr Brainin. 'He has her telephone number and address. In case. You know he comes in every day, to see if I'm dead. He is quite a good man but I will not speak German to him. One day he will find me dead, that is why he has my granddaughter's address. Though I don't want a funeral, just a few ashes in the canal. Why not?' She turned away and stared from the window. It was as though a curtain had come down between us and I knew the interview was over.

I had lunch in a gasthaus on the way back to the city and then took the Gurtel to the Cottāge. Frau Schidloff, Frau Nissel's granddaughter, lived in a large and rather grand house in Gustav Tschermakgasse, a lovely, tree-lined street. I suppose the Cottāge area was the equivalent of St John's Wood or parts of leafy Hampstead, though nearer the centre of the city.

The ornate iron gates were open and I went up a flight of marble steps to the front door. I realized Frau Schidloff did not occupy the entire house, for there were six names and six bells. I rang her bell and waited. And rang again.

'You waiting for Frau Schidloff?' a voice said. A young man was standing at the bottom of the steps. 'She doesn't get back til seven.' His accent was American. He was dressed in a plaid shirt, jeans and a pair of wooden clogs.

'I'll come back,' I said.

'Sure.' He watched me with cold eyes as I went to the gate.

I had an afternoon to fill so I drove out to Sievering and up Krotenbachstrasse where the European Youth Movement had had its camp. It looked different now. Then there were only the trees and the vineyards and the *heurigers* but now much of the land had been sold for housing. I had come here later with Fay and shown her where the camp had stood; even then I had hardly been able to recognize it, now it was a street of wealthy apartments. I went to the top of Krotenbachstrasse and here little had changed. I turned up on to the hillside and stopped outside a *heuriger* I had first visited more than twenty years before and again with Fay: Zietsman's. In the evenings the car park was usually full, now mine was the only car there. I went into the gate and walked up through the vines, past the benches and tables under the apple trees, to a wooden shack in the middle of the vineyard where one could buy smoked sausage, rye bread, sliced green peppers and cheese. A youth was sitting on a high stool at the cash register, reading.

'What would you like?'

'A *viertel* of white.' I took the flask and glass to a table. The heavy grey skies made it seem too lonely outside.

On a clear day the view from Zietsman's was one of the loveliest I knew. I remembered having saved it for Fay as one might a present. We had arrived there about five on a warm summer's evening. I had ordered wine for myself and *krakel*, a kind of lemonade, for her and we sat down in the shade of a tree and I said, 'Look down there.'

The ground fell away to the valley of Neustift am Walde where there was a church with a golden onion dome and white walls. Surrounded as it was by vineyards and huge leafy trees it was the kind of urban view I had seen nowhere but Vienna.

Fay had glanced down indifferently, then turned back to me and said, 'Why do we *always* come to places like this?' She'd had her dark hair close cropped and it seemed to sharpen her profile, giving her a nervous, tense appearance.

'Places like what?'

'Where all we do is drink.'

'And talk.'

'All right—and talk.'

'Don't you like drinking and talking?'

'I wanted to see the Breughels.'

I had been out to Linz that day interviewing refugees who looked more like characters by Goya and I was tired and depressed.

'I was at the clock museum in the morning and the catacombs after lunch. You said you were coming home early.'

Fay's idea of a holiday was a time for self-improvement. She had already been to Schubert's house, to the Bauern Museum, to the museum of furniture off Mariahilferstrasse, to the Kunsthistoriche, to Schönbrunn, the Hofburg, the Spanish Riding School; she had been to see the Hieronymus Bosch, Franz Joseph's gardening tools, an exhibition of painted furniture, one of Art Nouveau . . .

'Don't you think for once it's pleasant just to sit and relax without trying to improve yourself?'

'Don't sneer.'

'On the contrary I envy you your capacity. Only it's so remorseless.'

'How often do you think I'll get the chance?'

'Vienna won't go away.'

'But we will.'

'We can come back.'

'On what?'

That killed the evening and we spent it as we had spent so many, in a state of armed neutrality. The following evening I took her to a Heiler recital at the Stefanskirche and afterwards we strolled up to the Amhof and had a sausage and salad in a wine cellar. But instead of the usual Dubonnet she said she'd have white wine so I ordered a litre of Neuburger. She drank her first glass with a slight shudder and then, with the meal, drank four or five more and had a brandy with her coffee. I had never seen her drink so much and she was unsteady as we went out into the square. When we reached the hotel she began to undress in front of me; this too was unusual because she was modest to the point of prudishness. We made love as though it was something new for us, as though we were strangers who had found a mutual chemistry. But it was too good. She over-acted. Then I saw her face turn away and two tears squeeze from under her closed eyelids. It was such a sad, transparent sight that I stopped and fell away to one side. She made no effort to keep me and I switched off the light and lay in the hot darkness, a sick feeling in my stomach.

We never spoke about it; we went on with our lives as though nothing had happened but we both knew that something had and that it wouldn't go away and that it would be difficult to live with. In the end, of course, it became impossible.

I don't know how long I sat there drinking the slightly acid wine and thinking about the last time I had been there with Fay—perhaps half an hour—then something made me uneasy. I felt I was being stared at. I glanced at the boy but he was still on the high stool by the cash register reading his book. As I turned back my eye caught something in the window, just a flash and it was gone. For a moment I thought it might be a branch moving in the wind then the photographic image was recalled by memory. It had been a face pressed against the misty glass, a dark shape, with eyeless sockets, and something small and white in the foreground.

I got up and walked to the door. The air was heavier than ever and the low cloud was like mist. I might have been miles from Vienna, in the deepest countryside, for even the city sounds seemed muffled. I peered around the corner of the shack but could see no one. There was a noise of scraping behind me, like a leather sole on cement. I turned and saw that the boy had come to the door and was regarding me with interest. Somewhere on the hillside below I could hear a car engine start, the unmistakable rattle of a diesel.

'Auf wiedersehen,' I said.

'Danke sehr. 'Wiedersehen.'

I walked down through the trees and vines and wondered that it had ever been a place of gaiety and sunshine. It compounded my unease and I wanted to get out of it and out of Vienna as quickly as possible. The old ghosts were dead; others were haunting me now. It was past four o'clock so I decided to return to the hotel and rest for a few hours until it was time to see Frau Schidloff.

It was nearly eight when I drove to the Cottãge. I turned into Gustav Tschermakgasse and left the car some way from the house because of the heavy kerbside parking. Many of the cars bore CD plates.

There were lights on all over the house but I had no way of knowing which was Frau Schidloff's apartment. I rang her bell and leant forward to listen to the answer-phone but instead a door opened halfway along the front of the house and a little girl, about five or six, called 'Pappi . . . ! Pappi . . . !' and began to run along the gravel path towards me. Then she got a good look at me, stopped and said, 'You are not Pappi.'

'No,' I said.

'Who are you?' She spoke English with an American accent.

'I'm David. And you?'

'Maria. Pappi is away.'

'Hello, Maria. Is your mummy in?' She was confused for a moment, then shook her head. "Are you all by yourself?' I asked.

'She's with Uncle Ray.'

'Oh, where's that?'

She raised her eyes, indicating one of the upstairs rooms. I walked back with her towards their front door which had originally been French windows letting out on to the lawn when the house had been a single unit. The child had left the door open and I could look into a large sitting-room in one corner of which was an ornate colour TV showing a kids' cartoon. A man came down the stairs. I saw him first as a pair of wooden clogs; he was the young cold-eyed American who had spoken to me on the steps that morning.

'I've come back to see Frau Schidloff,' I said.

The child said, 'I thought it was Pappi, Uncle Ray. I thought it was Pappi.'

He turned to her and indicated the TV. 'Why don't you go on watching?'

A woman's voice called from the top of the stairs. 'Who is it?' She sounded tense and frightened.

The American said, 'It's no one.'

'I thought I heard Maria . . .'

'It's no one.' He turned back to me with his light blue, chilly eyes. 'What do you want?'

'I wanted to see Frau Schidloff.'

'Mummy . . . Mummy . . . his name is David. He is for *you.*'

'What does he want?' Frau Schidloff said.

'If I could have a word with you . . .' I called up the stairwell.

'What is it? Is it about my husband?'

'No, it's not about your husband. It's something from a long time ago. I'm trying to trace someone.'

She came down the stairs patting herself into place. Her hair was awry and the top two buttons of her blouse were undone. She was about ten years older than the American and good-looking in a sensual way, with thick lips and a big mouth; her hair, heavy and silky, reminded me of Christina's. As she came nearer, I saw she had a slight hare-lip on the left side. Strangely it did not detract from her sensuality, on the contrary, because of the fullness of her lips and the fact that her mouth was large, it gave an added attractiveness. 'I'm sorry to bother you,' I said, 'but I was talking to your grandmother this morning and she suggested I come to see you.'

'My grandmother! What were you doing with my grandmother?'

'Do you mind if we sit down for five minutes?'

I think they were both so relieved at my reason for calling that they were prepared to forgive the intrusion. Uncle Ray poured us bourbon and water and we sat at the end of the room farthest from the TV set. A photograph on a small table showed Frau Schidloff on the arm of a man in the uniform of an American colonel. I guessed he was the missing husband. The child wandered back to the TV, sat down and put her thumb in her mouth. I went into my routine, which was becoming almost second nature. Frau Schidloff held the photograph of Granek and said, 'There is something familiar . . .'

'Your grandmother said there was a man who used to take photographs.'

She bent forward, staring at the picture. In profile her high cheekbones shadowed her face but one's mind filled in the harelip. She nodded. 'Yes, of course! That's him. That's the man. I remember this chip.' She pointed to the picture. 'His tooth. He used to photograph the children. Sometimes he used to sell the pictures. I remember he gave me chocolate once.' She sat in silence for a moment as though everything was coming back to her. 'When I was about fourteen he wanted to take me nude.' She let the sentence hang there, then looked up under her eyelids at the young American and I wondered if I had interrupted him before or after; if it was before he had my sympathy.

'And did you let him?' he said softly.

She kept him briefly in suspense, then smiled. 'Of course, why not? I didn't have anything to be ashamed of. And he paid. One day he wanted to rub me with oil. He said it would photograph better. He said he could make me into a model.'

Again there was a pause. 'And?' the American said.

A dog barked outside the house. Frau Schidloff and Uncle Ray swung towards the door. Maria ran to a window, opened it and called out, 'Pappi! Pappi!'

I watched her mother. The tension was back in her face. There was safety in numbers but that didn't seem to help her much. She crossed the room and opened the door. 'Charles?' she called. 'Is that you?' No one answered. After a moment she closed the door and handed me the photograph. 'I'm sorry,' she said. 'I must get Maria her food.'

'Just a moment. You remember the man?'

'I told you.'

'What happened to him?'

She thought and then she said, 'They sent him to England.'

'England!'

'Yes, I remember now, there were many people who were angry. People who had waited longer than he, families.' Her tone was bitter. 'My mother died in the camp. She would have been all right if they had let us go, but they said he had lived in England before the war so he had priority. He was always talking about it.' She looked at her watch. 'I'm sorry, but that's all . . .'

'Do you know where in England he went?'

She shook her head. 'I must go.'

I went down the marble steps towards the street and as I did so I heard her say, 'No, not now—'

'But you said—'

'Charles could come back any time.'

'F'Chrissake he's not due till—' And then they shut the door.

I went through the iron gates into the street. Everything was still, even my footsteps seemed to be muffled by the misty darkness and the air was warm and heavy with moisture. Herr Brainin had said there had been no real summer yet, only rain followed by misty days, followed by rain. I began to make my way in the direction of the VW when I heard the noise of a car starting somewhere behind me. It was that unmistakable sound, pins being shaken in glass, of a diesel. I stood at the kerbside waiting for the car to pass before I crossed, but it didn't come. I could hear the engine idling somewhere in the mist away to my right. The street was packed with cars, mostly Mercedes and Opels. I turned and walked along the pavement and as I did so I heard the rising note of the car pulling away from the kerb. I should have stopped and turned and perhaps even walked back towards the house if only to satisfy myself. Instead I walked more quickly.

I didn't know who it was. I recalled the noise outside Frau Schidloff's flat: the dog barking, the child calling 'Pappi, Pappi.' Had her husband been waiting? Was he following me now? I walked even faster. This was ridiculous. It wasn't *me* he wanted.

I broke into a run, dodging in and out of the trees on the pavement. All the time I heard the car somewhere behind me. I reached an intersection, turned right and felt the ground change its slope; I was now running downhill. What I wanted was lights, people, crowds. Here there was only silence and the thud of my running steps and the clatter of the diesel engine as it churned through the darkness behind me.

I had abandoned my own car. I had even abandoned rationality. I was simply running blindly. I had no idea how far I ran or for how long. I was spurred only by the thought that there was someone in that car who wanted to damage me. Visions of a jealous husband holding a gun or an axe swept through my mind, a demented man, perhaps frothing at the mouth, unwilling to listen to reason.

An autobus was coming to a stop across the road. I ran to the far side and saw an old woman getting off with a heavy suitcase. My brain cleared sufficiently for me to realize the car's driver would expect me to board the bus. Instead I said in English, 'Please, allow me,' and I helped the old woman down the steps and took the suitcase and held her arm and walked along the pavement with her, bent over as though I was talking to her. The autobus pulled away from the kerb and then I saw the car. It was a Mercedes, not new, the sort they sometimes use in Vienna as taxis. It went on down the street, following the autobus. It passed close to me and I could see the driver plainly. He was hunched over the wheel, staring ahead of him. He had a cigarette stuck in one corner of his mouth and I realized it was the face I had seen looking in at me at the *heuriger*, the white thing in the middle of the face had been the cigarette. He was the man who always smoked cigarettes like this, the Algerian garage mechanic from St Claude-sur-Mer. I felt a tug at the suitcase and looked down to see the old woman pulling at it and shouting at me. She thought I was trying to rob her, so I put the case down. At that moment an autobus came along in the opposite direction. I climbed aboard and sat well down in my seat as we made for the centre of the city.

I didn't feel safe until I reached my hotel room and I looked out of the window before switching on the light. I saw the wet shining cobbles and the shadowy outlines of buildings and the lamps that hung on the wires swaying in the wind and knew there was something going on of which I had only the barest inkling and although I had conquered my panic I was still very much afraid. I closed the curtains, switched on the lights and took out my bottle of whisky. I sat down on the bed and had a stiff drink. I knew then that I couldn't go on with this alone. I would have to get help from someone.

London

'Of course you need help,' Victor Granville said shortly. 'I don't know why you didn't tell me all this when you came back from France.'

I had told him most of what had happened over the past two weeks. We were in his penthouse suite overlooking Victoria. It was lunchtime on Sunday and we had just finished one of his little 'bachelor spreads', as he called them: Persian caviare, cold game pie from Harrod's and a triple-cream cheese. Now we were at our coffee and he was dispensing Upmanns from a humidor. The thick white carpet, tubular steel and smoked glass furniture made me feel I was sitting in a photograph from *Maison et Jardin*. He was also dressed for *le weekend*: black Gucci moccasins, white pincord slacks, a dark blue Viyella shirt, yellow knotted silk square at the throat.

'Let's go back a bit. When you lost the Algerian in Vienna you went back to your hotel,' he said. I nodded. 'I can't think why he didn't pick you up the following morning. He must have known where you were staying.'

'I moved to a different hotel,' I said, remembering the flutterings of panic that had still affected me as I drank my Scotch in the bedroom. I had made my decision then and, having made it, felt instantly better. I had packed up immediately, paid and gone. Luckily I had picked up a cruising taxi and had told him to take me to the Hotel Casino-Zügernitz in Döblingerhauptstrasse where Fay and I had stayed. It was sufficiently remote to give me a feeling of safety.

'And then?' Granville said.

'The following morning I went to the Office of the High Commissioner for Refugees.'

He finished fiddling with his cigar, rose and walked to the huge plate-glass windows through which one could see the black shape of the Grosvenor Hotel. With its domed roof it gave one the feeling of being in Moscow.

'And you got nowhere, of course.'

'I wasn't Granek's blood relative.'

'I could have told you that. I could have helped you in several ways if only I'd *known.* What about this chap Schubert?'

'Schuman. Same thing. He's helped as far as he can.'

'Did you tell him why you wanted the information?'

'Part of it.'

He lit the cigar and stood staring out over the still Sunday afternoon. It was close and thundery. After a moment he said, 'You had no right to go off like that.'

'Why not?'

'You left me absolutely in the dark. I knew nothing. Not a bloody thing.' Granville liked to win and I had handicapped him by not giving him everything in the beginning.

'I don't like to discuss things when I'm writing. Everything gets talked out and stale.'

'I knew damn-all about what you found in France. Nothing about Dolland or Smithson or Granek.' All through lunch he had been hiding his irritation.

'You don't seem to understand what's happening. I'm investigating my *father*. For the whole of my childhood he was held up as an example of moral rectitude and courage. I was supposed to model myself on him. Now I find out all sorts of things aren't as they should be; the possibility that he was a total fraud even to the VC. You can't expect me to come running to you with all this undigested.'

'We had an agreement, David, and we'd advanced—'

'I thought we'd get around to that. Do you want it back?'

'Don't be so silly.'

The fact was that we both knew I had something

much more exciting and saleable than the original idea. If I repaid him the advance my agent could explore the market a bit more and get double or treble what he was thinking of paying.

He must have guessed what I was thinking, for he said, 'You're wrong if you think you've got a marvellous story or a marvellous book . . .'

'Let me repay you then, and we'll test it,' I said sharply.

He stopped me with his upheld cigar. 'It's not a marvellous anything and you know that as well as I do. It's a fragment.'

'All right, but it will be, once I get the ending. If I live that long.'

'I told you earlier, if they had wanted to harm you, they'd have done so. And I think Dolland's death was an accident. No, it's Granek they want. The question is, why? He either knows something or had something. It's got to be one of those two. And we have to find him before they do.'

'What about your policeman?' I said.

'My what?'

'Your porno policeman. You know. What's-his-name. Mightn't he help?'

'Billy Pearson? He's not *my* porno policeman.'

'He found the names of the buyer and seller of the VC.'

'It's an idea. And he owes me one. I'll get in touch with him.'

Half an hour later he saw me to the lift. 'By the way, does your . . . Swedish lady know all this?'

'Christina? No. Not all of it. She was worried enough by the burglary in the flat. I haven't wanted to load her with anything more.'

Going up Lisson Grove I thought I saw a Renault following me, but it turned left into the Euston Road. I used my rearview mirror a great deal now and when I was on foot I found I kept looking over my shoulder. When I got home I bolted the door. Whatever Granville said, I still felt naked and exposed and vulnerable.

He telephoned me two evenings later, sounding tired

and irritated. It had been a long forty-eight hours for me. I had spent much of the time at the window staring out at the road. Once I thought I glimpsed the garage mechanic, but when I studied the man through binoculars I found it wasn't. The fact that I could not see anyone did not mean I wasn't being watched. The houses opposite were rabbit warrens of furnished rooms and the road was filled with cars; there were many vantage points.

We never left the flat empty. When we wanted a pound of butter or a box of matches either Christina or I went out alone. Most of the time we stayed behind the double-locked door. It was a strange, troglodytish sort of existence, full of tension and shadows.

'We've got something,' Victor said. 'It's a start, anyway.'

'I'll get a pencil.'

'It's not that much, you won't have to write anything down. In fact, better not. Billy said it was more difficult to get information of this sort than a credit rating on the PM. Anyway, here it is for what it's worth: our Mr Granek came into this country on a refugee intake in 1960. He stayed first at a reception centre at Bordon in Hampshire, later on he joined a firm of industrial photographers in Basingstoke—I have the name if you need it—but he was not with them for more than about eighteen months. His last adress is Hay-on-Wye.'

'That's a place, not an address,' I said.

'It's the best Billy could do.'

"That's it?' I said. 'Granek, Hay-on-Wye?'

'That's it.'

'Do we know if he's still there?'

'Billy looked in the telephone book, but there's no Granek listed.'

'So he just gave up?'

'I couldn't ask him to go on. He had his own job with a security firm. You'll have to go there.'

We arranged for Brigitta to come and stay with Christina and I left early the following morning and was on the M4 by seven o'clock. It was a humid day, very still.

My eyes kept flicking to the rear-view mirror but it was impossible to sort out the pack of cars that stretched behind me along the motorway. All I could see were dark shapes. I could not make out size, model or colour, except when they closed on me to pass, and no follower was going to do that. Once or twice a car hung back suspiciously, keeping its distance, and my stomach contracted. But then when I slowed down it would pass me.

The countryside was lovely. The sun was streaming down and the trees were in full leaf. There was a special poignancy about it. Vienna had been different, so had France. They did not belong to me. But this was *my* territory. The flat in Hampstead, the road outside it, even the wider spaces of England, were mine. Anger came, because other people were using me in my own landscape. I welcomed it, because it blotted out other emotions.

I crossed the Severn Bridge and wound up the Wye Valley, passed Tintern Abbey, then cut off the main road and took a series of lanes until I hit a C road going through the mountains. I stopped on a rise and looked back; there was nothing in sight for miles. As I went farther into the Welsh Marches rain, light at first but becoming heavier, set in and it was pouring when I reached Hay-on-Wye.

It was like no other English town I had ever seen. There was a Continental quality about it, northern Spain or Italy, perhaps. It was built on rising ground with a small castle at the top. The crooked, narrow streets fell away, twisting and turning and worming their way into the centre of the town. It was not very big, half a dozen small streets with shops, crisscrossed by winding alleys where people lived above their businesses. It advertised itself as having the largest stock of second-hand books in the world, and certainly every third or fourth shop seemed to have dusty volumes in the windows. It was the sort of place where one might have expected a thriving artists' colony, but the only evidence I could see of craft work was one shop selling hand-made baskets and wood-burning stoves. In the doorway sat a young man wearing dungarees, with a Mormon beard and bare feet, who directed me to the police station in an accent acquired at one of the major public schools.

I checked with the police, and at the library, I went to the Town Hall, I asked a postman on his rounds and the driver of the refuse lorry. But no one knew of a man called Granek. I asked at the electricity board and the Co-op, I rang the Voter's Roll in Hereford but they would not give any information over the phone. Then I had an idea I should have had when I arrived; I asked to be directed to a photographer's studio, after all he might still have been in business.

Following directions I turned into one of the narrow lanes that burrowed into the centre of the town and found myself stopped by a parked hearse, its back doors gaping. It was so large and the lane so narrow that to pass it I had to turn sideways. I had my back to the hearse and my face to the glass window of a shop when I saw something that stopped me. The shop was in an advanced state of decay but there were a few dusty pictures behind the grimy glass. It looked as though it had once been a hairdresser's. One of the photographs was of a young girl. It was a portrait, head and shoulders, and had turned sepia with age. I stared at it for several seconds. There was something familiar about it. The girl could not have been more than fourteen or fifteen with high cheekbones and a large mouth.

The blind on the shop door was down and the cardboard notice said 'Closed'. I heard voices and the door opened to the jangle of a bell. Four men in black appeared, carrying a coffin. I had to move out of their way as they came to the rear of the hearse. I waited in the middle of the lane as they slid the coffin in and closed the doors. Then I stepped forward and stared again at the picture in the window. I cupped my hands on either side of my eyes to cut out reflected light. There it was, the faint shadow of a deformity. It must have been taken twenty years before, but the embryo face was there, the full sensual lips, the knowing eyes, and the faint shadow of the hare-lip. I was looking at

Frau Nissel's granddaughter; the lady who had been up in the bedroom with Uncle Ray. I stepped out into the middle of the lane again and read the name on the shop front. It said 'Cruikshank and Freeman. Passport photos while U wait.' I turned to the men in the hearse but the engine had started and it was rolling down the hill. Then the door of the shop opened again and standing in the doorway, wearing a tweed suit, strong brown brogues and carrying a bunch of flowers in her hand was the unforgettable woman I had first seen at Sotheby's sale and later in France. We stood staring at each other in startled silence. Then I said, 'Do you remember me?'

She had a strong, mannish face and, although she must have been over sixty, a big body that still looked powerful. She frowned as she tried to identify me.

'You were at Sotheby's sale,' I said. 'The medal sale.'

'Yes.'

'You sat next to me. My name is David Baines Turner.'

She seemed bewildered for a moment. 'You're not the son of the VC?'

'Yes.' I said. 'And I've been looking for Mr Granek for a long time. Could I see him?'

The name startled her. 'You're too late, Mr Turner,' she said coldly and went down the alley after the hearse.

They buried Stefan Granek in a small graveyard a couple of miles out of town. I stood under a sycamore in a lane leading to the church, feeling the drip of the rain on my green oilskin fishing-coat. There was only the priest, the men from the undertakers and the woman, whose name I was to learn later, was Miss Argyll. The service was short, the rain made everyone cold and wet. The coffin was lowered, the priest said a few words. Miss Argyll tossed sand on the coffin, the ropes were pulled up and the grave-digger began to shovel loads of wet red earth into the hole. The priest scuttled back to the church, his cassock and surplice flying, the hearse was driven off at indecent speed, and Miss Argyll prepared to squeeze behind the wheel of her Morris Minor Traveller. Stefan Granek, born in Lodz in Poland, photographer, prisoner, displaced person, had gone to his permanent resting place before I'd been able to talk to him. The question now was: had anyone else—Miss Argyll, for instance?

The shock of hearing my name had caught her off balance, but now, as I approached the car, she seemed to have regained possession of herself. She closed the door and started the engine and would have driven off had I not hurried forward and stood in the way. She wound down the window.

'I'd like to have a talk,' I said.

'I'm afraid I can't just now.'

'When?'

'There's nothing to talk about.'

I could feel the rain dripping down the inside of my collar and soaking my shirt. 'It has taken me a long time to find this place and to find Mr Granek,' I said. 'To get here I've had to go first to France, then to Vienna. You don't think I'm going to leave now because you don't feel inclined to talk to me?'

'But there's nothing to talk *about,*' she said. 'He's dead. You found him, but he's dead.'

'You don't know what I want to talk about. I'm writing a book about my father. It appears he may not have performed the act of heroism for which the VC was awarded. Perhaps the reverse. I don't know. I want to check. I think Mr Granek could have helped me, but it's too late for that. Now I find you here. You obviously knew him and it's possible you can help me. If you won't talk to me today, I'll be here tomorrow. And next week and next month. I haven't spent all this time and money and effort just to let the trail peter out. And there's one thing, I'm going to write the book anyway. If you won't co-operate, I'll go on digging. I'm not sure if you'll like that.'

She stared at me for some seconds, making up her mind, and then she said, 'So you want to know the facts, do you? All right. You shall have them, but first I want you to see something. Is that your car?' She pointed down the lane and I nodded. 'I'll wait for you,' she said.

I followed her along a series of damp country lanes for about twenty minutes. I lost all sense of direction as we twisted and turned and sometimes seemed to be going back on our tracks. The hedgerows grew higher, the lanes narrower, until I hadn't any idea where I was except that it was in the deepest and remotest countryside. We finally drove along a lane beneath a low hill, passed a sign which said 'No Through Road' and then the tarmac ended and we were on corrugated gravel, splashing in and out of puddles. Just when I thought we couldn't go on any farther because branches from the hedgerows were scraping the sides of the car we came to a pair of heavy iron gates which reminded me of those leading up to M. Mourass's house in France. She opened them, drove through, allowed me to follow, closed them and said, 'One moment.' I saw her go to one of the big granite gate-posts where there was the button of an electric bell. She pressed it and then returned to her car. I followed her up the long twisting drive between great banks of unkempt rhododendrons. I wondered why she had rung the bell since there had been no one there to let us in, and then I realized that the button was on the *inside* of the gate.

We came around a bend and there was the house. The first sight of it was something of a shock. It was a large place and must at one time have been the local manor. Its central block was three storeys high with large gables at each end forming separate wings. It was almost ruined. At some time there had been a fire and most of the roof had gone, leaving only blackened beams pointing up to the grey sky. What had once been a lawn was overgrown, grass and weeds sprang from the drive and from crevices in the steps up to the big front door. She led me along the side of the house and we parked at the back. Here things were slightly better; there was a chicken run and a vegetable garden and I could see several beehives. This section of the house was undamaged, the roof was sound and there were lights on in one or two windows. I was about to get out of my car when two large dogs came round the side of the house and bounded towards her like overgrown puppies. 'Stay where you are for a moment,' she said, 'they won't harm you. Let them get used to you.' She brought them over and said, 'This is Tilly and this is Crumpet. Rhodesian Ridgebacks. They are used for hunting lions, but they're gentle as lambs really.'

I followed her up to the house, the dogs flopping and gambolling about. She pressed the bell four times, opened the door with her key and we went into a big warm kitchen, one wall of which was taken up by an old-fashioned black range on which several pots were simmering. Seated at a pine table peeling vegetables was an old woman perhaps in her seventies. She was dressed in a dark woolen dress and a severe white turban of the sort worn in the forties. She was hung with necklaces, her wrists decorated with bangles, there were large rings on her fingers and her nails were painted dark red. She had a basket of swedes in front of her and she was peeling them on to a newspaper. She looked up as we came in and said something in a language I could not understand. Miss Argyll said, 'Now Sophie, remember our agreement.'

The woman went on in what sounded like Russian, but Miss Argyll turned her back, put both hands up to her ears and shook her head. After a moment Sophie stopped talking. Miss Argyll lowered her hands and turned round. 'Is everything all right?' she asked.

Sophie appeared not to be going to answer, but finally she said, 'Yes.'

'That's splendid,' Miss Argyll said. 'This is Mr Turner.'

Sophie held out her hand. I stepped forward to shake it and then realized it was not for shaking so I bent over it and touched the old skin with my lips. It gave off a strong smell of Swedish turnip.

'We're having soup today,' Miss Argyll said.

The outside door opened and a man came into the room holding a cabbage in one hand and a bunch of leeks in the other. He was dressed in a Welsh fisherman's smock, corduroys and Wellington boots caked with mud. He was thin and gnarled and also seemed to be in his seventies.

'Hello, Oskar,' Miss Argyll said. 'That's a lovely cabbage.'

'Savoy,' he said briefly.

'This is Mr Turner.'

Oskar inclined his head in my direction and then abruptly darted forward and stood over Sophie. 'You cannot cut like that! Look!' He held up a piece of swede to show Miss Argyll. 'It is waste! Always she is wasting.'

And in fact Sophie's idea of peeling swedes was to reduce them by about half. She ignored Oskar as he held up the thick peel. He threw it on the table and put down the cabbage. 'I will not grow more,' he said.

'Now Oskar, you know we couldn't live if you didn't grow so much,' Miss Argyll said.

'Look what she do, I will not grow more!' He was furious.

Sophie turned and snarled something at him in the language she had used originally. Oskar replied briefly in the same language and then he appeared to catch himself and he turned to Miss Argyll and said, 'So sorry. But she is talking always Polish. Always when you are out she is talking Polish. Never English. I am talking English to her and she is talking Polish to me. I go now.' He stomped to the corner, took off his Wellingtons and disappeared through a door at the end of the room.

'He'll be all right,' Miss Argyll said. She turned to Sophie. 'Can't you peel them a little thinner, dear? Such a waste.'

This seemed to enrage Sophie, for she stood up. She wasn't much above five feet tall. She flung the paring knife down on the table and said, 'I will not! I am countess. I will not peel more. Thin. Thick. Turnips. Ugh! We do not eat turnips. I am countess!'

'I know, dear,' Miss Argyll said. 'I know how you feel. But they're very good for you.'

Sophie stood for some seconds, her lips trembling, then she sat down and began to cry. I turned away so she would not be embarrassed. Miss Argyll was at her side immediately and patted her shoulder. 'There, there, dear. Don't you worry now. I'll come down and peel them a little later.'

Sophie, still with her head bowed, reached and took Miss Argyll's hand and brought it round and laid her cheek on it as a child might. 'So sorry,' she said.

After a few moments Miss Argyll disengaged herself and said, 'We'll leave her now.' She took me to what may once have been the second sitting-room. It was very bright, with strip lighting on the ceiling. An easel stood by the window and near it an old tattered arm-chair with its back to us. These were the only two pieces of furniture in the room. The walls were covered with pictures.

'Peter,' Miss Argyll said to the back of the armchair. I noticed a thin line of smoke rising from it. 'Peter!' The column of smoke rose unwaveringly. 'I have brought someone to meet you.' We went forward. 'This is Mr Turner.'

A very tall but shrunken man was sitting in the chair, all bony arms and legs. He was dressed in an old tweed jacket and grey trousers with a knotted paisley scarf at his throat. In his hand he held an onyx cigarette holder. He seemed very elegant until one saw the torn tennis shoes on his sockless feet. The cigarette was almost done and Miss Argyll reached forward, took it out of the holder and stubbed it in an ashtray on the window sill. The sill itself was covered in cigarette burns, the floor round the chair littered with burnt-out ends. Immediately the man took a case from his jacket pocket, fitted another cigarette into the holder and lit it. Then he said, 'Does he wish to buy?'

'I don't know, Peter.'

'Ask please.'

'He means his paintings,' she said.

'I'd like to have a look at them,' I said.

'He can look.'

I went round the walls. There were literally hundreds of paintings and drawings, some in old frames picked up at junk yards, some glued to hardboard, some painted on hardboard and some on paper. In all this mass of stuff there was only one picture; they were all the same. They showed a barbed-wire fence in the foreground. At the right was a guard-tower and one could just make out the figures with rifles. In the centre of the painting was the body of a man caught on the wire. The painting was done in blacks and oranges and greys but the man's face was yellow, with black eyesockets. His mouth was open and he seemed to be screaming. Some of the canvases were large and some small, some pictures done in charcoal, some in pencil; but the picture was always the same.

Miss Argyll said, 'He was Peter's friend.'

'Where did it happen?'

'At a labour camp during the war. He tried to escape.'

'And he does it over and over?'

'Always.'

'Does he wish to buy?' Peter said.

'Yes, I'll buy one,' I said.

'Not for sale!' he said sharply.

Then Miss Argyll took me up to her own flat at the top of the house. It consisted of a small bedroom and a small sitting-room; I think they had once been servants' quarters. It was sparsely furnished. I could see through the open door into her bedroom; there was an iron-framed bed and an old-fashioned wash-stand with basin and jug. Her sitting-room was furnished with a couple of armchairs and an old basket chair that seemed once to have lived in a garden.

'I don't like funerals,' she said. 'I'm going to have a whisky. That's all there is unless you'd like parsnip wine.'

'Whisky would be fine.'

She got out a bottle and two glasses, poured a couple of drinks and disappeared to get some water. The most garish object in the room was a large radiogram dating from the late forties or early fifties with a pile of seventy-eights on the top. I picked up several. Arte Shaw and the Gramercy Five, the Benny Goodman Sextet, Nellie Lutcher, Red Norvo, Big Sid Catlett, all on old Parlophone and HMV labels. It was like looking at someone's book shelves, a private and vulnerable side of character. I felt bad about having threatened her.

'Here you are,' she said, coming back.

'I see you like jazz.'

'That's not really what you want to talk about, is it?'

'No. Look, I'm sorry for what I said. It isn't true, I wouldn't have dug very deep, at least I don't think I would, and even if I had found something I wouldn't have used it without your permission.'

She looked at me over the rim of her glass, a forbidding, mannish face. 'Sit down,' she said. 'No, not in that one, you'll probably go through. Now what is it precisely that you want to know?'

'Let me tell you my side and the reason I was at Sotheby's sale and what has happened since, and perhaps we could go on from there.'

I began with Granville and then the sale and Smithson and Mr Blossom and my father's girlfriend, Rose. Once I started speaking, something rather strange happened, she seemed to draw things out of me. She was the best listener I had ever met. She didn't say anything, there were no sympathic noises or twists of the mouth or nods of the head; she sat quite still and I had the impression that every single word was being registered. I found myself telling her things in minute detail, recalling nuances that had arisen first in my search for my father and then for Granek. And I told her about Christina and the sort of life we led and I told her about Fay. I told her about Dolland and about France and about Mourass and the Algerian mechanic; I told her about the shrine in the house in St Claude-sur-Mer; about Madame and about how my father was alleged to have raped her; about Frau Nissel and Frau Schidloff and the photograph in the window; about the terror I had experienced in Vienna; there wasn't a detail I left out. I hadn't had a chance to drink my whisky and when I had finished I drained it in one gulp. She took my glass and for the first time she smiled and said, 'Now *I* can have another.'

We sipped these in silence and then she said, 'It's only soup but you're very welcome to stay.'

The five of us ate in the big kitchen and the meal was surprisingly good, the soup was rich and full of home-grown vegetables and the bread was home-made. It was followed by a strong country cheddar and yoghurt which they made themselves. Sophie and Oskar had recovered their composure, and Peter, who sat at one end of the table, drank soup with one hand and smoked with the other. When the three old people spoke it was mainly to ask for something and it was done in English and after each sentence they would look slyly towards Miss Argyll like children hoping for praise and she would nod approvingly. It was clear that they were devoted to her and she to them.

After lunch she said, 'Do you fancy a walk?' The rain had stopped, the wind had turned to the north-west and there were breaks in the clouds.

I'm not sure how far we walked, perhaps five miles along the tops of the hills, with the wind blowing at us and bringing occasional rain squalls. Once or twice we stopped to look down at the River Wye, meandering in and out of the rich fields; and sometimes the sun would come out and we would look down the other side into the Golden Valley; I can recall very little about it, for most of the time Miss Argyll was talking. 'Where do you want me to begin?' she had said as we started down the drive.

'I'm not sure,' I said. 'At the beginning, I suppose, but I don't know where the beginning is and perhaps you don't either. You said you wanted to show me something. It was the old people, wasn't it?'

'Yes.'

'Well, why not begin with them?'

It was not the best place to start after all because Sophie, Peter and Oskar came somewhat late in the story and although occupying the central position in Miss Arygll's life were really peripheral to my own investigation. But I listened and absorbed and it was only later that afternoon as dusk closed down on the countryside and I was racing back to London trying not to think of what I might find there that I employed the old journalistic trick of writing the story in my mind, of shifting paragraphs and trying to find the correct place for chunks of dialogue that remained fresh.

Her Christian name was Madge and she was sixty-two years old; she did not actually tell me her age, but I was able to work it out by other events she described. She had been born in the house and had spent her youth and young womanhood there, long before it was a ruin. The first interesting thing that had happened to her was the war, when she had worked for the Special Operations Executive under Colonel Buckmaster.

'Not in a glamorous way,' she said as we strode along the glistening lanes. 'I mean I wasn't dropped into France with a radio transmitter or anything like that. I worked at one of the training centres for agents in Buckinghamshire. General dogsbody. Making the tea, helping with briefings, typing, working on cover stories, checking that the agents had French labels in their suits when they were dropped into France, and that they weren't carrying Southdown bus tickets.'

It was at one of the centres that she had fallen in love. My mind needed some adjusting to this. I had to remove the tweeds and the brogues and the mannish grey hair and put her into something more feminine, but even so, even with thirty-odd years removed, I wondered what sort of man it was who had fallen in love with her, for there was no doubt, the way she told it, that her love had been reciprocated. And then she answered that too.

'It was a case of opposites,' she said. 'I was twenty-eight and he was forty-one, I stood nearly six foot in my stockinged feet and I don't think he was more than five foot five; I'd had a conventional country upbringing, private school, ponies, gymkhanas; he had been born in Brighton, into a theatrical family, with an English father and a French mother. From the time he was four he was touring the halls in Britain and the Continent. Of course he was perfectly bilingual, that's why they wanted him in SOE.

'We weren't supposed to fall in love. That was the

biggest sin you could commit at the Centre. They were going to be dropped into France to link up with the Maquis and already we were getting a high rate of casualties. I suppose you could say their chances were less than forty per cent. So everything was to be kept cool: Code, learn how to use the transmitter; learn how to be a Frenchman; learn how to kill; but don't, under any circumstances, learn how to love.

'It was a hothouse atmosphere, a forcing-ground, and there were affairs all over the place. You couldn't blame the men; they knew what was coming. You couldn't blame the girls either; they felt they were doing something to help. You have no idea how frightened some of the agents were. It was pathetic. Most of the girls were able to remain unaffected, but I wasn't like that. With me it's always been extremes: all or nothing. And that's how it was when Jimmy and I met. We tried to keep it a secret. Then, before he was dropped, they gave him some leave and I took mine at the same time. We only had four days. Most people went to London to do the shows and the nightclubs and have a good time, no complications. Learn your lines, learn the Morse but neither of us wanted that. We took a cottage in Scotland on the Findhorn.'

I thought of my own father and his leave just before he had gone off to fight. That had only been a weekend and he and Rose Crawley had taken a room in Portsmouth and spent a day on the Isle of Wight.

They had looked at birds, she said. 'It was June and I remember the oyster catchers trying to lead us away from their nests. Jimmy was amazed. I don't think he had ever been in the countryside. He'd never seen a hawk or a deer in his life.'

During that fortnight they had exchanged rings and told each other they would be married when he came back. And at the end they had travelled back to the Centre by different routes and he and his radio transmitter were placed on board a Lysander and he was flown to France and she never saw him again. He was captured less than a month after arrival. An informer had given him away, not to the Germans, but to the French *milice*. The only definite news that she had of him was that he was in prison in Lyons. But when the war ended there was no record of him there or anywhere else. So as soon as it was possible to travel, she had gone to France to search for him. It had taken her nearly three months to discover that he had died of pneumonia, brought on by a combination of cold, damp and malnutrition.

During those three months her life changed. While searching for Jimmy she encountered hundreds of other people also searching for husbands, wives, mothers, children, lovers, brothers, sisters. The more she travelled the more she met until she began to feel that the whole of Europe was one seething mass of people all searching for other people. She decided then what her life was to be about: she would help them, and the only way she could do it was by joining the Red Cross. For ten years she had worked in the Tracing Section, then her mother had died and the house became hers, so she returned to the Wye as a case-worker attached to the Red Cross's Hereford Branch.

It was soon after this that the house caught fire; the cause was never established but it was thought it might have been old, faulty wiring, unchecked since the 1930s. There was hardly any money from the insurance.

'It was one of those things I had been meaning to check,' she said. 'But mother hadn't been dead long and there were so many things to do that I hadn't got round to it. After the fire I found that no one had increased the assured sum since before the war; it was like the wiring, out of date. There wasn't much money, certainly not enough to rebuild the house; so it just stood there open to the weather and I took a flat in Hereford.'

Nineteen-sixty was World Refugee Year and in many countries there was a stirring of conscience about the thousands of people still living in camps fifteen years after the war had ended. The British Government increased its intake; the Red Cross moved into action and the search began for places where these displaced people could live and work.

'It wasn't easy to fit them into a new background,' she said. 'Some were already in their forties. I managed to place ten. One or two went to work on farms, one to a factory, a couple to shops. I found Sophie a job in a delicatessen, althugh she didn't know anything about food. She really is a Countess, you know, and all the cooking was done for her before the war; she didn't soil her hands. But the delicatessen owner wanted someone with a foreign accent who looked as though she knew all about smoked sausages and pâtés and pickled herrings. Oskar went to work in a nursery. Peter was a bit more difficult. All he wanted to do was paint and he really only wanted to paint the one picture. No one was going to employ him to do that so I had to find him something where he could use his talents, though not actually painting pictures, if you see what I mean. I got him a job with a sign-writing firm. He did rather well at that.'

'And you found Granek a job as a photographer?'

'Yes. He was already working somewhere in the south but apparently he didn't like it.'

'Basingstoke,' I said. 'He'd been working for a firm of industrial photographers.'

'Mr Cruikshank in Hay took him on. He was getting on and he wanted someone to help him with the dark-room work. I think he had been looking for a young lad, perhaps someone who would carry on the business when he retired, but I told him about Stephen and he took him on.'

'You called him Stephen?'

'He changed his name when he came here. Stephen Freeman. Free man.'

Freeman. Free man. It had never occurred to me. No wonder we hadn't been able to trace him. I should have thought of it. If Schuman had taken another name, why not Granek?

We walked on for a while in silence; she was deep in her own thoughts.

'And then?' I prompted.

'Then Mr Cruikshank died and Stephen took over the studio. The years went by and we all got old and some of us began to die. That was when I realized I had made a mistake.'

'What was that?'

'Bringing them to this isolated area. I should have let them go to the big conurbations where there were other Polish people. London, Birmingham, Manchester, Glasgow, Edinburgh. There are thriving Polish communities there, Polish societies, Polish clubs, monthly dances and get-togethers, marrages, funerals, a sub-stratum of life where people have intermarried and had children; a whole society. The point is, they look after their own.'

I hadn't grasped her point. 'I thought that's where the Red Cross came in?'

She shook her head. 'We try, but it isn't easy. What has happened quite simply is that they have got old. Like all old people they've become forgetful; they've regressed; they've gone back towards their childhood and can remember what happened sixty years ago but not what happened last week. And everything is much worse for the refugees. They never had a strong grip on the English language because they learnt it so late and in old age that's the first thing to go. They forget simple words and sentences. They find it easier to talk in Polish, and they become more isolated. That's why I keep my three at their English; I won't answer if they talk Polish; not that I can understand it anyway.

'And they get frightened. This is still basically a foreign environment to them, a strange environment, and they become frightened of that and frightened of the past. You must remember that they lived in camps. Before that their homes were ruined and in many cases they escaped either the gas chamber or a labour camp. They were constantly on the run. All those early terrors have come back to them. Sophie is afraid that *They* will seek her out and execute her because she comes from an aristocratic family. Peter escaped from a labour camp in Silesia when his friend was killed. He now lives in terror that *They* will come to drag him back. He has terrible nightmares. Sometimes I hear him screaming at night and I have to go into his room and calm him. Oskar is convinced that the British Government doesn't want him here and plans to deport him. I've tried to reason with him. I've told him that he's now a British subject, that no one can make him leave, but it's no good.'

'So that's why I had so little success with the Red Cross in London,' I said. 'They don't want anything more to upset these people.'

'I'm amazed you got as far as you did. They have rigid rules about giving information.'

'So you brought Sophie, Oskar and Peter to your house?'

'It was all I could do. I couldn't push them off to geriatric wards in London or one of the big centres when they were too old to work. They were used to me. They had even got used to this area. But they didn't know anyone; not in the sense of having friends to look after them. I was their only friend, their mother almost. I patched up the one wing of the house that hadn't suffered in the fire and I look after them.'

'Surely there are government agencies who could take over?'

She shook her head. 'You mean "Meals-on-Wheels" and organizations like that? Can you imagine what Sophie and Peter would be like if they were left alone? They would forget English altogether. They'd turn in on themselves. I had one woman, a Ukrainian, who had seven separate locks on her door. Think what they'd be like answering the door to a strange face every day. They'd be frightened out of their wits. Even I give them a warning on the bell when I have been out.'

'You hadn't told me what frightened Stefan Granek,' I said.

'No,' she said. 'I haven't. This is where it gets mucky.'

It was a word straight out of her childhood, redolent of stables and gymkhanas and points-to-point.

'You have a picture of him, haven't you?' she said.

I took it out of my wallet and gave it to her.

'When was it taken?'

'I'm not sure. Thirty-nine; early forty, perhaps.'

She handed it back. 'You'd never have known him.

The only thing remaining was the chip out of his front tooth.'

'Did he ever tell how he got it?' I said.

'He never told me anything, except once. He hardly ever spoke. He was the quietest man I ever knew. He used to spend a lot of time in the dark-room. Much more than he needed with the work he had. I think it gave him a feeling of safety being able to lock himself away and live in his own world.'

'Did he have any friends at all?'

'Not one. He was afraid of people. It was even difficult to get your photograph taken. You would have to knock at the door and sometimes he'd come and sometimes not. His fears were different from the others. Theirs grew with old age, and sometimes they spoke about them and one could understand. But Stephen was always frightened. He couldn't have been more than forty-eight or nine when he came and he was frightened then. That's really why he changed his name.' She looked down at the silver streak of the river as though getting her thoughts in order and then she began to speak and her whole involvement became clearer. The trigger was the fact that Granek had had a stroke some months ago, just after Christmas. It wasn't severe, but enough to make his speech difficult and Miss Argyll was worried about him and had brought him to her house. There he had lived a kind of twilight life. He would not move from his room, would not associate with the other old people and spent his days lying on his bed or sitting in a chair watching TV. He watched everything: programmes in Welsh, in Hindi, in French, Play School, news, current affairs, plays, old films, cricket, poetry reading, prayers. He watched from the moment the channels opened in the morning until the last glimmer at night. He even took his meals in front of the set.

'It didn't do him any harm,' Miss Argyll said, 'and it certainly kept him out of the way. But there was a problem. He had become somewhat deaf in his later years and he had to listen with the volume turned up and this began to get on Oskar's nerves. He had the room next door and he used to complain that he worked outside all day and was tired at night and wanted to get to sleep early and of course nine or half past nine was the peak of Stephen's evening viewing. I tried to shift the rooms around but Sophie wouldn't budge, nor would Peter. You can't blame them. In their frame of mind their rooms are their world, the one secure place. Oskar stood it for as long as he could and then one night he went in and smashed the front of the TV set with a garden fork. Stephen became hysterical. He must have thought Oskar was going to stab him. I thought he was going to have another stroke. I stayed with him and got him undressed and into bed and sat next to him and held his hand while he grew calmer. I don't know how long I sat there, perhaps a couple of hours. I thought he was asleep, and then he began to talk to me in English. It was very slow and indistinct, but after a while I got used to it.

'At first it had a lot to do with Oskar and Peter and Sophie and how they hated him and were spying on him. How they wanted to search his room—which is why he never left it, I suppose. Even in the slow articulated words you could feel his sense of terror. He thought everyone was spying on him. Then he began to talk about Mr Cruikshank and some photographs which the old man had been looking for. As far as I could make out they were Stephen's photographs and Mr Cruikshank was looking for them to give them to the police. But it was a jumble really, there wasn't much sense in it. I sat on and after a time he gripped my hand much more tightly and then he spoke about something that had happened during the war. About a Victoria Cross and a crime that had been committed in a village called St Claude. I couldn't make head or tail of it then. Later, when I went up to my own flat the few shreds that I had understood remained in my mind and so I jotted them down and I lay in bed that night thinking about what he had said, trying to form a picture in my mind.'

'Did you succeed?'

'Only partly.'

'What sort of crime was it?'

'A robbery and a murder.'

'In the village—St Claude?'

'Yes.'

'You're sure? Not on the outskirts? Perhaps in the farmhouse?'

'No. He mentioned a square. But the two things might be separate.'

'And he mentioned the VC? Did he say my father was implicated in the crimes?'

'I don't think so. He talked about Frenchmen.'

'Frenchmen!' I was beginning to lose what slender grip I had on the facts.

'Mourass says my father didn't enter the village,' I said. 'He didn't mention a robbery. But Dolland did. Dolland said my father *was* in the square. Mourass says he raped his sister at the farmhouse and he was shot there and taken to the boats from the farmhouse. Dolland says he was in the village, Granek says he was in the village. Let's say for argument's sake that Granek was in the village when my father and Dolland entered it. That would place the three of them there. Now Granek was working for a British picture agency so he would have been interested in a picture story about British troops. He sees a British captain coming down the road in the middle of an action helping a wounded comrade. It's an absolute natural for a picture story. He probably stuck with them. You say he spoke about photographs.'

'That's the whole point. As far as I could make out he had photographed a murder.'

'Jesus!' I said, and all sorts of thoughts began to tumble round my mind. 'You mean he sat on photographic evidence of robbery and murder for nearly forty years? No wonder he was frightened. I mean if anyone involved in the crime knew he had pictures . . .'

'Yes, I'd worked that out,' she said.

'And did he have them?'

'I don't know.'

'Didn't he say something about Cruikshank looking for them?'

'Yes, but I had a feeling that was all mixed up with people he thought were spying on him, like Sophie and Peter and Oskar, that it was part of his paranoia. I said why didn't he report it to the police, but he was afraid of them, too.'

'Let's assume for the moment that what he said about the robbery was true. He was in St Claude. He saw a crime being committed and photographed it. Somehow—and this takes some believing—over all the years to come, in prisons and camps, he kept the photographs intact. Then assume that the people involved in the crime knew he still had the photographs. That also takes some believing. But it would explain quite a lot. Granek photographs a robbery and a murder; possibly the murder of my father in the barn. He keeps the pictures. The Frenchmen who committed the crime know he has them and come after him. Except, why didn't they search for him earlier? And what was the robbery all about? The only one I know is the one Dolland mentioned in the square. If my father was shot in the barn how was he robbed in the square? Unless it was a different robbery. Or a different murder.'

'I can't answer those questions,' she said, and I could hear mild irritation in her voice.

'I'm sorry. I didn't mean to interrupt. It's just that I'm trying to place everyone in the framework; you included. Let's go back to Granek. What happened after that night when he told you about the robbery and murder?'

'It became impossible for him to stay on at the house. He was terrified of Oskar. It was holding back his recovery. So I took him back to his studio. Then a couple of months later, it must have been in the spring, I saw a piece in *The Times* which said that your father's VC was coming up for sale and it gave one or two details. It mentioned St Claude-sur-Mer. Naturally I wanted to know more so I went to Hereford Library and got out a book on VCs in World War II.'

'Was it written by a Colonel Smithson?'

'I think so. Anyway, the upshot was that I had to go to London on private business so I timed my visit to coincide with the sale. I had no idea people paid that sort of money for medals. It made me very angry. I kept thinking about my old people and all the other refugees living on the poverty line. It made me see red.'

'I remember,' I said, the picture of her at bay still fresh in my mind.

'It's a terrible thing to say, but I *want* them to die at the same time as I'm keeping them alive. I told you we were running out of money. I've known for a long time it was going to be a race between what money I had and the length of their lives. I want them to go to bed one night and go to sleep and not wake up. If they linger on the money's going to run out and there'll be nowhere for them to go except an institution and who is going to look after them there? Who's going to have the time to translate what they're saying? Who is going to understand their fears? I've tried to sell the house, but no one's interested; I've applied for grants but haven't got them. We've fallen through the Welfare net in some way. Things have been getting worse and worse. Bills unpaid. The electricity people want to cut us off.

'When I was driving back after the sale an idea began to form in my mind. I call it an idea but it was a sort of madness. I began to think about what Stephen had said: the robbery and murder and the photographs. If he really had such photographs they'd be valuable, wouldn't they?'

'Yes,' I said. 'But you're talking about blackmail.'

'I know. I told you it was a sort of madness, but when you're desperate anything seems reasonable. I thought: someone must have made a lot of money; why shouldn't *we* have some of that money. So I asked Stephen to the house for a few days and while he was there I went to the studio. I searched it over and over but there was nothing at all that resembled the sort of pictures he had mentioned.'

"Then you went to France,' I said. She turned in surprise and I told her about seeing her in the dunes. I did not mention the man with the binoculars. I had no wish to frighten her.

She told me she had stayed for several days and my

mind drew a picture of this large Englishwoman badgering the secretive villagers of St Claude.

'There was a bar in the square and I spoke to the barman,' she said. 'And I asked at my hotel.'

'Which hotel? There were two, the Relais and the Miramar.'

'The Relais. People told me how fierce the fighting had been and how the village had been awarded the Croix de Guerre, but no one seemed to know anything about a murder or a robbery.'

'So you gave up and came back?'

'I had the idea of continuing the search back in Britain but soon after I returned Stephen had another stroke, and this time it killed him.'

We walked on along the shining lane for a few minutes then I said, 'Assuming that there *are* photographs, and you haven't got them and I haven't got them, where the devil are they?'

She shrugged.

'There is an alternative,' I said.

'What's that?'

'That Granek dreamt the whole thing. What if there are no photographs? That there never have been any?'

'Why would you have been followed?' she said. 'Why would anyone have searched your flat?'

'Maybe they *think* there are photographs. Look, we've already heard three stories. One is that my father raped Mourass's sister and killed a German in the barn. That's Mourass's story. Then there's Dolland's story: that Granek robbed my father's dying body in the square. The third is Granek's story: that there was a robbery *and* a murder, but that it was committed by Frenchmen. Granek was unbalanced. You said so yourself.'

'Only in certain areas. In others he was perfectly sane.'

'All right, but when I spoke to Dolland I questioned him again and again and he always said the same thing. He remembered my father bringing him into the square. He remembered being put down on the ground. He saw a British officer taking photographs. He heard shots which didn't sound like rifle or machine-gun fire. He saw my father's body and a falling something'—I didn't mention 'it', whatever that was—'and he saw the British officer with the camera, i.e. Granek, rob my father's body and run. Now that's Dolland's story and it came out that way every time.'

'But rob your father of *what*?' said Miss Argyll.

'I don't know. What would he have of value? And how would Granek have known anyway?' And then I felt a hot flush on the surface of my skin. 'My God!' I said. 'What if he wasn't robbing him? *What if he was putting something on his body?*' We stopped in the lane and stared at each other and I had a feeling of light-headedness that comes with the absolute certainty of having guessed correctly.

'Photographs? Where are they now, then?'

'Don't you see?' I said, thinking of my father's things that had come down to me through my mother. '*I* must have them.' And even as I registered this, another thought came into my mind. My flat had been only partially searched by the man I had passed on the stairs. There had been no opportunity for him to have another try. Until now. I remembered my smug feeling on the mountain road coming to Hay when I had assumed I had lost any pursuers. What if they had not bothered to follow me at all? *What if they had only been waiting for me to leave?*

I told Miss Argyll and we turned off the lane, stumbled back through the soggy fields and hurried through the mud and over the stiles. I phoned Christina from the house but there was no answer. I visualized the flat with shadows creeping through the rooms. Where was Christina? Where was Brigitta? 'I must go back,' I said. 'Would you please keep ringing?'

I drove as fast as I could, ignoring speed limits but hampered by the twisting and turning of the road as it followed the river down towards Chepstow. Tintern Abbey fled past, its gaunt buttresses lit by a watery sun, then the Severn Bridge and I was on the M4, with the wet Welsh Marches left behind. I switched on the radio news at five o'clock and listened to the usual roll call of strikes. I tried to be interested, tried to keep my mind off the flat. The exit signs for Swindon flashed past and soon I was beyond Newbury and the traffic coming towards me was getting heavier all the time as the rush-hour picked up momentum. I knew that the centre of London would be jammed, so at Chiswick I cut up through Acton and Harlesden. The Edgware Road was solid but I managed to worm across, then through the smaller streets of Swiss Cottage and finally into Englands Lane and Haverstock Hill. I left the car on a yellow line and raced towards the flat. I thought there was a light behind the curtains but could not be sure. The lift was out of action as usual and I ran up the stone stairs. The lights went out halfway up but I didn't wait to switch them on again. I thought I heard a sound, strained to listen, but all I could hear was my blood pumping in my ears. I came to our landing. There was a strip of light under the door. This time I did hear something; it sounded like the second act of *Rosenkavalier*. I felt myself go limp with relief. I rang and knocked and in a few moments the letter box flap was pulled open from the inside. A heavily accented voice said, 'Yoh?'

'It's me.' She opened the door and we fell on each other like wrestlers. At the time I phoned Christina, Birgitta and Elisabeth were having coffee and cakes at the Swiss Café, but Miss Argyll had kept on ringing until they had come in, had told Christina I was on my way back and Birgitta had left. Now she poured me a drink and sat beside me—almost on my lap—and I told her everything.

'*You've* got them?' she said at last.

'Not *them,*' I said. 'It. A roll of film, not pictures. He must have taken it out of his camera. If he did put it on my father's body, it must be around somewhere. My mother never threw out a single thing of his. She would have kept his nail parings if she could. Give me another drink.'

What mother had called my father's 'things' were scattered over the flat and it took us the better part of an hour to find them all. First there was an old wooden cigar box in the bottom of my right-hand drawer, which contained among other things several World War I medals which *his* father had been awarded, then there were brass buttons from both wars; I couldn't tell which had been his or which had been my grandfather's. There was an old Conway Stewart fountain pen, a glass marble which must have been mine, and a locket. I hadn't looked into this box for twenty years or more and when I picked up the locket I half expected to see Rose Crawley's face staring at me, but it was my mother's, aged I suppose about twenty-two, with her hair caught firmly back and a prim expression on her lips. His wedding ring was there and a pair of rolled gold cuff-links engraved G.B.T. which my mother once told me she had given him for a wedding present. We looked through my desk thoroughly and also my shelves and cupboards. No film.

There was no point in looking in Elisabeth's room or the bathroom or the kitchen or the dining-room and I knew there was nothing in the sitting-room. I looked through my wardrobe, top and bottom. And then Christina said, what about the cupboard in the hall? This is where I kept golf clubs, a photographic enlarger, tank, dishes, several pipes, cricket boots, tennis rackets and things I would never use again but which I was loath to throw away. At the back of the cupboard we found an old Val-Pak which had been given to me by my mother when I had won my scholarship to Cambridge and was now covered in patches of mildew. It contained several things which had belonged to my father and I realized that I must have put them there meaning to give them away. There was a grey suit and a tweed jacket, three white shirts without collars and a brown dressing-gown. I went through all the pockets of the suit and jacket and found nothing. Tucked in the bottom flap of the Val-Pak was an expanding cardboard wallet about the size of a foolscap file. It was one of those concertina-like things which tie up with tape. You pull them open and there is a pocket for each letter of the alphabet. I had used one as a filing system for newspaper cuttings and notes until I needed something bigger.

We took it into the sitting-room. The tape tying it was brown with age and the knot had been tightened fiercely. I made some ineffectual tugs at it, then Christina fetched a pair of scissors and cut it. We crouched next to each other as we opened it. It was half full of various things, mainly vegetable seeds. There were packets of peas, broad beans, lettuces, one marked 'Tomatoes: Ailsa Craig'. All were filed under their letter. Very neat; very like a bank clerk. In the section marked XYZ was a Sutton's seed catalogue and several tear-sheets from magazines and newspapers on the best way to cultivate this and that. We looked at it in disappointment. It had never occurred to me to think of him as a gardener.

'I'm sure there was more than that,' I said. 'There was his uniform and I remember a pair of boots and other things. I gave some to Oxfam but even so . . . my God! The tin trunk!'

'What tin trunk?'

'The one that my fir . . . the one that Fay's got.'

'Oh.'

We never talked about Fay; now her name dropped into the room like lead.

'You've never mentioned it,' Christina said.

'I'd forgotten all about it. I used to keep one or two of my things in it too. There's nothing sinister about not mentioning it. I just haven't thought of it, that's all.'

'Why does she have it?'

'When we split up I forgot to get it and I've never needed anything from it.'

'Do you know where it is?'

'The last time I saw it was in the loft.'

'She is still at the same place?'

'As far as I know.'

I went into my study and looked in the telephone directory but there was no F. Turner or Fay Turner in Wimbledon. So I looked under her maiden name. And there it was: Fay Bryant, 28 Maxwell Road, SW19.

'You have to go there and look,' Christina said.

'Yes, I'll have to look. I'll phone.' The line was engaged and remained engaged for the next half hour. I looked at my watch; it wasn't eight yet.

'You must go there,' Christina said.

I hesitated, then I said, 'For God's sake, don't open the door to anyone.' She nodded. I kissed her and held her close for a moment then I went out. She closed the door and I heard the rattle of the chain and the slam of the bolts.

I hadn't been to Wimbledon since Fay and I separated, but 28 Maxwell Road, what I could see of it in the dark, looked much the same. It was one of a row of houses that faced the Common and had been split into two flats before we moved in. The bottom flat comprised the basement and ground floor, ours had been the top maisonette. The lights were on upstairs. I rang the bell and waited. Thunder rumbled over central London and there were flashes of lightning. A light came on and the door opened and I found myself facing a tall young man with long dark hair and a rather solemn face dressed in a heavy fisherman's jersey and corduroys. I might have been looking at myself fifteen or twenty years before.

'Good evening,' I said. 'I'm David.' He looked puzzled. 'David Turner . . . Fay's . . .' I made a sort of movement with my hand.

'Oh.'

Fay's voice called from upstairs. I would have known it anywhere: crisp, clear, firm. 'Is that the insurance man?'

'No,' he called in reply. 'It's not the insurance man.' Then to me, 'You'd better come up.'

We were halfway up the stairs when she came to the top. 'David!'

'I'm sorry to barge in,' I said. 'I tried to ring but the phone was engaged.'

'I thought you must be the man from the insurance,' she said as we moved into the flat. She looked much as I remembered, small, dark, with her hair cut short, neatly dressed in a jersey and skirt and plain sensible shoes. She looked so . . . my mind groped for a word but all I could think of was the word *capable*. She must have been nearly forty but looked twenty-eight.

She turned to the young man and said, 'Darling, this is David. You two haven't met before.'

'No,' I said, putting out my hand.

'Dennis Oakfield,' she said.

We looked at each other. He appeared uncomfortable, as I was myself, but there was no antagonism; there was no feeling of any sort, not when I looked at him and not when I looked at Fay. I had often wondered how I would feel when I saw her again. I had missed her dreadfully at first, now there was nothing. Whatever feeling I had once was dead. The flat was entirely different. It seemed to have come directly from a catalogue, all pine and white melamine; a mixture of Eames, Bauhaus and Tiffany. It was formal and neat and clean and unlived in and reminded me of Fay herself.

But things were not quite so neat and tidy when I looked more closely. One of the pine shelving units had been torn away from the wall. I could see the screws and the rawlplugs and the holes in the plaster; the door of a cupboard had been yanked off its hinges and was resting against the wall. One of the table lamps no longer had a shade. With a bitter twist of her mouth Fay went to the sofa and picked up one of the cushions, holding it up so I could see the bottom. It had been slashed. She dropped it back. 'They're all like that. And our pillows, and the mattress.'

'What happened?'

'We had a robbery.' She said it savagely. 'Yesterday or last night. I'm not sure which. Dennis and I were in Oxford. He was doing some research. We came home this morning and found it like . . . well, not quite like this. I've tidied up the worst.'

'What did they take?'

'That's the strange thing,' she said. 'They didn't seem to take very much. I suppose there wasn't much worth stealing and that made them angry so they broke the place up.' I thought of Christina washing down our flat with disinfectant. This must have been much worse. 'Portable TV. Dennis's typewriter. The radio. That sort of thing. None of it very good but it's the typewriter that was the worst. Dennis and I are writing a book on the relationship between working mothers and delinquency and half our notes were tucked into the lid of the typewriter. That's why I thought you were the insurance man. He was supposed to be here at half past six.'

'Do you mind if I sit down?' I said.

She arranged herself neatly on a hardback chair and I sat on the ruined sofa; Dennis hovered. 'I think I can explain about the burglary,' I said. 'It has to do with why I've come.'

They looked at me as though I had taken leave of my senses. I told them what had happened as briefly as I could, too briefly, I suppose, because I could see their eyes full of question marks when I had finished.

'What I don't understand is why you think *I* have the film,' Fay said.

'Not you. I just think it is *here*.'

'But why?'

'Because if I did have it, I'd have left it here in the tin trunk.'

'What tin trunk?'

'The tin trunk in the loft. Is it still there?'

'I didn't even know there was a tin trunk.'

'It had some of my father's things in it, and some of mine.'

'Are you sure?'

'Positive.'

It was apparent that no one had been up to the loft for a long time because it took us a good ten minutes to find the pole you hooked the ladder down with. We finally found it behind the hot water cylinder. I went up first and switched on the light. The area near the top of the ladder had been floored as storage space. There were one or two old rugs, a couple of broken suitcases, a metal folding bed, two cardboard boxes filled with university textbooks, and standing a little way behind them was the tin trunk. The lid was badly dented and the whole thing had taken a battering but the name and address in white-painted capitals were clearly legible: 'Lieut. G. B. Turner, RHF, Stoner Barracks, Hampshire.' Everything was covered in the dust of years.

Fay stood at my side. Dennis stood on the ladder itself, his head just visible. There was no padlock and the lid came open with a groan. The first things I saw were several old copies of the *Granta* which had carried articles of mine, and then part of a thesis on Gerard Manley Hopkins which I'd never finished. I took them out and put them on the floor. More manuscripts, short stories this time which I had never sold; a play I'd written when I was seventeen; a rugby jersey and a dirty kneeguard. The pile grew. And then I came to my father's stuff: uniform, cap, swagger stick, shoes; a framed letter from the bank; a box containing cap badges of other regiments. There were two or three other things lying in the bottom of the trunk: a ceremonial sword, an old-fashioned piggy-bank with nothing in it and the old camera that had once hung on the wall of mother's room.

'Well, that's about it,' I said.

Fay squatted down next to me and went through the pockets of the uniform but found nothing there either. We stared down at the pathetic pile that was all that remained of my father and then she reached into the tin trunk and picked up the camera. 'Is this yours?'

'No, it was Dad's.' It was a small brown leather case worn and scuffed by much usage. 'It was with his things when they brought his body back.'

'Does it still work?'

'I don't know, I've never used it.'

I began to pack the stuff back into the trunk.

'It looks quite a good camera,' she said. 'A Leica.'

'Rubbish. He'd never have had a Leica.'

'Look.' She had opened the case, something I'd never done in all the years it had hung on the wall. I took it from her and stared at it. There were patches of rust on it.

Then I said, 'Christ Almighty! It was the camera! Not a film! It was the *camera* he put on the body.'

That's what Dolland had seen. That was the camera he had mentioned. Granek had not been putting a film on my father's body. He hadn't had time to remove a film from the camera. He'd got rid of the camera itself. Then I looked down at the film counter. It was reading zero. There was no film in it. I showed her. I crouched there, holding the camera in my hand, and said bitterly, 'Well, we gave it the old college try.'

Then another thought came to me, out of the mists of my own photographic experience, which wasn't wide but which had been sufficient to carry me through a dozen or more freelance jobs. What would *I* have done? I tried to place myself back in the village in June 1940. Say I had photographed a murder and a robbery and the people who had committed them knew I had. I wanted to keep the film but had to get rid of it. What would I do? First of all I'd—*I would have rewound it into the cassette.* And if I hadn't had a chance to take it out of the camera that's where it would be still.

My hands were shaking as I took the camera out of the case. It was bottom loading and there was a twist flap that opened it. I turned it and the bottom came away. There, nestling in its little compartment as it had for nearly forty years, was a 35mm 36-exposure cassette. 'Bingo,' I said softly.

I sat in the car outside Fay's, not quite knowing what to do. Each time I looked down at the camera I felt a pulse of excitement. It was a classic case of the invisibility of the obvious. For years and years it had been living on the wall of my mother's room but because of my attitude to my father even his belongings had been anathema. Poe would have understood. But what now? I couldn't trust the film to a chemist; nor could I trust myself to process it. I needed an expert. I remembered Mr Peel.

Going up Queensgate I knew I had company. A Ford Granada. I had first seen it on West Hill, but then it had been ahead of me. The only reason I'd noticed it was because it had one of those black furry spiders hanging from the rear-view mirror. The storm had broken and the rain was lashing down and I could not make out the driver's features but there seemed to be only one person in the car. At the top of Queensgate traffic turned either right, the way I wanted to go which would take me through the park, or left into Kensington High Street. I turned into the left lane and when I reached the top the lights were green. I turned left and the Ford turned after me. There was a gap in the traffic on the opposite carriageway. I swung the car into it and in a couple of seconds was travelling in the opposite direction. The Ford slewed round in the centre of the road trying to follow but the line of traffic was bumper to bumper and it was unable to force its way in. The lights at the Alexandra Gate were with me and I turned left into the Park and in a matter of minutes was outside Peel's house. I sat for a few moments but there was no sign of the Ford.

I rang, but no one answered. There were lights on inside and I could hear noise. I rang again. At the third ring the door opened a crack and Peel's voice said, 'Julius?'

'No, it's not Julius. It's David Turner.'

'Who?' His voice was thick and slurred.

The noise behind him increased in volume. I said, 'I came to see you recently about a photographer named Granek.'

'Granek?'

'We found a picture of him in one of your rooms. In a box.'

'Yes. I remember.'

'I want you to develop a roll of film for me,' I said.

'I don't develop film. Take it to Boots.'

'This is rather special. It's the film I was looking for.'

Behind him, in the studio, something fell over with a crash. He would have closed the door if I hadn't been leaning against it.

'Boots,' he said. 'They'll do a good job.'

'The film is forty years old. It's never been out of the camera.'

There was a slight change in his expression. 'What sort of camera?'

'Leica.'

'Forty years old?'

'Well, almost.'

'What film?'

'Kodak. Super Double-X.'

There was another crash in the background and the studio door opened. A boy, perhaps twelve or thirteen, wearing heavy make-up and a shorty towelling dressing-gown, came out into the hall. A voice from the studio called, 'Donald! Donald! Come on, darling.'

The child opened his carmined lips and said, 'Piss off, you shitty old bastard.'

'It's a Kodak film,' I repeated.

Only part of Peel's mind was concentrating on me. 'Give Kodak a ring,' he said. 'They've got a customer relations place. They'll tell you what to do.'

'It's urgent and important. It must be done privately. I'll pay, of course.'

Again there was a flicker of interest. 'How much?'

'Fifty if it's done right—and that includes the printing.'

'All right. Leave it with me.' He put out his hand.

'No,' I said. 'Now.'

Behind him the boy had lit a cigarette. The figure of a man burst out of the studio. He was short and burly and dressed only in a pair of pants. He had hair on his chest, shoulders and arms and was holding a Hasselblad in one hand. 'Come on, Donald!' he said.

'I don't feel like doing it again,' Donald said.

The man turned to Peel. 'Listen, old mate, for what I'm paying you'd better get this snotty-nosed little git back in the room.'

'Don't be a spoil-sport,' Peel said to Donald.

'Get knotted,' the child said.

'Give us a minute,' Peel said to the hairy man.

'Just get him back! I haven't finished yet. And Gary's ready.' He went back into the studio.

'The local photographic society. Their monthly meeting,' Peel said to me.

'About the film . . .'

'I want to go home,' Donald said.

'Not yet, darling.'

'Yes, now.' He dug his long manicured finger nails into Peel's arm. Peel shook him off and turned to me. 'Some other time,' he said.

'What do you think would happen if I phoned the police?' I said softly, so the child could not hear.

We stared at each other. 'Look, Mr Whatever-your-name-is, I couldn't do a proper job. Not with all this going on. Be reasonable. Don't you know anyone else?'

'No.'

'You could do it yourself in half an hour.'

'If I knew how.'

'You said you'd done a bit of processing.' His memory wasn't as bad as he had been making out. 'You never forget.'

I thought of the enlarger in the cupboard at home, the old dishes, the tank.

'Peel!' The voice from the studio was filled with anger.

'Look, I can let you have chemicals and paper,' Peel said desperately.

'But the film's forty years old.'

'That makes no odds. A film's a film.' He knew he had me and said, 'Give me two minutes . . .'

When he came back he had developer, fixer and paper. 'That's my Dad's old manual,' he said, pushing a book into my hands. 'That should help.' Then he slammed the door and I heard it lock. There were suddenly a hundred things I wanted to ask him but I knew it would be useless to go on. I ran through the rain to the car and drove back to Hampstead.

With Christina's help it took me less than half an hour to set up a ramshackle dark-room in the bathroom. Fortunately, it was dark outside and a blanket at the window kept out the street lighting. We ransacked the cupboard and found my old Gnome enlarger, a Patterson developing tank, three plastic dishes and a thermometer. I had commandeered two measuring jugs from the kitchen as well as Christina's large baking tin and chopping board. My safe light wouldn't work, but

Christina found a red scarf and I tied it round a low wattage light so everything was lit by a dull red glow. It was warm and sticky in there and I could hear thunder rumbling outside.

I put the enlarger on a small folding table next to the bath, and the dishes containing the print developer, the plain water stop-bath, and the fixer on the baking board, which was large enough to bridge the bath from side to side. Underneath the board I could run water into the bath to wash the prints. I had no changing bag, so I loaded the film from the cassette into the tank under our bedclothes.

Now we were ready.

I was nervous, unwilling to begin. But I *had* to know what was on the film.

'If we're lucky we're going to get some sort of picture and a lot of fogging,' I said. 'The picture's likely to be flat and faded. If I use a long developing time I'll bring up the picture but I'll also increase the fogging. So we have to be somewhere in between. Long enough to bring up the picture, but not the fog.'

From time to time as I worked I glanced at the dog-eared Kodak manual, explaining to Christina what I was doing. 'Even then they were recommending D76 as a developer,' I said. 'So we're in luck. That's the one Peel gave me. Normal developing time for Super Double-X was twelve minutes, but I'm going to increase that by half. Got the watch?'

'Yes.'

'Ready?'

'Yes.'

'Don't forget, tell me every sixty seconds.' I poured the developer into the tank. As the last drops went in I said, 'Now.'

Christina stood under the red light where she could see the clock that usually sat on my bedside table. 'One minute,' she said.

I picked up the tank, inverted it, and put it down. I would have to do that at the end of every sixty-second cycle to make sure the developer reached all parts of the film.

Eighteen minutes is a long time. We stood in the red glow with the clock ticking away the seconds and could not find anything to say. At the end of each minute Christina warned me and I lifted the small developing tank, inverted it and put it down again.

The minutes dragged. It was hot in the bathroom, claustrophobic, almost foetal. I thought of Granek who had spent so much of his last years in the dark-room at Hay and I could understand that someone might feel safe in such a place: enclosed, warm, shut off from the outside world.

Finally Christina counted: 'Sixteen . . . seventeen . . . eighteen . . . stop!'

I emptied the tank into the hand-basin, filled it with cold water, inverted it, poured out the water and poured in the fixer from the second measuring jug. I kept the fixer in for five minutes, inverting the tank about every thirty seconds and then poured that out. I poured more fresh water in and opened the tank. As Peel had said, you don't forget the process. I held the spiral between two fingers and gently drew out the film. Holding it delicately by its edges I looked at it against the red light.

'Can you see anything?' Christina said.

I ran the strip through my hands. 'Yes!'

I plunged it into the running water, held it up again and stared at pictures that had been taken nearly forty years before. I let the film run between two fingers, using them as a squeegee and got most of the water off. I put one end into the negative carrier and switched on the enlarger light. An image sprang on to the white paper holder below the light but it was a negative image with the blacks and whites reversed and I could not 'read' it as a professional could. I could see two faces and a background that looked like part of a house but who the faces belonged to I had no idea. Parts of the negative were blank and I thought water, from the time my father's body was in the boat, might have seeped into the camera and eaten away the emulsion.

I switched off the enlarger, took a piece of light-sensitive paper and placed it on the paper-holder. 'I'll give it ten seconds,' I said.

I switched on the enlarger light to burn the negative image on to the paper and counted up to ten. I switched off the light, put the paper into the dish of developer and stood staring at it. It was simply a blank piece of 10 × 8 paper lying in water until, slowly, a shadow on one part darkened and began to grow. The paper became mottled by greys and blacks. Then I saw parts of a picture. Suddenly, it was there, and we were looking down at two British soldiers standing at the side, not of a house, but a wrecked tank. The next picture showed one of the soldiers climbing on to the tank. The third had both men on the tank. There were blank areas on each.

'Are those the pictures you are looking for?' Christina said.

'No, this is out in open country. What I want is houses, a village square.'

I moved the film through the enlarger carrier. I was clearly looking at part of a series Granek had shot of two soldiers rescuing a third from a tank. There were fifteen or sixteen frames, about half the film. Water had only affected the first three or four.

'Here's something different,' I said. There were buildings now, one of which had lettering on its facade. In the foreground were two figures, one standing, one lying on the ground.

Just then, as I was about to print, we heard a noise, a heavy thump. We stood still, listening. Then there was a cry. 'My God, Elisabeth has fallen from the cot!' Christina said. She opened the bathroom door and I could hear her running along the corridor. I stood like a rock, as I had on many occasions before, waiting to hear what the damage was. Usually Christina would call that all was well, but this time there was only a cry that was instantly muffled. 'Are you all right?' I shouted, and turned to look into Mourass's square white face.

He stood blocking the doorway, legs astride, hands thrust deep into his coat pockets. I tried to push past him.

'Christina!' I shouted.

'She is all right.'

I grabbed him by his coat and tried to throw him to one side. He was like a rock. He took his right hand from his coat pocket and I saw the pistol.

'I told you . . .' he began.

'Christina!'

He hit me, then, on the neck. The gun barrel was like an iron bar, and I went down on my knees.

'She is all right. So is your daughter. Yussuf is with them. If you co-operate he will do them no harm.'

He hauled me to my feet. I felt weak and dizzy.

'Where are they?' he said.

'What?' Slowly my head cleared. I was very frightened.

'The pictures, of course. You're not a child!'

I pointed to the enlarger.

'Give them to me.'

'They have not been printed yet.'

'What?'

'They were still in the camera.'

'Where was that?'

'In my ex-wife's flat.'

He frowned. 'Yussuf spent five hours there.'

'How did you find her?'

'You have a publication that lists writers and their books, and their addresses. Fortunately for me, it is only published every few years. Where in the apartment was the camera?'

'The loft.'

He gave a small, mirthless laugh. 'Yussuf did not think of that. Perhaps they have no lofts in Oran.' He followed me into the bathroom, closed the door and looked at the negative strip hanging down on either side of the enlarger. 'Go on with your work. I'm going to destroy the negatives, of course. But after all these years I would like to see the pictures.'

I made no move.

'You have no choice, Mr Turner.' He moved his head in the direction of Elisabeth's room.

I turned towards the enlarger and saw my hands.

They were shaking. I thought of Christina and Elisabeth and I thought of Yussuf. I could visualize the three of them in Elisabeth's room. Had he hurt them? All I could do at the moment was co-operate: that might give me time. As long as I followed instructions there was no reason for them to hurt Christina or Elisabeth. I wanted time to think; time to create an opportunity.

I took a piece of paper, placed it in the enlarger's carrier, switched on the light and counted to ten. Light off. Paper into developer. Watch for image. This time we were looking at the square in St Claude, with the two figures in close-up, one standing, one lying on the ground. The prostrate figure was indistinct but in size and shape it could have been Dolland. The standing figure was sharply in focus, but grainy. It was my father. He was half facing the camera, with his left hand flung out, pointing, I thought, to the far side of the square. It was a shock seeing him, even though I had been expecting it. The square had taken a terrible beating. A car away to the right was burning. One opposite had been blown on to its roof. I could see craters where bombs had hit, and some of the buildings were in ruins.

The building at which my father seemed to be pointing was the one with lettering on its façade. There was the letter E then blank, then an I and a T, then several more blanks and a Y and more blanks. The remainder of the letters had been blown off by bombs or shellfire. The ones remaining made no sense. There was a figure standing, hands in pockets, below the central letters, but it was too far away to be clear.

I put the picture in the fixer and began to print the next. This was similar, except that my father had moved halfway across the square and Dolland was no longer in shot. My father was nearer the building with the broken lettering and Granek must have taken the picture from the middle of the square. The figure with his hands in his pockets was still there but his head was partially obscured by my father's shoulder. The letters on the façade were big now. I stared at the picture, trying to imagine the present square as I had seen it. Standing at the bar, looking across . . . E blank . . . IT blank

. . . a Y . . . more blanks. Then I recalled that from that position in the square I would be looking at the bank. IT. It. The 'it' that Dolland had seen! Not it. But IT. Part of a word. Part of CREDIT LYONNAIS.

The fourth and fifth pictures gave me the secret, though I could not interpret them then. Swimming up out of the developer I saw the murder of my father. He was in the road outside the bank. He had turned and was running back toward the centre of the square. The figure standing near the building was now holding something to his shoulder and sighting along it. I looked more closely, conscious of Mourass leaning against my arm. It was a shot-gun. Granek must have taken the picture at the precise moment the gun was fired, for some sort of discharge, flame or smoke, was coming from the right-hand barrel and my father's body was leaning just too far forward for a running man; he was a falling man. This was Dolland's gunfire that didn't sound like gunfire; this was the thing he had seen falling.

I looked back at the three earlier pictures washing in the bath. It was all there, like a movie. There was only one thing that bothered me, and that was the identity of the figure standing by the bank itself. It was too far away to be clear and yet there was something about the stance, something about the thrust of the hands in—
'You!' I said.

'Yes,' Mourass said.

I printed the remainder of the pictures, another three. The others on the roll had not been exposed. When I had finished Mourass said, 'The negatives, please.'

'You killed him,' I said.

'Yes. I killed him. There was no other way.'

'Why?'

He stared at me. He must have been wondering what harm I could do him. I was wondering myself. The answer was none. It was only the stance that had given him away to me. Without the negatives he would be untouchable.

He lifted the gun. 'The negatives!'

I drew them from the carrier on the enlarger and gave them to him.

'Why?' I said again. In spite of our situation I needed to know.

He must have thought then that he was safe, for after a pause he gave a slight shrug and began to talk.

Again I was carried back in my imagination to that day in June 1940 when the beaches of Dunkirk were packed with what remained of the British Expeditionary Force and every lane and small country road was choked with tanks and armoured cars and men. Down one of those, the wind-swept road through the dunes, had come my father, helping the wounded Dolland. But now I had to readjust the picture, for there was a third man. Somewhere behind the railway line or the far side of the canal my father had picked up a German prisoner. So there were three men who came down the sandy road. Dolland was not the only one who was wounded although his was the most severe. The German had taken a machine-gun bullet in the calf of his left leg and was using a heavy stick as a crutch. My father brought the two of them to the Mourass farm. Some of the family and their farm-workers had already thrown up a defensive cordon around the house. They allowed the three men through and escorted them to the barn at the back of the house. The German, a corporal in the catering corps, was left in the barn, hands tied behind his back. My father and Dolland were taken into the house itself, where an attempt was made to change the field dressing on Dolland's face. But the bandages had stuck to the skin so they decided not to disturb the wound. My father used some water to wash Dolland's neck and chest. Mourass remembered that well. He remembered wondering why my father took so much trouble for a man who was almost a corpse. The two men were given food and wine, which Dolland could not swallow and then, after resting for a while, they left in the direction of the river where the wounded were being embarked in fishing boats. But at that time German planes were strafing the river road heavily and my father must have changed course and gone into the village, perhaps hoping to find an assembly point in the square. The village was almost completely deserted; everyone had taken to the dunes to avoid the bombing and shelling: almost deserted, but not quite, for when my father and Dolland had reached the square they met Stefan Granek and that was where his picture story had begun. It must have started in Granek's mind as a simple war story of two comrades, but before he could even begin it, it had moved into an inevitable chain of events which included a bank robbery and a murder.

According to Mourass, there had been an arrangement among the banks of the nearby villages to bring all cash reserves to the Crédit Lyonnais branch in St Claude. There was a rumour that the money was then to be sent to Dunkirk.

'We had known about it for two days,' Mourass said. 'When I say *we*, I mean my father and two older brothers—I was fifteen at the time. Early on that last morning a truck came through from Canadelle with the money from the bank there. We had decided to take the money. Why not? It belonged to Frenchmen, not Germans.'

They had gone to the bank while my father and Dolland had been trying to get to the river and so the robbery was already under way by the time Granek began to use his camera. Mourass's father and his two brothers and two other men from the village had gone into the bank while the young Mourass was told to wait outside on guard with a shot-gun. He had stood near the door and what he had not been able to see he could hear.

'The manager of our bank was M. Charles Bellange,' Mourass said. 'My family had known him since he came to St Claude twenty years before. We banked with him. He was then an old man, ready to retire. He was not a man of flair, but of great trust. Everything in its place, all things precise. They used to say that at twelve o'clock each day the barman across the square would pour a glass of beer and place it on the zinc and before the froth had time to settle M. Bellange would be raising it to his lips. You could set your watch by his movements. I heard the men in the bank arguing with him. It went on like that for many minutes, but he would not give up the money. I heard him say it was in his trust and he could not give it up.'

He paused again, remembering, ordering his thoughts. 'I did not see, but they told me what happened. They said he tried to open a drawer and one of the men thought he might have a pistol there, so they shot him.'

'What was in the drawer?'

'Indigestion tablets.'

'No gun?'

'No gun.'

It was then that my father complicated the affair. He must have heard the shot and known it was a shot-gun. He had been looking for help and I imagine he had gone to investigate. Mourass had waved him away but either he misunderstood or his need for help was so desperate that he disregarded the youth. For he came on and reached the door of the bank. It was at this point that M. Bellange, who was still alive, was shot for the second time.

'So my father saw it,' I said.

'Naturally. The money was there in bags. M. Bellange's body was on the floor. Blood was coming from his head. It was obvious what had happened.'

'And he turned and ran,' I said.

'Yes.'

'And you shot him in the back.'

'What else was there to do?'

I could see my father stumble and fall. Get up. Stumble. Fall again. And lie in the dust of the square, for this is what the other pictures had shown. Then young Mourass had realized there had been a witness, a man with a camera. He had fired his second shot at Granek, but had missed. He ran into the bank to tell his father, but when they came out, Granek had gone. It must have been during those few moments that he had hidden the camera on my father's body.

'Why didn't he keep it?' I said.

'He knew we would search for a man with a camera.'

I had thought he'd been motivated by panic, but if Mourass was right, Granek had been thinking clearly. He must have gambled on British troops coming into the village and taking my father and Dolland to the boats. He could then have reclaimed his camera with its valuable pictures. Instead, he had been picked up by a German patrol and had started on the long road that led to Mauthausen, the DP camp in Vienna and a grave on the banks of the Wye.

They took my father, now dying, and Dolland, almost as bad, to the farmhouse again. Mourass didn't say so, but I had the impression they would have killed them both and buried them if they'd had the chance, but they did not have the chance, for what was left of a regiment of British troops which had fought its way past the Germans on the canal had almost reached the farmhouse. There was no time to do anything before the soldiers arrived except to decide on their strategy. It had meant taking a gamble but in the circumstances it had been worth it and it had paid off. The British captain had been only too happy to believe a French account of British bravery. I could imagine the hurried questions, the almost illegible scrawl as he put down what they said. I could imagine too the pleasure it had given him, as it did the whole of Britain, that at such a desperate time, when France was blaming us for leaving them in the lurch, one English soldier was being honoured by one French village.

Mourass stopped and lit a cigarette and I waited for him to go on. But he kept his silence and after a few moments I said, 'What about your sister? The story of her being raped by my father. She wasn't, was she?'

He shrugged. 'Not by your father. By a panzer officer the following day when they took the village.'

'And the German from the catering corps my father had brought in? The one with his hands tied behind his back. He didn't shoot him either?'

'No.'

There was a bitter irony about the German's death. He had been left by my father in the safe-keeping of the Mourass family because there was no way my father could look after a prisoner and none were being taken to Britain. The man must have thought it would only be a matter of hours before his release by the German forces and he had crawled into the straw of the barn and fallen asleep. They had forgotten him and I imagined him being woken by the noise of picks and shovels, for he opened his eyes and saw the one thing he should never have seen: they were burying the money under the floor of the barn. They shot him where he lay and took his body out into the dunes and buried it. But according to Mourass, the starving village dogs dug it up and by the time the German tanks reached the farmhouse the following day, parts of the man's feet and legs had been eaten. His hands were still tied. It was for this that the heads of families were shot.

'And so you lied to the village as well,' I said. 'You told them my father was responsible for the death of the German and therefore responsible for the reprisals against their families.'

'Of course,' he said matter-of-factly. 'It was a mistake not to have buried the German deeper. But remember, it was *our* resistance that allowed the British troops to be taken off. It was *our* resistance that allowed so many wounded to be saved. It was *our* resistance, the resistance of the Mourass family that brought the village the Croix de Guerre.'

'So that is why you bought the VC.'

'We deserved it.' I thought of this fifteen-year-old boy whose first act of war was to rob a bank and shoot an ally in the back. And I thought of the years that had followed. At seventeen he had become head of the Resistance cell in St Claude; at nineteen head of the Resistance for that entire section of the coast. After the executions he had been the only man left who knew about the bank robbery. He had used the money secretly for bribes, pay-offs, ammunition and guns. And when the war ended he must have been the most powerful man in the region—and the richest.

'You weren't defending a village,' I said. 'You were protecting your loot. The war made you.' He was staring at me coldly. 'You became lord of the manor, with your money under the barn floor. Did you ever think of returning any of it when the war ended?'

'Only a fool who has never had money would ask a question like that.'

'There was only one thing wrong,' I went on. 'The photographs. What if Granek had turned up with his photographs and his story? The village would have wanted an accounting. The photographs were the dark clouds, weren't they? But when nothing happened all those years you must have felt safe. Then I came along.'

'Yes, M'sieu Turner, you came along.'

'You and your sister almost convinced me,' I said angrily.

'We hoped we had. But then the woman arrived—the big English woman in hairy clothes.'

I could imagine her asking questions about a robbery and talking about photographs, and I remembered his splendid house, the drive lined with lime trees, the elegant wife, the sister who owned the Relais, the garage owned by Mourass, the buildings owned by Mourass; the whole way of life he had built for himself since the war was endangered.

'So you had her followed back to England,' I said. 'That's how you found Granek, and you killed him like you killed Dolland—or had him killed.'

'Dolland was mad. Swings. Ice-creams. Higher and higher. That was an accident.'

'And was Granek an accident?'

'There was no need to kill him. He was like an old dog, shaking and trembling. He could not speak properly. The saliva dripped from his mouth. It was disgusting. I would not have touched him.'

'But you searched his place and found nothing.'

'Nothing.'

'Did he tell you what he had done with the film?'

He shook his head. 'He was unconscious by then.'

'But you still had me.'

'Yes. You.'

Mourass was smiling now. It was a smile filled with contempt for me and my father and for Granek and

Miss Argyll and all of us who had come into his sharp-edged world. The contempt had been there from the time of my visit to St Claude.

From the moment I had put my name and address on the *fiche* I had been watched and followed by him and his Algerian gunman—and who knows who else, for a man like Mourass would not only have one man on the payroll, there was too much at stake for that. They had come to London. To Vienna. To the beautiful valley of the Wye. Again I remembered the twisting country road where I thought I'd dropped them. I remembered feeling smug. But he'd had no need to follow me, for he had already been to Hay; he had already found Granek.

But none of this really mattered; what did was here and now. What mattered was what they were doing to Christina and Elisabeth and me.

He put the gun on the cistern and his hand went to his pocket. He took out his cigarette lighter, but no cigarettes. I knew that in a matter of seconds he would flick on the lighter and hold the negatives over the flame and there would be a burst of fire and the smell of burnt celluloid and only wisps of ash floating to the floor. That would be the final remaining fragment of my father's life. I saw again the two men, Captain Turner and Sergeant Dolland, the one cherishing the other. I saw them at the farmhouse; among the dunes of the river road; in the square. My father with Dolland, never leaving him, obsessive. And then the picture changed and I saw Christina with Elisabeth in her arms, staring at the Algerian, frightened of him.

As Mourass's thumb came down on the lighter and the flame sprang up, I picked up the bath of acid fixer and threw it in his face. He gave a cry and dropped the lighter and the negatives. He groped for a handkerchief and at the same time tried to get the gun. It fell to the floor. I made a dive for the negatives. Mourass, one hand rubbing his eyes, was feeling on the floor with the other for the gun. I kicked it under the bath and switched out the light.

I had taken my bearings and was able to open the

door. The light from the passage shone through for a moment and I could see Mourass still on his knees, searching for the gun. I knew the fixer would sting his eyes for a time but was basically no worse than strong vinegar. I closed the door, put the negatives in my pocket and ran softly along the passage.

They were in Elisabeth's room. I stopped short of the doorway, not knowing what I was going to do. I couldn't rush in, he would have a gun. From my position in the passageway I could see the mirror that hung above Elisabeth's cot. It showed the inside of the room. Christina, with the baby in her arms, was hunched on the edge of a straight-backed chair. The Algerian was sitting on the arm of an easy chair behind the door, the gun hanging loosely from his right hand. From his position he couldn't see me. If I was able to get up to the door I might be able to surprise him. I might be able to use something. But what? I could hear Mourass in the bathroom. He had found one of the taps and turned it on and must be washing his eyes. In a minute or two he'd be able to see again. I thought of my golf-clubs, but to get them would mean noise. Then I saw the Leica on the hall table. I'd left it there when I had taken out the cassette. It was no longer in its leather case, just a small, chunky, heavy piece of metal with a long carrying strap. If I could get to the doorway and swing it . . . even as I considered the possibilities Mourass shouted for Yussuf. I grabbed the Leica by the strap and flung back the door. Yussuf had been getting to his feet and it unbalanced him. I swung the camera with all my strength. I think it hit him in the throat for he fell back, trying to get his breath.

Christina was on her feet. 'Come on!' I said. There was only one thought in my mind: to get us all out of the flat. We ran to the front door. Mourass and Yussuf must have come up in the lift, for it was on our floor. We darted in and closed the door. As we reached the bottom I heard their footsteps on the top landing.

'Give her to me,' I said, but Christina shook her head. We ran to the car. She said, 'The keys!'

'Oh, my God!'

I caught her hand and we ran along the road. The rain was lashing down. There was the short, explosive bark of a handgun. The bullet hit the railings near by and whined off into the night.

'The Heath!' I said. 'Run!'

We ran as hard as we could. I heard a car start behind us. We turned the corner at the end of the road and there before us was the great black ocean of trees and grass that marked the edge of Hampstead Heath. As we plunged on to the grass I could feel the mud under my feet. Christina slipped and half pulled me down. This time I took Elisabeth from her. The child seemed too shaken to cry. Christina kicked away her shoes and we ran on. I knew the Heath well. It was more my territory than theirs. Like an animal, I felt safe there. Somewhere ahead was a patch of heavy wild willow and I thought if we could get into that we might throw them off. But they did something I had not thought of. Instead of leaving the car in East Heath Road they drove on, smashing through the bracken and low bushes. I could hear ripping sounds as branches were torn away. The lights swung crazily as the car swerved in and out of the bushes. Above the noise of my own heart-beats I could hear Christina's ragged gulping. The ground was so slippery with mud that it was difficult to keep our footing.

Then I saw a more intense blackness. We were nearly there. Branches whipped at my eyes. Christina cried out. I buried Elisabeth's face in my shoulder. We burrowed into the willow branches like animals and the leaves closed behind us.

The car stopped but the lights stayed on, their beams drilling two holes through the bushes about twenty yards from where we were hiding. One door opened and Yussuf got out. He began to search the great bank of willows. Cleverly Mourass moved the car backwards and forwards letting the powerful beams light up the trees just ahead of the Algerian. I knew it would only be a matter of minutes before he found us.

'We can't stay here,' I whispered. 'You take Elisabeth. I'm going down that way.' I pointed in the darkness to the bottom of the Heath.

'No.'

'Please! Give me about three minutes. Then you go there . . .' I pointed in the opposite direction. 'You'll eventually come to the Vale of Health. Go to the pub and you'll be safe.'

She put out a hand as though to stop me but instead I took it and kissed it and then I leant forward and kissed Elisabeth. 'I'm going now.'

I wormed my way downhill away from them and then stood up. Yussuf was making so much noise he couldn't hear me. I went on. Still he didn't hear. I smashed a branch. The cracking caused him to turn in my direction. He shouted and pointed and Mourass turned the car so that the lights played on me. I was blinded for a moment and then I saw the path ahead of me and began to run. I heard a car door slam as Mourass picked up the Algerian and then they came after me. The ground fell away very rapidly. The rain was still coming down in buckets and the ground was like a quagmire. When the car was about fifty yards behind me I knew I'd have to get off the path or be run down. I sprang away to the left. The ground was fairly level. The car followed. I could hear the swishing noise as it swept through the grass. The bouncing lights were little help to me and the night was so black I didn't know where I was. I ran on and on, jarring my body as I tripped and floundered. Then I was in bush again and on a much steeper slope. I knew where I was, or thought I did. I was on the outskirts of the Hampstead Ponds. They were fenced but if I could get over I'd have a chance. I crashed into the fence hurting my shoulder. The car was about thirty yards behind me when it hit the slope. Mourass braked; the wheels locked on the wet ground. The car slewed sideways and moved down the slope as though on grease. I turned and saw it plough into the fence, sweeping it away, and career on. For a second I glimpsed the two figures in the front seat. Mourass was slumped over the wheel. Then the car hit the water and was gone. It simply wasn't there any longer.

In my panic, I ran on, almost down to Keats Grove before I stopped. I looked back towards the ponds. There was no movement, no light, no sound. It was as though the car had never been.

But there must have been someone else on the Heath that night for I heard a shout and the sound of running footsteps. I let him go and then I paralleled East Heath Road to the Vale of Health. The pub was closed. I passed the little fishing-lake, calling Christina's name.

'David!' I stopped and looked to my left. She was crouched under a bush, hugging Elisabeth. I slithered down the muddy bank and put my arms around them both. 'It's all right now,' I said. 'It's all right.'

There was nothing in the morning papers about an accident on Hampstead Heath. I went down to Pond Street about mid-afternoon and both the *News* and *Standard* were carrying short reports on page one. The car had been lifted by crane. Two men had been found dead inside; they were thought to have drowned. No one knew why or how the car had come to be where it was. Over the following few days the story gradually diminished in size and receded into the inner pages. Fleet Street lost interest, for it appeared to be nothing more sinister than an accident. The men had been identified as foreign business men on a brief visit to England. What no one could tell was why the car had been on the Heath in the first place. It was suggested that the men had been drinking. In a week there was nothing in the papers at all.

At first I had wanted to go to the police; I had thought it my duty. But I'd soon got over that. What good would it do? I thought of writing to Miss Argyll but decided to postpone a letter until I knew exactly what action I was going to take. That there had to be some action was obvious. I had the negatives. But I was in a curiously indecisive state. We simply existed inside the walls of the flat, never going out, jumping if the telephone rang, keeping together in unspoken need; we kept Elisabeth with us whenever we moved to a different room and she slept in her cot by our bed.

For some weeks I did not quite understand what was happening; Christina and I were closer than we had ever been and yet we were strangely frightened. Granville phoned, but I put him off. I told him I wasn't sure about the book. He was angry. But it was true.

I had the negatives locked in my desk drawer. I had the whole story. I had a marvellous book. I could have destroyed Mourass, except that he was already destroyed. I could destroy his wife and his sister. But did I want to? If I did, I would also destroy my father. You don't get a VC for looking after a wounded comrade. What was it Smithson had said? '. . . Outstanding gallantry in the face of the enemy.'

The days passed. The negatives remained where they were. Finally, I could not face going into my room. Then one morning I unlocked the drawer, took them out and burnt them and I felt a great weight of fear and depression lift off me. I couldn't write the book now, not the way I had planned it, and that was a relief in one way and a disappointment in another. I hated losing a story as good as that.

And then a different thought came to me. It was still possible to write it. Not as fact, but as fiction. I sat for a long time probing the idea, trying to see how it could be done. Slowly I began to feel its shape. I felt excited and went to find Christina. She was lying on her tummy in the sun in the sitting-room, drinking coffee. Elisabeth was balanced on Christina's bottom, chewing one of my cassettes. The others were strewn all over the floor. It was such a familiar picture that I felt a lump come into my throat.

I told Christina about my idea. 'Do it!' she said.

And I have.